THE

TURNING

A.L. NOBLE

This is a work of fiction. Any names or characters, businesses or places, events or incidents, are fictitious. Any resemblance to actual persons, living or dead, or actual events is purely coincidental.

Copyright © 2017 A.L. Noble

Printed in the United States of America

ISBN: 0-692-85471-1

ISBN-13: 978-0-692-85471-6

www.alnobleauthor.com

DEDICATION

For my family.
Without your love and guidance, this would not
Have been possible.

CONTENTS

PROLOGUE

"No! Please don't take Robbie away. He hasn't done anything. Get your hands off him," I scream, summer's humidity causing my hair to cling to my tear soaked face. The half dozen, hulking men, dressed in dark combat fatigues, either don't hear me or don't care. Through my sobs, I struggle to formulate more words to express my anguish, but nothing but garbled sounds will come out. My family and I knew this day was rapidly approaching, but none of us were prepared for the moment it became reality.

Speaking gently, as is her natural way, mom replies, "Zayda, you must let The Healers take Robinson to the safe zone. We are running out of time." Although her soft, velvety voice suggests calm, the perspiration on her brow and her stiff shoulders betray her.

Becoming unhinged, I say, "How could you just give up on him like this, Mom? He can beat this. I can help." In a frantic attempt to free my brother, I begin clawing at the Officers' arms. Sensing my opportunity rapidly passing, I desperately try to tear their hands off Robbie.

"Zayda, stop," my dad abruptly interjects, roughly grabbing my hands and cutting off my next plea.

Dad has always been the strong one in the family, but even I can see he is on the verge of breaking in two. The sadness in his eyes makes me suck in a sharp breath. Foolishly, over the past year, I have allowed pity only for myself. Faced with the reality at hand, I am forced to recognize everyone is hurting.

"He must go. We all know what will happen if he does not," dad says, still clutching me gently, yet firmly enough to hold me in my place.

"It's okay, Zay. I don't want to hurt you or anyone else. I've made my peace, and you have to as well," Robinson says. Throughout this ordeal, he has been the most calm-a testament to his entire existence and kind heart.

Looking at my brother for the first time since the men showed up, I cannot help but focus on the drastic change the last year has produced in him. His once beautiful, blue eyes-the same shade as mine-have been replaced by the monstrous yellow ones we are all too familiar with. Blemishes and festering sores mar his previously flawless complexion, and his sparse, platinum-blonde hair does little to conceal the unusually pale skin and the large, bulging veins on his frail head. Where has my brother gone?

None of those things matter, he is still my brother. As I turn to him and speak, my voice quivering with each syllable, "I can't be okay without you. It has always been you and me, Robbie. Who will play chess with me? Mom and dad don't know how. Who will laugh at my stupid jokes? You are the only one who understands me. I love you. *Please* stay. We can fight it together. Please. Don't. Leave. Me."

Tears well up in Robinson's eyes, and he turns hastily away from me. Facing his escorts, his face grimacing in a combination of pain and sadness, he shouts, "I need to leave here now. I can feel the change speeding up. Get me out! Now!"

Hysteria peaking inside me, and fear over the very real possibility I will lose my brother welling up, I plead once more, "No! Please don't go?"

Robinson just looks at me sadly and smiles. "No matter what, I will always love you." Doubling over in pain and emitting a low growl, Robinson yells once more, his voice much raspier and harsher this time, "Please, take me NOW!"

Grabbing him by both arms, the men escort him outside, where at least ten more Officers wait. My parents and I stand in shock, sadness cascading freely down our faces, none of us daring to move just yet. Knowing it will be the last time I ever see my brother, I wish I could think of something better to say while he is being shoved into the back of the reinforced truck. Instead, I just run to the door and yell, "Happy birthday!"

***

In the year 2019, a plague ravaged the world wiping out all but one percent of the entire population. In the year 2020, The Cure was given to the survivors. Every great accomplishment comes with consequences; however, no one could have imagined that a cure for all disease would lead to such dark days. It has. For every living being over the age of eighteen it was a blessing, for the rest, a curse.

Welcome to my world; the time of The Turning.

THE TIME BEFORE

My parents often speak of The Time Before, but I have no memory of those dark days. For that, I am thankful. For many other reasons, I am not. Like all the children in my community, I was born after The Cure had been given, and the world was reborn. We are saved, they claim. We are free, they cheer. I don't know who 'they' are, but I do not feel any of those things. My friends and I are now the oldest youth in our camp, and like hundreds before us and hundreds to come, we will be leaving here very soon.

Looking around our peaceful and remote village atop the levee in the southeast region, I find it hard to imagine humanity being on the verge of extinction like they describe. We will not likely forget, but as a reminder to us all to obey the laws of The Great Healers, and to never slip back to the selfish ways that led to The Unraveling, The Council mandates each child must hear The Truth Tale at least three times a year. Mom loves to tell the story late at night while we wait for the last embers of the fire to die down. The stars above twinkle brightly on this cool, August eve as we rush to claim the spots closest to the warm fire.

Taking her place on the log reserved for the night's orator, in her most dramatic cadence, the flames dancing playfully in her clear, blue eyes, mom beautifully pulls long gone spirits from the heavens and casts their shadows upon us all. "In The Time Before, disease ravaged the world, consuming any and everything it desired. People were constantly warring with one another because of this. Man, woman, and child were at the mercy of illness's relentless, unbiased grasp. You could be healthy one day, and poof out of existence the next.

Living in a constant state of chaos, and waiting for their turn to dance with the reaper-no one knew how or when it would strike-humans became obsessed with sins of the flesh. The Old City was a conduit for these activities. Nightly, you could wander up and down the cobblestone streets and witness depraved acts. Women stripped down to nothing while we watched from afar and offered rewards for their boldness. Establishments sold spoiled ales, so everyone could blurry their minds and forget about their impending doom. Soon, even these desperate activities could not keep death from calling and disease overtook the town.

To keep from washing away in the floods after hurricanes, bodies by the thousands were buried in above ground crypts in The Old City. Waiting for their families to join them in darkness, the people lie; their flesh slowly rotting away until their bones become dust. And that is why we have Rule 1: Everyone, regardless of the side effects, must be given The Cure.

Our village was once a large municipality, humming with thousands upon thousands of people. So many, in fact, that housing was inadequate and some were forced to sleep on boxes in the street. These poor souls, referred to as bums, spent their days begging for money from the more fortunate citizens; some days they made a profit and ate, other days they lay their head on their cardboard home with an empty hole in their tummies.

People used whatever talents they possessed to perform for the wealthy: statue men, future tellers, spirit advisors, and history tellers lingered on every corner. Willing the crowds to join them and contribute to their livelihood, these humans stalked the night in hopes of surviving one more day. In this way, they became like the vampires in old lore, skulking in the shadows.

Like us now, the old one's held music in high regard, and some were able to sing songs and earn a living. It is said, their melodies permeated every inch of The Old City, and the magic conjured by the notes illuminated the darkest recesses of the mind and soul. However, these endeavors took away from the important tasks and upkeep of the city, and soon it all began to crumble.

All of this was because resources were too scarce to maintain the rapidly swelling population, and people became too desperate for their own survival to care about their fellow man. And that is why we have Rule 2: The population of all villages must remain under 500 people at all times, and The Healers must monitor the surplus food. Any village containing more than the allotted number of inhabitants will be removed from the supply list until the issue is corrected.

Violence used to be commonplace in every city around the world. You could be shot and killed for no reason, or while simply eating your morning meal. Renegades with guns ran up and down the streets shooting people at will. It is said that you could not walk more than fifty feet without stepping upon a gun of some sort. In order to prepare them for the world, babies were given replicas of machine guns as their first toy. Eventually weapons outnumbered humans 100 to 1. Disease of the mind led people to slaughter one another in the manner we do our food. Regard for human life was cast aside; man, became man's worst enemy; genocide was as common as waking with the morning sun. And that is why we have Rule 3: No one, outside of The Healers, may possess a gun or other weapon.

Unlike now, the world used to be so bright and colorful you could not see the stars-even on the clearest night. Man-made fire burned brightly in every window in the village, allowing terrifying shadows to leach out into nature. People spent their days and nights watching false realities flash rapidly on the large mechanical boxes in their homes. Often, these boxes and their mesmerizing stories consumed the minds of the villagers so much they could no longer separate real from make-believe, and thus their minds were lost to madness. Even the young were susceptible to the enticing glow of the other world. In fact, they were so enamored with it they carried around small versions of the mechanical boxes so they could access its magic at will. It is believed this is why The Unraveling spread so quickly. And that is why we have Rule 4: No man-made fire or as they used to call it, electricity.

Besides the mechanical boxes, there were also paper versions of untruth circulated in numbers by the millions. This practice was so widely accepted, even the teachers used them to educate the young ones. Everyone had access to these words at will, and it only took a moment to find one. People began to believe more in this fantasy world than in the world around them, thus causing the seeds of unhappiness to blossom in their minds. They were always looking for ways to make the world into a perfect utopia, failing at every turn. This failure enraged people so completely they began to rebel against the leaders and fight them. In this way, words became more dangerous than guns. And that is why we have Rule 5: No one, besides The Healers and One Elder from each village, shall be taught how to read.

Our world used to be made up of many different, large villages all run by different people. Often, the rules from one area to another varied so greatly people would commit crimes by accident and then be subject to incarceration or other punishments. Travel outside of our world carried with it the possibility of never returning to your loved ones because of an accidental mistake. It became increasingly more difficult to know how to behave without fear. The Healers stepped in, began governing all villages, and thus created The Rules to help us avoid these problems. The Rules are universal across the land, so no one must worry if they will break one without knowing. Life became easier and more controlled when they established our boundaries. And that is why we have Rule 6: Never leave the village, and above all else, obey The Healers and follow their rules at all times." At this point, mom pauses and looks longingly toward the river. "Okay, that is enough for tonight," she says.

"But you forgot the most important rule," Posy says. Posy is my best and most trusted friend. We have known each other since birth.

"Not now," mom replies, standing and brushing the dirt off her brown, work pants.

Mom has been doing this since last year when Robinson left us. It isn't that she believes it to be an unimportant rule, just that she cannot bear to speak about him without choking up. We have all been struggling with the unimaginable, gaping hole in our lives where Robbie used to be, but mom has struggled the most. I think that is because I am not far behind him, and then she will be all alone with Papa.

Sensing another protest coming, mom gently says, "It is getting late, Posy. After chores tomorrow, we can reconvene, and I will finish the story. For now, please get some rest. We have a busy day of harvesting awaiting us, and the Officers will be here for our weekly check day after next."

We all know, tomorrow night, mom will be absent from the fire. She will find some unavoidable and important task and vanish into the shadows until morning, when she feels our curiosity and need to hear the ending will have waned.

Posy just smiles knowingly and lovingly, her brown eyes reflecting the flames from the fire, "Okay, mama Iris. We can finish tomorrow."

She has called my mother mama since we were six, and her own mother was relocated to another village. Our numbers had grown five people above the allotted, and June's name was randomly selected to be among those sent away. We all hate when someone close to us is picked in The

Transference, but it is the only fair way The Healers have for redistribution of population. Still, Posy was incredibly close to her mom, and still harbors resentment toward The Healers for taking her away. Some days when they are here, I make Posy hide out in my tent, so she does not do something crazy like charge them and claw their eyes out. We have no choice but to follow The Rules. However, we don't have to like it. That is one thing they can't take from us-resistance.

Walking back to our tents in silence, shivering as the warmth of the fire quickly leaves our bodies, the six of us internally fret about the year to come. I do not need any of my friends to tell me what we have already discussed dozens of times before; the end is approaching-fast. When we first learned about our fates, we all felt like we had all the time in the world, but now we realize just how utterly and completely wrong we were. It is easy to imagine, when you are seven, how slowly a decade will pass. Now I know, it was just a simple blink of the eye.

Viola was the first to break the tension and speak, "Do you think she will ever be able to finish the story again?" she asks.

I can hear the sudden intake of breath from Reggie as he walks beside me. Reggie is my second oldest friend, and he knows me better than anyone else in the world-well, almost anyone, but I don't think Robbie officially counts as a person anymore-and he knows how sick and tired of Viola bringing up my brother I am. If she were not such a great friend, I would swear she hates me.

"Seriously, Vi, would it be possible not to have the exact same conversation every time we hear the story? You must be getting tired of asking the same question. I know I would," Reggie huffs.

"Yeah, sorry," Viola replies, while playfully pulling the back of Reggie's brown hair, "I didn't mean anything by it, Zayda. I just can't help but feel guilty and nervous every time we leave. You guys all know I'm a nervous talker. When I get upset I just talk and talk and talk. I don't even have to have anything specific to talk about to start rambling on. It is a curse really. I just ramble and ramble and..."

"Vi!" we all shout in unison.

"Sorry," she says, a bit more quietly, while ducking her head so her flaming, red hair hides her blushing cheeks.

"It's all good, sis," Camden says, as he wraps his strong arm around his twin's shoulder, "We all still love you. Even if you do have diarrhea of the mouth a lot."

"Gross! Seriously, Camden, that is the most disgusting figure of speech ever," Posy says playfully.

Sticking his finger in his mouth, wetting it, and trying to rub it on Posy's face, "I never claimed to be anything else," Camden teases.

Changing the subject, I say, "Do any of you know why The Healers are coming again so soon? It has only been two days since they were here last, and if they come the day after tomorrow that is three days early. I don't remember them ever being early before."

"No clue, but I'm sure it is nothing to worry about," Kyle says.

I have almost forgotten Kyle is with us because he has been so quiet. As the oldest in our group, Kyle is usually the most composed, but he is rarely this silent. Something tells me it has everything to do with his birthday coming up in just a few months. The symptoms, which were unusually slow at first, had recently sped up so quickly I wonder if Kyle will even make it to eighteen. I hope so; it is already tough enough on him to be the first of the group to Turn. Man, I do not envy Kyle right now.

"I guess you are right," I reply to him. I know I am probably being paranoid, but lately this flicker of uncertainty has started to blossom in the back of my mind. Tonight, that flicker has ignited into a full-blown forest fire, and I have no idea how to put it out.

"They *have* been early a few times before," Camden states matter-of-factly.

"Yeah, last year before the big harvest they came to offer us more farming supplies. Maybe they are coming to help again," Viola adds.

"Well, the good thing is we will find out first thing in the morning, two days from now. I for one am happy for that," Posy says.

I open my mouth to contribute to the conversation, but we have already reached the campsite. Besides that, I don't feel like showing the rest of them how completely crazy and paranoid I am becoming. Instead, I just say, "Good night, guys. See you in the morning."

The others all turn around and wave silently, except for Reggie. He stands and looks at me for a few seconds longer as we split off to go into our respective tents. I can tell he wants to talk more, but I am not in the mood for one of our midnight, friend sessions. He really is one of the best friends ever, and always makes me feel better, but tonight I just want to be alone in my own thoughts.

"You okay?" Reggie asks.

"Yes," I lie.

Taking a step toward me and brushing the platinum locks out of my eyes, "Okay. You know where to find me if you need me," he says.

Shocked by the gesture and taking a small step back, I simply say, "Thanks, Reg," When I see the hurt flash across his face, I immediately regret my unintentional slight toward his kindness. The look only lasts for a moment, anyone who did not know him better would have missed it, but it is there.

In his normal chipper tone, as if I had not just wounded his pride, "Good night. I'll come get you for duty as soon as I wake up," he says, ducking his head into his small tent.

Walking away toward my own home, "Good night," I say.

Finally alone, I relish the time it takes to finish the short walk to our family tent. I get so few moments to myself, so I cherish them when they happen. On the way there, I look around our small village. Tents are crowded so close together, it appears to be one, large, intertwined mass instead of hundreds of individual structures. Despite it being a late, summer night, there is an unusual chill in the air, and I long to be back by the fire. I casually rub my hands up and down my arms to generate some heat. Normally, this time of year, I would be sweating profusely. However, like so many other things in my world, that is also changing. My mind is a torrent of thoughts, most of which revolve around the upcoming year, and as usual Robinson's fate. Where did he go? What did The Healers do to him? Did he die right away? Is he in pain? Where is my brother now? Is he still my brother? My brain, as is customary lately, runs through this list of questions over and over as I walk. However, tonight I have a new worry to add to the list-Reggie's bizarre behavior, but I push it back down to the bottom where it belongs. For now, I want to think about Robinson. I try to focus on the happy times. Small glimpses of his face, smiling and jubilant flash into my mind, as the two of us run down to the river to help dad catch fish for dinner. Sadly, after just a few moments, like every other night, his visage quickly morphs into my last memory of him, and I stare bewildered into his now yellow eyes. In an instant, Robinson is taken from me again, and I'm left alone standing at the entrance to our tent.

Arriving home and slipping out of my day clothes and into my wool pajamas, I sink quietly into my down-filled sleeping bag, warmth finding me once more. The last thought of the day enters my brain; in just a few days, I will be seventeen. The village will all gather to celebrate, pretending it is a happy occasion. We all know what the number signifies, and it isn't a cause for celebration. Still, as is custom, we will eat, drink, and sing until the early morning hours. How pathetic and ignorant. Then the next morning, like my friends before me, I will officially begin turning into a monster. Shuddering, I attempt to push this thought aside, but it is no use. As has been the case every single night since Robinson left, I will spend the better part of my time staring up into the dark void above my head, praying for salvation.

SPECIAL VISIT

Commotion from outside of my tent wakes me at dawn. We are early risers, but rarely is anyone, besides the night watcher, up before the sun. Alarm shoots through me as I hastily grab my wrinkled clothes and put them on, not even pausing to pull my long hair up into its customary ponytail. The last time so much activity had been going on in the early hours was when we had been compromised a few years back. One of The Turned from a nearby village had escaped before The Council could take him into custody, and he ended up here. We lost two of our own that day.

"Please don't let this be like that," I mumble to myself, grabbing my secret stick from its hiding place. Months ago, I found the sturdy piece of wood, gathered enough sharp stones to shape the tip, and made myself a spear. It is strictly forbidden, but I feel better with it on me. I don't think anyone suspects me of carrying it, but once I thought Posy might have spotted it when we were sitting around the fire. She never brought it up, and I doubt she would ever rat me out for having it. I mean, she is my best friend. Wedging the dull end down into the recess of my boot, I reposition my pantleg and check to make sure it is concealed. Satisfied, I make my way outside.

When I exit the tent, my eyes struggling to adjust to the darkness, I faintly see Reggie jogging toward me. He looks alarmed, but not afraid, which makes me relax a little. He is buttoning up his shirt on the way, so I guess he was just as caught off guard as me. Behind him, I can see a few other of our friends emerging from their slumber. They all appear as confused as I am.

"What is going on?" I ask Reggie.

As he stops in front of me, breathless and huffing, "They are early. The night watcher spotted them on the river a few minutes ago. He said there were only two of them, but it was definitely The Council's men. I'm going to run down and see if I can get a closer look."

"Okay, I'll go with you. Just wait a minute while I grab my binoculars," I say. He nods in agreement and pauses to catch his breath. I return the gesture and spin around to gather my supplies.

Back inside my tent, I rummage around looking for my council issued binoculars. I can't help but recall the feeling of foreboding I had last night. Sleep was hard to come by, as I predicted it would be, and I tossed and turned more than I rested. My brain is not currently working on all cylinders. However, the feeling is still very much present. In fact, it is growing exponentially stronger. Something big is about to happen. Finally, I find my binoculars in the large cabinet by the sink and rush outside. "Got 'em," I say, but no one is paying me any attention.

Reggie is bouncing from foot to foot, anxiously looking around at the other tents. No one appears to be emerging yet. I'm sure he is also impatient for us to be on our way; he hates to wait, but the behavior seems to be more suggestive of nervousness. The rest of the crew has joined him and are gearing up for the recon mission to the edge of the water. Like Reggie, most of them are still dressing in some manner: Viola is tucking the top of her jeans into her boots, Camden is tightening his belt, and Posy is pulling her black hair up into a bun. Man, I wish I had grabbed a hair tie. As usual, the twins stand mere inches apart. They rarely go anywhere without each other, and on the uncommon occasions they are separated, their twin senses are activated-linking both minds as one. Robinson and I used to be super close, but nothing compared to the twins' connection.

Apparently, I walk out right in the middle of a conversation between the group.

"...super early this time, and why are there only two of them? Doesn't make any sense," Kyle states.

"Those are just rumors. You know Andy has terrible eyesight and didn't get a good look," Posy says.

Noticing me for the first time, "Oh hey, Zayda. We were just trying to figure out what all of this could mean. I for one, think it is probably just a mistake. Maybe they got confused on what day it is. Or what village they are supposed to be going to today. I mean, it doesn't have to be a big deal. Why does everyone always freak out when they show up? I for one, think it's not that serious. And..."

"Vi!" we all shout in unison.

"Sorry," Viola replies, "I'm just nervous is all."

Walking over to touch her on her arm for comfort, I say, "I know. We are all a bit spooked. There is only one way to find out, and that is to head to the water and get a good look."

With that, we all begin making our way to the water's edge. Our boots crunch loudly on the rough ground beneath our feet, the sound echoing off the nearby, abandoned buildings down the hill, announcing our approach to everyone nearby. Not seeing or hearing an objection, I decide it doesn't really matter though, we don't seem to be waking anyone. Seeking answers like us, the rest of the villagers are probably already up and getting dressed to come out and greet the guests. For now though, things are pretty quiet. Looking out over the water, I am reminded how lucky we are to be stationed here. I think this every time I walk along the levee during the day, I am amazed at the beautiful view we were all granted, but nothing compares to watching the sun rise over the large river. Many other villages are not as lucky. I've heard of some of them being in the middle of the woods with nothing around but trees and squirrels. I would go mad if all I had to see each day were merely a few feet in front of me. Luckily, that is not a problem for those of us who dwell in Alon.

From the highest peak on the bank, the remnants of the old town stretch out for miles. My favorite thing to do, in my few moments of freedom in the winter, is stare down and imagine what life might have been like when the city was still alive. In my dreams, I am always casually strolling through the narrow alleyways, my hands intertwined with a handsome man. Unlike life since The Unraveling, I get to choose my mate, and we are together because we love one another. We pass shops filled with amazing artwork created by local residents. The colors are bright and vibrant, filling the world with splendid beauty. I can smell the sweet pastries baking in the nearby restaurants, and the prospect of consuming their warm, puffy deliciousness delights us both. We laugh and smile as we meander all day long; nowhere to be, no work to do, only fun to be had.

"Zay. Zayda. Yoo hoo, Earth to Zayda," Posy says, waving her hand in front of my face and startling me back to reality.

Shaking my head to clear away the thoughts of a life I will never have, I reply, "My bad. I'm here. I was just zoning out."

"I'll say. I've been trying to ask you a question for like two minutes. I was beginning to think you were ignoring me on purpose. Does Camden need to remind you what happens when I am ignored?" Posy scolds.

"Um, no way. Who could ever forget that week of hell. I'm not trying to get put on the Posy shit list." Out of the corner of my eye, I can see Camden shiver at the memory. He has made it a priority to never cross her again after that day.

"Good idea," Posy says with a wink, "Now, do I have your undivided attention?"

Brushing my windblown hair out of my face, and again internally scolding myself for not grabbing that dang hair tie, I say, "Hit me, Pose. I promise not to let my mind wander again."

Interjecting and casting a knowing look my way, Reggie says, "You seem to be doing that a lot lately. I'm worried about you, Zayda."

"No worries, bro. I'm all good. Promise," I say dismissing him with a friendly nudge on the shoulder with my knuckles. I then turn back to Posy, "Now, what was your question?"

"I was just asking if you have seen any of the elders this morning? When we all woke up, they were nowhere to be found," Posy says.

Come to think of it, I hadn't seen any of the elders, including my parents. They were always in the tent waiting and preparing breakfast when I woke up, but not this morning. That would explain the lack of yelling about the noise. "Um, no. I guess I haven't" I reply.

"That can't be good," Viola says.

We all nod in agreement. Worried, we walk in silence for the remainder of the time it takes to reach the bank, each of us swiveling our heads to survey the camp. No smoke comes from the tents or the breakfast fires. Aside from us, the young ones, and the night watcher, it appears to be deserted. The forest fire inside me begins to rage uncontrollably again, and I grab my stomach in an effort to extinguish it. Scanning my friends' faces, I see they are just as worried as I am; however, no one dares verbalize their concerns.

At the bank, we all gaze west through our binoculars. I adjust mine for several minutes, still not quite getting a clear view, but managing to see a half-mile or more. Thankfully, the sun is behind us and doesn't cause me to have to squint. Still, a dense fog is just beginning to burn off the top of the water, further obscuring the bend we are focused on. The craft will have to be relatively large for us to see it from this far away.

"Do you guys see that?" Reggie says.

I adjust my lenses more, trying to find what he sees. "No. I don't see anything past that flock of birds."

"Me either," Camden says.

"I think I see something," Viola states. It is hard for me to miss the hint of pride in her voice. Viola is always competing with someone, so I'm sure she is ecstatic to be seeing something we could not.

"Wait...I see it too. Coming around the bend of the river. It looks like a small, motorized boat.," Posy says.

"It's a boat, but not a small one. It just looks like it from this far away," Reggie says.

"Holy cow, it is huge," Viola says, "Looks like The Council's boat all right."

"Yes, but those are not Officers. They don't have on any of the normal fatigues. You know The Four would have their heads if they made an official call without the proper uniform," Kyle adds. I shudder at the thought of the four members who make up The Council of the Southeast. Rumor has it that they are brutal and ruthless, but I have never met them before.

In response to his statement, we all squint our eyes tighter to take a closer look. Kyle is right; these are not the normal guys. The boat is manned by an older man with long, silver hair. Beside him, sits a younger man with hair the color of a raven's feathers. Even from my position on land, I can see the resemblance between them. They appear to be engaged in conversation, the younger man seems upset, but it is difficult to tell with certainty from this distance.

"Do you recognize either of them?" Camden asks.

Shaking our heads, we all lower our binoculars and wait for the boat to come ashore.

***

"Well, don't just stand there," the older man barks, "help us tie up the boat."

Camden, Kyle, and Reggie move forward and begin following orders. They grab the lines and tightly shore the boat to the dock, while the men exit the vessel and make their way toward us. Up close, the relationship between the men is even more obvious. I can't stop myself from staring at them. Both have amazing bone structure, their jaws set in a muscular way that implies either a strict workout routine or tremendously kind genetics; I am going to guess both. However, that is not the most impressive similarity; that title belongs to their eyes-amethyst mined directly from the earth would not have been as beautiful of a shade of purple. Guilt washes over me as I find myself staring at the younger man in awe. He is the most handsome being I have ever laid my eyes on.

Finished tying up the boat, and as if he had been reading my mind, Reggie makes his way to stand defensively by my side. He has yet to come out and say it, but I am beginning to suspect Reggie is developing feelings for me. I say a silent prayer that, if he ever decides to make his feelings public, I will have the right words to let him down gently. Don't get me wrong, Reggie is extremely attractive, in a boy next door kind of way; he is muscular and fit, has a nice, square jaw-line, and kind, brown eyes. However, there is no point in us getting involved-especially with only one year left.

To help plant the seed that I do not need to be protected, I take a step forward and extend my quivering hand to our visitors. "Hello, my name is Zayda. Welcome to Alon."

Both of the men appear taken aback by my gesture, but the younger one-Mr. Perfect-places his hand in mine. At the exact moment our palms meet, a shock travels up my fingers and goes through my entire body. Startled, I pull back quickly. His arm remains extended, but the look in his eyes tells me all I need to know; he felt it too.

"Pleased to meet you. I am Brighton, and this is my father Eli," the stranger responds.

"Holy shit!" Camden says.

"Excuse me?" Brighton says.

"Sorry, man. What I meant to say was, I can't believe you are here. This it totally cool," Camden corrects.

From the gaping mouths surrounding me, I would say we are all equally as surprised as Cam. None of us really know what to say next, so we just stand there, awkwardly waiting for the two most important members of The Council to speak.

Eternities seem to pass before Eli speaks, "We are here on official Council business, and time is of the utmost importance. Can you please direct us to the meeting place of The Elders?"

Well, that at least explains the quiet. The Elders are never in a meeting this early, and with the panic over the incoming vessel, none of us had suspected an emergency meeting. My friends all appear to have been turned into statues, so I step forward, avoiding eye contact with Brighton, and offer to escort them, "Please follow me," I say.

The walk to the gathering place is only a short distance away, but it feels like miles. I remain silent while the two men flank me. Occasionally, I chance a glance toward them both. Brighton always appears to be studying me intently, a small smile hinting at the corners of his lips. Conversely, his father is glowering at me like I have recently stabbed him in the heart. Boy am I happy when we finally reach the elder cabin.

I knock on the door and open it, exposing the faces of our most cherished villagers. My mother and father sit nearest the door in the positions of highest respect.

"Pardon my intrusion, but I have brought our guests," I say quietly.

"Of course, dear. Please do come in, great Council leaders," my mother says, as the entire room rises and then quickly kneels in the customary greeting of respect for our leaders.

Brighton and his father casually enter the building.

"Phew! That was intense," I accidentally say aloud. Embarrassed and blushing, I quickly turn and hurry away.

As I am walking, I hear a small chuckle and turn to see Brighton smiling at me as he pulls the doors closed.

***

When I arrive back at our special spot in the middle of camp, everyone is eagerly awaiting me on their respective stumps. Judging from the expectant looks on their faces, they are ready for some juicy gossip.

"Sssooo? Lay it on us. What did they say?" Posy inquires.

"Um, not much. In fact, nothing at all," I reply.

"Oh, come on! You can't expect us to believe they said absolutely nothing, Zayda," Viola snaps.

Becoming defensive, she really pushes my buttons sometimes, I reply, "Well, it's true."

"Whatever. You just want to be the only one who knows what it was. You are always like that," Viola snorts.

"If she said they didn't say anything, then they didn't say anything. Why don't you chill out, Viola?" Reggie chides.

Not really wanting to justify her snotty comment with a response, but being irritated nonetheless, I say, "Actually, the only person who said a word during the entire time I was with them was me, and that was really just a mumble to myself. I guess they were too focused on their task to make small talk with a random villager they just met. Imagine that, two very important men not giving a crap about an almost seventeen-year-old."

"Dang! You don't have to be rude about it," Viola states. As she continues speaking, she moves over to sit closer to Camden, like she always does when someone calls her out on her attitude. "We are all just curious about what went on. Maybe if you would have asked one of us to go with you, we wouldn't be so in the dark."

"To be fair, none of us jumped at the chance to go with them. I'm pretty sure Zay was the only one who even flinched when they asked," Kyle states.

"Always the rational peacekeeper," Viola says, rolling her eyes.

"Can we all just chill for a minute?" Camden asks. "I know we are all on edge because of the surprise visit, but going after each other is not going to make any of us feel better. Relax, breathe deeply, and shut up with the attacks already."

"Camden and Kyle are right. Sorry, Viola. I didn't mean to be a bitch. I just have this terrible feeling that something is really wrong here," I say.

"It's all good. I'm sorry too. I know I can be a bit much at times," Viola responds. The roll of her eyes suggests she is a not quite as sincere as I am, but I was telling the truth when I said I didn't want to fight anymore, so I let it go. There is enough going on without the six of us losing our cool with each other.

"Now that we have settled all of that," Reggie asks, shooting daggers at Viola, "what do you guys think they could be doing here?"

"Surprise birthday party for Zayda," Kyle jokes.

"Came to help with the harvest," Posy laughs.

"Spending a few days here learning how the common man lives," Reggie adds.

"Maybe the young one is looking for a girlfriend," Viola coos.

"Pick me," Posy laughs again.

"No way, he's all mine," Viola replies, wagging her eyebrows and making a kissing face.

We all laugh out loud, thankful for the brief comic relief. That is the great thing about our group, we can erase away most of the world's problems with a five-minute conversation. I for one am extremely grateful for the reprieve from the torrent of conspiracy theories rolling around in my head. However, it doesn't last long because the sound of footsteps approaching snaps us all back to reality. Turning toward the noise, we stare at my parents and several other elder's walking directly toward us, behind them are Eli and Brighton. I can't help but notice his eyes lingering on me. I look away several times to break the awkward tension, but whenever my gaze meets his again, he is always locked on me. In anticipation of whatever news they are about to share with us, and something else I dare not acknowledge, my heart races a thousand beats a minute.

***

"This isn't fair! They can't take you both away from me! Why does it have to be you guys?" I sob into my mother's arms. The Council has just left us alone to discuss their plans, and I am beside myself with the news.

"We do as The Council wishes, Zayda. You know it has always been this way. The other village is in disrepair, and your father and I are the best people to fix their problems. Eli promised it wasn't going to be forever, just a few months at most," mom replies while gently stroking my hair.

"I only have a year left, mom. You are going to miss most of it. How can The Council leave me alone for my last year?" I shout.

"This is not about you, Zayda. In order for our world to function, we have to all work together as a team. Sometimes, that means doing things that make you, as an individual, unhappy," mom says.

Sitting up and rubbing the tears off my face, "How long do you have?" I ask.

"We leave at first light," my dad answers.

"First light? On my birthday? They are monsters! I hate them, and they will pay for doing this!" I shout, a fresh stream of moisture running down my cheeks.

"Zayda! You can't say such things," my dad spits. "If they find out you did, they will punish you harshly. You know this as well as anyone else here."

"I don't care! Let them punish me. It is better than being alone," I reply.

"You aren't alone, Zay," Reggie says gently.

In my despair, I had forgotten the others were still here. They had been too stunned to leave when my parents delivered the news of why we were granted this early visit. Wiping my nose on the back of my sleeve, I sit up straighter and look at the faces surrounding me. Camden and Viola hold each other tightly, tears threatening the corners of their eyes. Kyle and Posy hold hands as they cast their glances anywhere but on me and my family. I survey the five of them for many seconds-my best friends in the world-before allowing my gaze to settle on Reggie. His face is twisted in anguish. He knows how much my family means to me, especially over the past year, and that losing them will shatter my world to pieces. I love him so much in that moment; not because he pities me, but because he completely understands my soul.

"Thank you, Reggie. I know you will be here for whatever I need, but you have to get that it won't be the same," I say, trying not to hurt him.

"Of course it won't, but I will make sure it is okay. That is all any of us can do, just make it okay," Reggie replies.

"Can you at least try to understand? For us?" mom asks.

Lifting my face to meet hers, "Yes, momma, I will try," I say.

Sliding over gently to hug us both, Posy whispers, "I love you guys. We will get through this."

"I love you too, Pose," mom replies, kissing us both lightly on the head. "My girls. I will miss you both so much."

At that moment, my heart breaks for us all; my mom-who would be leaving her entire village, Posy-who is losing her second mom, and myself-who is becoming an orphan. I want to hold them both forever.

"Like Reggie said, it will be okay," my father says, trying to ease the situation. He is truly awful with words and has never mastered the art of timing. The comfort I felt moments before is shattered, and my reality comes crashing down on me. I can't explain it, but something inside me explodes when I hear his words. Red shrouds my eyes and everything I see in a blanket of blood; my anger consumes the world around me. I pick up a nearby, wooden bucket and hurl it as far as I can, splintering it when it hits the hard ground. My friends and family stare at me in utter shock, but I don't care. I continue to find things to throw, each one like a tiny piece of my sanity flying through the air. Piece by piece a new me is forged, and she vows to make things right again.

My hands are trembling with both exertion and rage, and I struggle to keep them from hitting the closest thing to me. "Zayda, you have to calm down," mom says. She has moved closer to me, and is extending her hand to touch me. I can see she means well, but I am still so angry, and I flinch away. "Please, baby, you've got to relax. Your dad is right, everything will be okay," she says.

"Oh yeah? Just like it was okay for Robbie?" I spit, knowing it is a low blow, but being unable to control myself. "Please, tell me how everything is going to be okay. Nothing will be okay. Ever! I hate them, and I don't know how, but they are going to pay for this," I say, before turning and huffing away.

OUT WITH THE OLD/ IN WITH THE NEW

Wanting to spend as much time together as possible, we wake well before dawn. I pull on my light pants and shirt this morning because the heat has already become almost unbearable. That is how it is in Alon, freezing one minute, burning to death the next. Internally, I vow not to make the same mistake as yesterday, and pull my hair up into a tight ponytail. The breeze on my neck offers immediate relief from the stifling inferno of our tent.

"Morning, mama," I say, while kissing her cheek.

"Good morning, beautiful, birthday girl. Feeling better?" she asks, a knowing look in her eyes. I nod in silent acknowledgment of the unasked question floating between us. *Are you finished throwing a tantrum and making insane threats?* Satisfied with my response, she continues, "Are you ready for your special breakfast?"

"Are those beignets I smell?" I ask playfully.

"Now what else would I make for my baby's special breakfast? They *are* still your favorite? Right?" she teases.

Trying to sound as chipper as possible, "You know it," I reply. "Too bad we can only have them once a year. Although, I probably wouldn't be able to run as fast as I can if I weighed fifty pounds more," I laugh. Resources are scarce in our village, but each family is allowed one special meal, per person, a year. We have to put in the request for the food weeks in advance because it comes from the special reserve in The Sacred City.

"You know before The Unraveling; the people of the Old City could walk into a café and order them any time of the day or night. Can you imagine that? Unfortunately, we aren't that lucky," mom states.

As I watch her small frame move slowly around the tiny space, her platinum hair swishing with her steps, I can't help but think of how much I truly love her. She is my rock, and I have no idea how I will survive without her.

"Mama?"

"Yes, sweet."

"Are you afraid?" I ask.

"Not afraid. More of a nervous feeling. I want to do a good job and help all of those people because that is what's right, but I'm worried about you being here so far away," she replies.

"Where is the other village?" I ask.

Looking at me skeptically, still frying the sweet dough, "A day's walk away," she states.

"Can I come and visit you?" I question, averting my eyes because I already know the answer.

"Now, Zayda, you know travel to another village is strictly prohibited unless The Council gives you permission," she states harshly.

"Do you think they would give me permission?" I ask.

Mom spins and looks at me sternly, "I forbid you leaving this village. It is too dangerous out there in the wild. You must promise me you will stay put." I drop my eyes to the floor. Every inch of my body and soul is tired of following rules. "Zayda, I mean it. You can't go wandering around out there. Promise me," mom demands.

"Mama, I have never lied to you before, and I am not starting on the day you leave," I reply.

"Oh, Zay. What am I going to do with you?" she asks, softening a bit and grabbing me in an embrace.

I am getting ready to reply with something terribly witty, but my father comes into the room. Conversations like these have no place in front of my dad. Not that he is a tyrant or anything, but he and I do not always see things the same way. "Smells good, Iris. Man, am I glad Zayda loves these things, so I can get some for my big belly," dad says with a wink. He is always making silly comments about his "big belly". When in fact, the provisions not being enough for us, he is skinny as a rail.

"Dad, do you ever get tired of making the same silly jokes?" I tease.

"Nope. If it weren't for these old, silly jokes, I wouldn't have any material," he laughs.

"I'm pretty sure nothing you say can qualify as a joke, Stephen," mom says. We all laugh at the truth behind her statement.

Despite our differences, I have to admit, I am going to miss my dad just as much as I was my mom. Silently reflecting on the moment, the three of us stand quietly, our bodies nearly touching in the small, cramped part of the tent that serves as our kitchen. Most of our meals only take some minor heating up to prepare, so it really isn't necessary to give up more of our precious space. On days like today, with the heat and humidity already oppressive, I long for an outdoor place to cook. However, none of us mind the closeness right now. We are all more than happy to just be near each other for this special time.

After the nostalgia passes, we all sit down and begin eating my birthday meal. Stuffing the fluffy pastries into my mouth as quickly as possible, I eat until I feel I will burst open.

"Slow down, Zay. You're going to choke," dad laughs.

"It's just so good," I say with powdered sugar falling down my chin. I am still gleefully enjoying the meal when a light rap sounds on our door. "I wonder who could be here so early in the morning?" I ask, rising from the table to answer it. Probably one of my friends rushing to be the first to tell me happy birthday, I think, smiling at the thought. I wonder which one it will be? I'm not sure who I truly expect, but when I open the door it is the absolute last person I ever would have thought of- Brighton. He stands in the doorway, the rising sun casting a halo around his head and making him even more handsome. Too shocked to say or do anything, I just stare at him. Looking equally uneasy, Brighton stares back.

Abruptly standing from the table and motioning with his arms to offer Brighton his seat, "Welcome," my father says.

"No thank you. Please continue your meal," Brighton replies.

As I squeeze myself into the farthest corner of the room, trying to put as much space between the two of us, I can feel his gaze searching me again, and I immediately begin to flush. I try my best to ignore his presence, but there is this undeniable connection tethering the two of us together. "Do you always have such lavish meals?" Brighton asks innocently.

"Oh, goodness no. We usually have oats, but today is a special occasion. Our Zayda is seventeen today," mom replies.

Something briefly flickers across Brighton's face. It is gone too quickly for me to discern what it is exactly, but I could have sworn it is anguish. Recovering his composure completely, and leaving me to wonder if I were imagining things, Brighton says, "Well, happy birthday. I know we met momentarily on the dock, but allow me to properly introduce myself. I am Brighton Nash. My father and I serve on The Council of the Southeast."

Remembering that despite his beautiful and perfect face, he is responsible for sending away my parents, I spit, "I know who you are."

"Zayda!" my father scolds. "Do not be rude to a member of The Council. I am so sorry, Mr. Nash. Zayda has not been herself since hearing of our relocation."

"Think nothing of it," Brighton replies sincerely, "I'm sure it was a lot to take in. Especially, for one who is about to begin her year of Turning. Had I realized, I would have tried to persuade Eli to make a different choice to rehabilitate the other village."

"I just bet you would have," I respond. If I don't leave here right away, I am going to say or do something that will land me in a great deal of trouble. "Mom, I'm suddenly not feeling very hungry. May I be excused?"

"But, Zay, your mom has been killing herself in here all morning," dad replies.

"No, it's okay. Go ahead. I will put some on the table for you to have later. Don't wander off too far, we will be leaving soon," mom says.

I know I am being a brat, but I can't stand to be in the same room with that disgusting monster. Who was he trying to fool with his nice guy routine? "I'll just be over at Reggie's," I say. I swear, with the mention of Reggie's name, Brighton's posture changes again. What was this guy's game, and why was he playing it with me, I wonder?

On my way out the door, I hear the conversation pick back up. I can't make out many details, but I do hear Brighton say, "I wanted to make sure they made it here safely. He is the best doctor..." All the rest was lost to the wind.

***

"What the hell?" Reggie says. The two of us are sitting in the grass on the edge of his tent. I absently pull blades out and toss them lightly into the air. Reggie just looks casually into the distance, trying to wrap his head around the news. "I don't think I've ever heard of a council member making a private house call before. This is crazy."

"I know. In my kitchen. Can you believe that? Brighton Nash in Alon two days in a row What could all this mean?" I ask.

"I have no idea. And you said he was acting like a decent human being? I figured anyone on The Council would have to be a complete monster to do the things they do," Reggie says, shifting his weight so he is leaning closer to me. Despite the heat, it is comforting to have him close. We are being careful to keep our voices low, but both of us are on edge knowing one of them is lurking about.

"Something about him feels off. I can't quite put my finger on it, but I don't think he is exactly who he claims to be," I say, tossing my latest handful of earth absently in his direction.

"What do you mean? Like he isn't from The Council?" Reggie asks, wiping the grass off his brown pants.

"No, not that. I...I don't know. You have to just trust me on this one. Mr. Nash has a secret," I reply.

"Did I hear my name?" Brighton asks, emerging from the side of the tent.

"Dang! You scared the crap out of me," Reggie yells, standing up and running his hands nervously through his hair. "I didn't hear you arrive. I'm Reggie."

"Pleased to meet you," Brighton says, reaching out to grasp Reggie's extended hand. I watch carefully for any indication that Reggie is being shocked by the exchange.

Nothing. Neither one of them appear to have traded anything other than a normal handshake. I just add that to my growing pile of Brighton Nash questions.

"What are you doing, stalking me?" I quip.

Brighton laughs; it is a husky sound but not unpleasant, and the smile accompanying it makes his face look younger than his twenty-two years. Brighton is one of the lucky ones who was already eighteen before The Cure was given. Despite my undying hatred for him, I find myself once again admiring his flawless face. He is, without a question of a doubt, the most beautiful person I have ever seen. I desperately wish those intense, purple eyes would stop looking at me; I can feel my face blushing with every pass.

Remembering his manners and the position of the man in front of him, "Would you care to come in for a drink?" Reggie offers.

"Sure, I could go for a drink." As Brighton looks around the room, he appears to be intrigued by everything he sees. "Nice tent. I've never spent much time in one. I guess I thought they would be different somehow," he says.

"Like with dirt floors and such?" I ask sarcastically.

Again, he just laughs.

"Do I amuse you?" I question.

"Not amuse. You just always seem to surprise me," Brighton replies. He seems to be sizing up Reggie and me, as if trying to figure us out. "How long have you both been at Alon?"

"All of our lives," Reggie answers, handing Brighton a cold glass of water.

"Are you together? You know, like a couple?" Brighton asks before taking a long sip. His intense eyes stare over the top of the raised glass, searching my face for a response. I just maintain my grimace and ignore the question.

Surprised by the directness of the question, Reggie stammers a bit, "Uh...well...no...I mean...we are best friends, but...you know."

Handing the glass back to Reggie, "Thank you for the hospitality," Brighton says. He seems happy with Reggie's response, and begins to walk toward the door.

I just continue to glare at him, hoping my death stare will finally work on someone. "Did you have a specific reason for coming in here and interrupting yet another part of my day, and asking questions that are none of your business?" I ask him, crossing my arms over my chest. Brighton asking about our relationship just didn't make sense. Why would he care? Seriously, didn't this guy have some important things to tend to?

As if reading my mind, Brighton says, offering us both another smile, "Well, it was nice visiting with you both, but I really must get back to business." He turns to leave the tent, but right as he is about to exit he faces me again. His purple eyes smoldering, "I am truly sorry I interrupted your birthday celebration. Please forgive my ignorance." With that, he walks out and is gone.

Ducking his head outside to make sure the coast is clear, and drawing out his words exaggeratedly, Reggie says, "Oookaay. Whhaatt just happened?" Despite his playfulness, he looks upset.

"I really wish I knew," I reply, shaking my head to clear away the barrage of feelings I am experiencing, "I really wish I knew."

"Weird, but it doesn't matter right now. Let's go see your parents before they take off," Reggie says, reaching out to take my hand.

Sucking in a deep breath, "I almost forgot about that," I say, grabbing his warm palm. For like the fifth time in my life, and third in the past few days, tears threaten to spill over onto my cheeks. Reggie lets go of my hand and sweetly wipes the moisture off my cheek. This small gesture makes me remember just how lucky I am to have him in my life, and I smile despite my immense sadness. "Thank you," I say.

"I would do anything for you, Zayda. Please remember that," Reggie says. The sincerity in his eyes matches that of his tone.

"I know you would," I say. Reggie would go to the end of the earth for me, and every part of me knows this. I just hope that he understands it is Reggie my friend who is supporting me, and not Reggie my boyfriend.

"Shall we?" Reggie asks, while bowing and offering up his arm for me to take.

The motion is extremely exaggerated and ridiculous looking, and I laugh loudly. "Oh, such a proper gentleman," I say, as we walk out to say farewell to my parents for what might be the last time.

**

Everyone else has already gathered, so Reg and I have to fight our way to the front of the crowd. My parents are hugging everyone around them, as they are presented with gifts for the journey. The citizens of Alon are incredibly humble people, and having a large group fawn over you tends to make you a little crazy. I can see my mom trying to hold it together, so I jump in as soon as there is an opening. "You guys are quite the celebrities," I joke, putting my arms around her neck. She hugs me back for a moment, and then we release each other. I know she would embrace me longer if we were alone, but neither of us want to make a scene in public.

"What do you mean, you guys?" dad laughs, situating his travel pack on his arm. "I'm the one they really want to see."

"Sure, Stephen. They have all been swooning over you all morning. One of the older ladies even asked me if she could have your autograph," mom snorts playfully. Returning her attention to packing last minute items in her bag, she sighs and shakes her head playfully.

Relieved they can be at ease during this time, I begin to feel better. We spend the next thirty minutes mingling with every member of our community, many of whom I rarely get a chance to engage with. Whenever someone leaves our village, we make a big deal out of it. Going out into the ruins is always dangerous, and my parents will be passing at least two dead cities-plus many more dead towns-before reaching their destination. I shudder thinking about the real perils they will face. However, looking out into the crowd of my people, my heart begins to feel lighter; I really am not alone. My friends and their families are front and center, as usual. I even manage to get a non-snarky smile from Viola. She'll make up for that, I laugh internally.

"Stephen, the sun has risen over the edge of the river. It is time to go," mom says.

I turn to watch the last rays of light emerge and cast golden ripples onto the murky water. "What a beautiful sight," I say aloud. Mom puts her arms around my shoulders, and dad puts his around us both. Like this, we stand for several minutes; lost in independent thought, yet connected as one in our grief. "I don't ever want to let go," I whisper.

"Me either," they both respond.

"You are strong, Zayda. So much stronger than I ever imagined. It is because of your strength, I am confident you will not only survive this but blossom from it," dad says.

Struck by his uncharacteristically moving words, I hug him even tighter. "Thank you, daddy."

"Uh hum. Sorry to interrupt, but we must get going if we hope to make it before nightfall," one of the escorts says. He is a man in his forties, probably one of the youngest adults in our village, and not someone I am all too familiar with. I make a conscious effort to memorize his face, so that if needed, he can take me to my parents.

"We are ready," mom replies. She turns to me one last time and places her hands on my face, cupping my cheeks. "I love you more than anything, Zayda. Be strong. We will be back soon."

My father does not speak again. Instead, he offers me one of his trademark winks, and then they are off. I watch them walk for as long as I can still see their silhouettes. Even long after that, I yearningly gaze down the hill at The Lost City, hoping this is all a joke and they will reappear. It is not a joke, and they do not come back.

***

I walk alone back to my tent. My head is hurting from the tears that I finally allow to flow, and I want to lie down. As I walk, I pass many of the villagers, but none of them speak to me. I know this is not out of disrespect. In fact, it is there way of showing me that they understand my mourning. I kick at the dirt to keep my mind from dwelling too much on the situation; I am on the edge of totally melting down, and I would rather do that in the privacy of my own home.

Finally, I arrive and go inside. Too tired, and too upset, I do not even bother to take off my dusty boots before sinking down into my sleeping bag. I stare at the ceiling for many hours, allowing myself to give in to the grief.

At some point, I must have fallen asleep because a few hours later, a light sound outside of my, now very, large feeling tent wakes me. Normally, we are not given such indulgences like sleeping during the day, but considering the current events, I was allowed to sink into solace for most of the morning. Groggy and still not fully awake, I open the door to see what has caused the sound. Standing there with a note in his hand, is a boy whom I have never seen before. He is about my age and with no symptoms of The Turning visible.

"I didn't mean to bother you. I was just going to leave this letter and go. I'm Kieran," the boy says.

I just stand blinking at him. My brain is too clouded with residual sleep, and my eyes too swollen from my pity party to aid in any coherency. Unsure of what to do, he just continues to stand there looking at me awkwardly. Trying to wake up more, I wipe my hand across my eyes; it does not work.

Obviously nervous, Kieran begins chattering away. "My father and I were just transferred here this morning, and I heard about your parents being relocated. I couldn't help but feel guilty, so I wanted to give you this apology note. Well, not really a note, just a bunch of drawings. I can't read or write, but you already know that. Duh! Why am I being such an idiot right now? I'm sure if I were you, I'd hate me completely. I don't blame you for that, but still, I wanted to say sorry. I guess there really isn't a reason to give it to you now since I already said everything and all. Well, not really everything, but most things. If you want it, you can have it. Geesh, sorry. I talk a lot when I'm nervous. I've just heard so much about you, and you sound really cool. I don't want to get off on the wrong foot with you. I...,"

All I can do to stop his babbling is hold up my hand. Thankfully, he takes the hint and shuts up. This guys would give Viola a run for her money. I turn around, walk to the wash bin, splash water on my face, and then return to Kieran, who is still standing in the doorway. "Thanks for the note," I say, snatching it out of his hand and shutting the door.

"Dear God, this day just keeps getting weirder and weirder," I mumble to myself. A few minutes later, I am back in bed planning on sleeping off the rest of the worst birthday ever.

THE RUINS

"This is crazy! You know what will happen if we get caught leaving the village. I know you are having a hard time dealing with your parents leaving, but that is no reason to go all suicidal on us," Posy says. She is standing in front of me blocking my path.

"I'm not suicidal. Come on, don't be stupid, Posy. I'm just tired of sitting around here doing nothing all the time. We only have one year left, and I do not plan on spending it picking potatoes. Tonight is the perfect night to do it; Bobby is on night watch, and he falls asleep after the first half hour. Besides, I've kind of already been down there a few times before," I reply.

"Say what? When did this happen?" Reggie asks angrily.

"The first time was right after Robinson...you know, and the others were last month. I know it sounds insane, but I just couldn't stand sitting here waiting for my life to end. There has to be so much more to the world than this damn levee. Don't you guys want to see at least some of the rest before we...you know?" I say, trying to sidestep Posy. Despite her small size, she is doing a great job of keeping rooted to my spot.

"You know, avoiding saying it will not make it stop," Viola states. "We are all going to start showing symptoms soon, even you. Hell, Kyle has over half of them already."

Kyle lowers his yellow eyes to the ground, and runs his brittle nails through his thinning hair. We all know how hard it is for him to be the first to begin the transition, and most of us-with the exception of Viola-do our best not to mention it. She seems to forget that Kyle is still a person and doesn't want to be reminded of what he is going through. I guess it is easy for her to forgot what will happen to even her when she is sitting there with her perfect, thick, red hair and beautiful, blue-eyes. Some days, I really hate her.

"At some point, Viola, you might decide to be a bit more considerate and watch your big mouth," Camden snaps.

Shock runs across Viola's face. "Cam? How could you say that to me?" she questions, her shoulders slumping with the verbal slap. We all just stare bewildered. Camden has never corrected Viola's behavior before, and we are all just as surprised as she is. In the past, no one could convince her to bite her tongue, and we have all tried many times. Maybe he will succeed where all of us have failed a thousand times before.

"Someone has to say it. You walk around here spewing insults at everyone like you are above us all. You aren't above us! You are *exactly* the same as *all* of us! And soon, you will be a monster just like the rest of us! Until then, why don't you try pretending you aren't already one!" Camden yells.

"Woah, that's a bit harsh, Cam," Reggie says, trying to diffuse the situation.

"No, it isn't. You don't have to hear all the vile things she says at home. I can't sit by and ignore it anymore. Especially considering...," Camden pauses and lifts his pantleg, exposing a giant sore on his calf.

"But that isn't possible," Posy states, "your eyes haven't changed yet. What does this mean?"

"I think it means the rules have changed," I say.

Everyone looks at me waiting for me to explain my comment, but I haven't completely processed it yet.

"What do you mean, Zay?" Viola asks. Judging from her soft touch on her brother's shoulder, I would say she has already forgiven him for his outburst.

"I mean the virus has mutated. It looks like the symptoms can skip around in order, and that means we may not have as long as we originally thought," I say.

"You're right," Kyle says. "I had my first craving last week."

We all gasp, and then instantly regret it. The shame on his face when he says the word "craving" drives a dagger through my heart. We have all heard about the cravings from those who have turned before us, and it sounds like the worst thing ever. Robinson described it as smelling frying bacon any time you got within ten feet of another human, and wanting nothing more than to rip their throats out to find the treat inside. If Kyle is already having the cravings, he has less than two months left.

"Dude, no wonder you have been acting so freaked out lately. You should have told us," Reggie says, taking a step closer to Kyle. I think this is his way of showing he isn't afraid.

"Yeah, we could have helped you deal," Posy adds.

"Sure, I should have just said, 'hey guys, you are all looking and smelling quite tasty today.'"

"Well, if I'm looking particularly delicious I would love to hear about it," I joke.

"Me too," Posy adds smiling.

"Maybe, I'll start putting gravy behind my ears to mess with you," Camden laughs.

"Ha ha, guys. I get it. You all think this is hilarious," Kyle says with mock irritation. He can't fake his anger too long, and his smile is back in a few moments. "Thanks for trying to make me feel better."

"There is one thing I know for sure now," I say teasingly.

"What?" Kyle asks.

"We are definitely going to The Ruins now."

Everyone smiles and nods in agreement.

"Get your gear and meet me at our spot in an hour," I state.

***

Night has settled over our camp like an onyx blanket by the time we all meet up again. That is good; we will be able to sneak away easier this way. In the past, I was always alone, so getting away unnoticed was not difficult. More people means more risk.

"We must be extra cautious to make sure we don't get caught," I say quietly. Everyone is looking at me nervously awaiting the game plan. I guess I saw it happening, but I don't recall the exact moment I became the unofficial leader of our little motley crew. My best estimate would be when Kyle started shying away a few months back. As the oldest, he was the natural fit for the longest time. When the transformation took hold, he lost that part of himself. "I believe the best thing for us to do it split up into groups of two. We can rendezvous at the cathedral in the middle of town," I add, hoping the uneasiness is not evident in my voice.

"I call Camden," Viola blurts.

I am secretly happy to see her choosing her brother; that means they have really made up during their time getting ready. Tension would only make this adventure more dangerous, and it is already risky enough.

"Okay, great. I'll go with Posy. Kyle, you and Reg can team up. Does that work for everyone?"

"Do you think it is safe for two girls to go alone?" Reggie asks skeptically.

"Well, if one girl can make it several times, then I think two will do just fine. Right, Pose?" I say, winking at her.

"Darn right!" Posy says, high-fiving me.

"Girl power!" I laugh.

Genuinely smiling for the first time in days, "Dorks!" Viola says. She walks over and nudges me on the shoulder, "This is pretty exciting. I can't believe you are such a secret badass and have been down there alone. I think I might have underestimated you."

"Only one way to find out," I say, nudging her back. "Let's get going. Posy and I will go first. The rest of you watch our path from over by my tent, and then follow when we disappear into the park. You ready, Pose?"

"As I'll ever be."

Carefully, the two of us make our way down the steep embankment. I've almost fallen on this hill many times before, but thankfully, the weather has been dry lately. Normally, this would be much more difficult. The last time I went down was after a two-day rainstorm, and the hill was incredibly slippery. Climbing down on dirt is much easier, especially for everyone else's first time. Posy is taking small, careful steps, pausing every few feet to readjust her gait. She never has been one to embrace adventure, but right now, I sense she is enjoying herself a little.

"Why didn't you tell me about this before?" Posy asks, pausing and glancing at me momentarily. She doesn't seem angry, but I can sense the hurt in her voice.

"I guess I wanted to keep it my own thing for a while. Plus, I didn't know if you would try to stop me. I've had such a hard time this past year, and this made me feel in control again," I reply.

"I get all of that, but I'm one of your best friends. Don't you know I will always support you? And, I get what it is like to lose someone you love. You don't have to be tough," Posy says.

Despite her words of support, something else seems off with her, but I do not have time to dwell on whatever it is. "I'm sorry if I hurt your feelings. I know you have my back. I think I just lost myself for a little bit. I'm back now for good," I say, smiling to ease her pain. Tears rim her brown eyes, and she looks on the verge of losing it. "We can work all of this out later. For now, we need to focus. Do you see the building with the green and white canopy?" "Yes, I see it."

"Okay, that's where we are going first. Sneak around the back and then wait for me," I say.

"Alone?"

"You've got this. I need to make sure no one has spotted us from camp before we go any farther. Girl power, remember?" I whisper.

"Girl power," she replies, hesitation marring her soft voice.

I watch her stumble a few times as she descends the remainder of the hill. Once, I think she is going to go down, but she steadies herself and continues. When she reaches the bottom, she turns and flashes me a thumbs-up. Relief washes over me. I will feel terrible if Posy hurts herself embarking on a crazy mission with me. I peer down the hill at her, waiting for her to reach the building. It feels like hours, but I know it has only been a few minutes. Soon, Posy's head, and all her black hair on top of it, are slinking into the shadows behind the building. I turn around and look back up at camp. I can barely make out the images of four figures where we had left the others; they appear to be looking down upon us, waiting for their turns. Straining my eyes to canvas the rest of the village, I try to pick out any signs of movement. Among the hundreds of tents, families crowded together for their night's rest, all is quiet. The last dying embers of the fire are fizzling out in the middle of them all, so it is becoming progressively more difficult to see the outlines clearly. For several minutes, I pan left to right repeatedly. Once, I think I catch a glimpse of activity toward the elder's meeting place, but as soon as I see it, it is gone. Probably just a stray dog. Satisfied that we have not been found out, I head down to meet up with Posy.

***

"What is this place?" Posy asks. She is staring in awe when I meet up with her. Totally entranced by the sights of the city, she hadn't even heard me approaching.

"My mom told me that it used to be a café."

"What's a café?" she asks.

"A place where people used to gather to eat. Mom says they could come here at any time, day or night, and the people inside would feed them," I reply, kicking packed dirt off my shoes.

"So, someone else cooked for them? That's wild. I wish someone would cook for me; I'm awful," Posy giggles.

"You don't have to tell me that, I've had your food," I respond, holding my nose and sticking out my tongue.

"Hey! You weren't supposed to agree," Posy says, putting her hands on her hips, mocking irritation.

"Can you picture it? I mean like it was back then?"

We take a few moments to look around the abandoned structure. I close my eyes and imagine the metal tables, all crowded with people from the old days, full of life. Families eagerly chatting away about the day's events while they stuff their faces with beignets dusted with white sugar, waiters and waitresses, dressed in white aprons, bustling about refilling coffee until everyone has their fill, and laughter permeating every inch of the space. Part of me didn't believe the stories were true, but another part-the one who knew my mother would never spread falsehoods-lived in awe of that time.

"I wonder if they knew how good they had it?" I ask, more to myself than to Posy.

"Probably not. I think we always take things for granted in the moment. I know I sure do," Posy replies.

Glancing at Posy, I can see she is far away in thought, and I'm sure it includes her time with her mother. As much as I want to stay there consumed by our memories, we have to get going. "We should make our way toward the cathedral," I say, "The others are waiting for us to make it across the street before they come down."

Visibly shaking off the last tendrils of her daydream, Posy replies, "Okie dokie. Let's go."

"Okay, stay close to me. We will be out in the open for a minute, so we need to move fast."

We crouch low, and hurriedly making our way across the cobblestone road. Running in this position is difficult, and I catch myself wobbling a few times. The road is uneven and several times I smash the front of my boot on a raised stone. Judging from the grimace on Posy's face, I'd say she is having the same issue. Pausing, a few times, I listen carefully for any sounds of approaching danger, but all is quiet. This part of the Old City is my favorite; the buildings all transport me to decades past. On the lower levels, restaurants, shops, and bars look out toward the street. A few trinkets can still be seen hanging in some of the windows; beads, novelty T-shirts, and alligator heads are among the most routinely spotted.

"There sure are some weird things in there," Posy states, pointing in the window of a nearby shop.

"I know," I agree, "These particular customs of the old people are a mystery to me."

"How far into the Old City have you gone?"

"Only eight blocks or so each direction. I've always wanted to explore more, but it is kinda freaky in here alone. Plus, I had to worry about mom and dad waking up and missing me in the middle of the night. Guess that won't be an issue now," I reply sadly. Posy doesn't respond. I know it isn't out of spite, but rather out of respect for my feelings still being worked out. "I think tonight would be a good night for us to venture out a little farther," I add, faking cheerfulness.

"Whatever you say, boss lady," Posy chimes back.

We abandon our spot in front of the shop window and head left toward the square. I can see the large, overgrown trees silhouetted against the pitch-black sky. Gazing upward, I search for signs of the moon, but it is currently sleeping behind a large bank of clouds. Moments later, we pass through the enormous iron gates into the park. Although the brick path remains intact inside, nature has reclaimed most of the once well-maintained area; flowers and shrubs threaten to knock us off our trail, and tree roots penetrate the concrete, causing small uneven ramps to jet out. Most of the times I had been in here before, the unkempt trees overhead blocked out most light, but nothing compared to the complete darkness we were in now. This part of the walk would be difficult and treacherous. Posy and I grip each other's hands firmly, so we do not get separated in the dark mass.

"The others should be on their way now," I say to fill the silence.

"At least the first group," she replies.

I can hear the shakiness in her voice. "Don't worry, Pose. We will be back out where it is clearer again soon," I say attempting to comfort her.

"I'm not worried. I'm scared out of my mind."

"I promise there is nothing to be afraid of out here. I have never encountered another living being in all of the times I have explored the Old City," I say as we round a corner and come into the last half of the square.

"That is one of the things that worries me. Where are all the animals? It is far too quiet out here," she states.

"Yeah, you're right. Until you mentioned it, I hadn't noticed how unusually silent it is."

"Was it like this last time?" Posy asks.

"No, there were lots of birds chirping and other nighttime sounds. It is one of the things I usually enjoy the most."

"This doesn't feel right, Zay," Posy says.

"Let's just hurry up and get out of here."

We grab each other's hands tighter and beeline for the exit that has just come into view in front of us. I don't want to admit it, but Posy is right; something is off. We walk only a few more feet when suddenly, a small shuffle sounds behind us. Both of us stop dead in our tracks. I drop her hand and hold my finger up to my mouth. She nods in understanding. Listening carefully, I focus on detecting any sound in the dark night. Nothing. The noise has stopped. Holding my breath and speaking as quietly as possible, "Maybe the others have caught up with us. We did stop and look around for a minute, and they are probably moving faster because they are nervous," I say, trying to calm her down.

"They wouldn't just creep up on us. They would say something," Posy declares, mirroring my near silence.

"Maybe, but maybe not. They are probably freaking out."

"Look, I can see the entrance to the church," Posy says, relief flooding her voice.

I must admit, I am relieved as well. This is the first time I have been in the Old City and felt threatened. Even though I cannot see our pursuer, I know they are there. We resume walking, picking up the pace exponentially, and exit the park through an exact replica of the gate we entered. Not daring to pause, we make our way over to the front steps of the large cathedral. Both of our shoes clunk loudly on the pavement, announcing our location to anyone within five blocks. I openly cringe, but do not slow my pace.

Within just a few moments, we are standing directly in front of the massive structure. A brief break in the clouds illuminates the front of the building in a soft glow. I find myself, despite my fears, becoming mesmerized by the sight. Even though nature is beginning to reclaim the building, and the paint is peeling away like a layer of burnt skin, it is beautiful to behold. The white building stands over four stories high with three large steeples pointing toward the heavens. A clock, stuck at twelve on the dot, adorns the middle of the building on the largest spire, and decorative glass, a rainbow of colors, ornaments each window.

"Wow! It is even prettier up close. What kind of glass is that?" Posy asks, releasing my hand.

Shaking my appendage to get the blood flow back, I reply, "Stained glass. Isn't it magnificent? Mom said it was used in all the old houses of worship. I wish we could see it during the day. I bet it is even more spectacular."

"I'm sure when the sun hits it just right, it is amazing."

"Perhaps that can be our next adventure?" I suggest.

"If we survive this one, I will consider it."

"Deal," I reply.

After looking around the front of the church and enjoying its splendor, we sit under the outside canopy, shrouded in shadows, and wait for the rest to join us. Finding a hiding spot is not difficult; there are deep recesses on the porch where we easily slink away and became one with the night. As we sit here, I concentrate on the sounds around us. There are not any animals near us still, nor any animal voices, but occasionally I can pick up on the faint sounds of walking; like whispers in the night, they are not loud but ever present. I want desperately to believe it is the others, however, the location of the noise makes it seem improbable. Most of the clamors come from our left or right and some even behind us, but never from inside the park where our friends should be. They are spread out enough in time that I am confident it is only one person sizing us up from as many angles as they can, but I can't be one hundred percent sure.

Posy is listening closely also, "Do you think they took a different way in?"

I just shake my head and hold a finger to my mouth. Someone is right by us. I can hear their breathing to my left. Panicky, I stifle my breath, grab my weapon out of my boot, and rise to my feet. Registering the item in my hand, Posy's eyes grow wide with shock. Crap! I probably shouldn't have grabbed it out, but I can't be defenseless out here. The last thing I want to do is come face to face, unarmed, with a Turned; they are vicious foes, and we will not stand a chance. Even though I know staying quiet won't do any good-they can smell us-I make myself a statue and pray for the best.

Just as the clouds again mask the moon, casting us in complete darkness once more, rustling can be heard in front of us and directly to our left. It is pointless to try and see more than two feet in front of my face. Posy and I are totally helpless. Petrified, I squeeze my eyes shut and reach for her in the dark.

UNINVITED

"What are you guys up to?" a voice booms from the darkness. Posy and I both scream and jump out from our hiding spot, ready for a fight.

"Posy, Zayda!" a voice yells from in front of us.

Again, we both scream at the top of our lungs.

"What the hell is all of the yelling for?" Viola asks, stepping out of the park. "Have you both gone mad?"

"Zay? You ok?" Reggie asks, emerging from the foliage, out of breath and gasping for air.

"I'm fine," I say shakily.

"Thank god," Kyle says, exiting the park.

"I know, right?" Camden adds. "You guys just scared the shit out of us. Why are you screaming like that?"

My mouth drops open as I count my friends standing in front of me. One...Viola, Two...Reggie, Three...Kyle, and Four...Camden. If they are all there, who spoke to our left? Posy must have had the same thought because she runs toward the voice and makes an amazing tackle. The duo is rolling around on the ground for several seconds before any of us realize what is happening. Jumping in to help, Camden and Reggie begin to flank the figure and pin its arms to the ground.

"Hey man! Let me go!" a semi-familiar voice shouts.

"No way," Cam screams back. "Who are you and what are you doing here?"

Making my way over to where the scuffle is underway, I can't help my brain from scrambling to place the voice. The source is someone I know, but not well. It is obviously a he. He sounds about our age. All my friends are here. I only know one other teenager our age. "Kieran?" I ask suspiciously.

"Yes, Zayda, it's me. Now please call off your boyfriend," he pleads.

"He's not my...Oh it doesn't matter. Guys, let him up," I say.

"Who is this guy?" Reggie asks, annoyance permeating his voice.

I don't know if he is annoyed by the fact that he had to practically fight a random guy, or if it was because I almost said he isn't my boyfriend. Either way, he is pissed, and it is obvious. Passing my eyes back and forth from Kieran to Reggie, I notice the many similarities. Both are muscular and tone. Both are classically handsome. Both are really irritating me right now.

"This is Kieran. He and his father moved in yesterday when my parents were relocated," I state coldly. "I think the more important question is why is he here?"

Kieran sits up and takes us all in. Besides his wrinkled clothes and tousled hair, he looks to still be pretty coherent. This is the first time I have actually looked at him without tired swollen eyes. He really is stunning. His face is very well sculpted, his eye color is difficult to see in the dark, but looks to be a deep shade of brown or even black, and his ebony hair is still very lush and full. I can tell from their expressions that Viola and Posy are on the same page as me.

"I saw you guys sneaking out earlier, and I wanted to see what you were up to. I know I shouldn't have, but you are the only kids my age at camp. I was nosey," Kieran says sheepishly.

"Nosey! You scared the crap out of me because you were nosey!" I shout.

"You? What about me? At least you have been out here before," Posy yells. The look on her face shows how much she instantly regrets her statement.

"You have done this before?" Kieran asks, awe showing in his expression.

I hate the way he is looking at me, like I am some sort of hero. I'm not a hero. "That isn't important," I reply sharply. "What is important is that you are out here being all creepy stalker on us, running around the building and circling us from left and right."

Sincerity washing over his face, "What are you talking about?" Kieran asks. He truly looks dumfounded. "I snuck ahead of you while you were in the park and then waited on the left side of the cathedral for the right time to come out."

"But? If that wasn't you, then who is it?" I ask, terror building in my veins.

We all slowly swivel our heads to the right and listen. The faint sound of feet moving toward us can still be heard, only now it is combined with a low growling noise.

"Is that one of The Turned?" Kyle whispers.

"I. Don't. Know," I mouth silently, not daring to make a sound. Pointing at the far corner, away from the sound, I try to guide my friends to a safer place.

Reggie, shaking his head no and flattening himself against the front of the building, begins to make his way over toward the uninvited guest. He has always been blessed with the ability to move undetected when he wants, but I am much better. Still, I try to be at ease with him slinking, and pray he will make it without being noticed. My stomach clenches when I think about him coming face-to-face with one of those monsters.

Once he is at the edge of the building, he turns to us and puts his finger up to his mouth to tell us to be completely quiet. No problem. I think we are all about to pass out from holding our breath and my head is beginning to spin. Reggie leans his head around the building, and then abruptly snaps it back. Even from a distance, I can see his frame shaking. He holds up three fingers.

'Three?" I mouth back. My body tenses with the news. We will never be able to fight off three of them. Not to mention, there hasn't been a turned in the wild for a few years. He just nods his head. Behind me, I hear someone sniffling in fear. One Turned is bad enough, but three is a death sentence for us all.

Reggie slowly and silently makes his way back toward us. "They are a few blocks away. If we go through the park right now, we might make it," he faintly whispers.

We all nod at him and rise to make our way across to the park. The journey itself is only about thirty feet, but it might as well be a mile. Viola is hyperventilating, and Camden is having to half carry her. Posy is stifling sobs, and I doubt she can fully see where she is going through the torrent of tears. Kieran appears to be limping from his welcome into our group. Reggie won't stop looking back at me long enough to keep up a good pace, and Kyle keeps sniffing the air every few steps like a bloodhound. I didn't think we would ever make it to the camouflage of the park.

Somehow, we do.

Once inside, we all take off in a dead sprint for the other side. None of us care about our ailments, or the multitude of scrapes we are getting from the brush; we are running for our lives. I clear the gate first and immediately go across the street to hide behind the café. My friends follow my lead, one by one, and soon they are safely by my side. We will wait here for several minutes; some of us need to catch our breath before heading up the hill. I am not out of breath, so I spend my time scanning the town for any sign of The Turned. I can't see any.

After about five minutes, we are finally convinced we are alone. We all hurriedly make our way back up the levee. The journey up is not as covert as the one down, and to be honest, it is much more difficult because I have spent all my adrenaline reserves running. Plus, I think we have all individually decided that whatever punishment the elders or Council dish out is much better than the alternative behind us. I do not chance a look back until I am all the way to the top. There are no words to describe the horror I feel when I do. Standing directly in the middle of the street, are The Turned, and they are staring right at us.

***

"We have to tell someone," Kieran says, for the one millionth time.

"No. We. Do. Not," I snort.

We are all sitting around trying to discuss our next move. The Turned are gone from down below. A few minutes ago, we watched them disappear behind one of the buildings. I am relieved a bit because of this, and that apparently, no one but Kieran is aware of our departure, so there will not be a punishment from The Council. However, some in the group still believe we should rat ourselves out. I'm a survivalist, and, to me, that sounds like the dumbest idea in the world.

"Look, I know we messed up by leaving camp, but what if they come up here? We are putting people's lives in danger," Kieran says.

"I get where you are coming from, bro, but we can't just tell the elders we snuck out. They will kill us," Camden says.

"At least that would not be a literal death," Kieran snaps.

"No, but we will wish it was," Reggie says.

"I'm going on record as saying we need to tell," Kieran protests.

"Noted, and noted, and noted," I growl.

"I think we are all forgetting the most important thing," Viola states.

Camden looks at her quizzically, "What is that?"

"Why are there turned in the Old City at all? Shouldn't they be dead? The Healers come and take everyone away before they can fully convert, right? And then they kill them. This makes no sense at all. I mean, three wild turned, that's not even possible. So where did these guys come from?" Viola adds.

In our haste to get back to the village, none of us has even taken the time to fully process the situation until now. Viola is right; there shouldn't be any turned, anywhere, but what does this mean? "I don't know," I say.

"Short answer, The Turned are either turning before The Healers can get to them, or The Healers are lying about destroying them after the change. Either way, we have to find out," Kyle states. He looks extra pale tonight, and I can see the veins on his face beginning to swell. He is getting dangerously close to the end.

"There is only one way to find out, and that is, go to The Sacred City. Which, in case you have forgotten, is forbidden," Posy warns.

"True, but didn't we decide to start breaking all of the rules?" I ask, wagging my eyebrows.

"Ugh! You are impossible," Posy replies.

"So, we make a plan to go off and figure out what is happening?" Reggie asks.

"I think that is our only choice," I reply. Man, I wish I was more sure of what I am saying. My friends are looking to me for guidance, and I am possibly steering them into peril.

"I get all of that," Kieran says, "but we need to take care of one problem at a time, and right now that problem is them getting into camp."

"Kieran is right; we need to make sure we haven't put everyone in harm's way. How about this? I will sit up and look out tonight. If there is any sign of them again, we will tell the elders in the morning. Deal?" I ask.

"Fine! But I am waiting with you," Kieran replies.

"Don't you trust me?" I ask, sarcastically making a face at him.

Picking up on my sarcasm and returning it, "To be honest, I trust you less than anyone I have ever met before."

"Fair enough," I say, shrugging my shoulders dismissively. "You don't have to trust me, and I don't have to trust you." I stand up to position myself close to the edge, so I can be at the best vantage point. Kieran follows me over, a look of satisfaction on his face. Apparently, he is used to getting his way and quite enjoys it. "Let's set up post," I say, trying not to smack the grin off his face.

"Sure thing, boss lady," he says, repeating Posy's words from before. Rolling my eyes, I turn away and begin setting my things down. Kieran Just might be the most annoying person I've ever met.

***

While the rest of the group, except for Reggie-who has run back to his tent to pick us up supplies for the night-head back to their tents to get some sleep, Kieran and I set up our sleeping bags on the edge of the village. Posy pauses twice to shoot me nervous and knowing glances, and I know she is going to give me hell about the weapon tomorrow. For now, I must put that out of my mind and focus on our task. We have a great view of The Old City from this spot, and I am confident we will be able to see anyone who tries to breach our perimeter. I honestly hope that does not happen, but if it does, we are ready to sound the alarm.

"What are the chances they will make it up here? Kieran asks.

"Probably pretty slim. That hill is tough enough when you *aren't* one of The Turned," I say, trying to convince myself as much as him.

"What will we do if they do? Kieran says.

"I guess run and get the guards. There really isn't much else to do," I reply. Before he asked me these questions, I hadn't really considered the likelihood that they might actually breach the perimeter. "Let's hope it doesn't come to that."

"Sorry again for scaring you down below. If I had known...well, I wouldn't have tried to freak you all out," Kieran says.

"It's okay. But...next time...why don't you save the spy routine and just ask us what's up," I reply.

"Sounds like a deal to me," Kieran responds. He is smiling at me with a big goofy grin, and I can't help but smile back. Despite his previous mess-ups, I think I might actually learn to like him. That is, if he doesn't start irritating me again. I laugh at this thought and Kieran says, "You are really pretty when you smile." Caught off guard, I just duck my head to cover the pink in my cheeks. "Sorry, I didn't mean to embarrass you. I just had to say it before I lost my nerve," he continues.

Pretending to just be returning with the supplies, Reggie interrupts us and asks, "Do you want me to wait up with you guys?" A few minutes ago, I saw him walk up and then hide away to watch us, but I ignored him and continued making my preparations for the night. While I wouldn't mind the extra set of eyes, Reggie is beginning to annoy me with his hovering, and obvious spying just now. Don't get me wrong, I appreciate him looking out for me, but sooner or later he is going to have to realize that I am not some fragile, little girl who needs his rescuing. At one time, I was and would have loved to have him watching over me. However, that helpless girl died when Robbie turned.

"Nope. Kieran and I have got it covered. Thanks for the offer though. If we are still worried tomorrow night, you can take a shift then. In the meantime, go get some sleep so you aren't a waste tomorrow. We don't want the elders to realize something is off, and if we all shuffle around like the dead, they will be on to us for sure," I reply, setting my canteen down next to my makeshift bed.

"Good thinking," he says, mumbling unconvincingly.

"I'll come fill you in first thing in the morning," I say.

"Okay," he says. His tone is a warring mixture of sadness and hostility, but I think the hostility is quickly winning the battle. He shoots a death glare in Kieran's direction before he begins walking away, and I can't help but feel bad about the way I treated him. Maybe, I'm the one making things weird between us. He hasn't confessed any feelings for me or anything like that. It is possible that I've imagined the change.

"Hey," I shout. Reggie turns around and faces me. I can see the anger extending up into his eyes. "Thanks for worrying about me. And, thanks for having my back down below. You're the best. Night."

"Night," he says back, without any emotion. He then quickly turns and walks away.

The minute he is out of sight, the guilt begins to consume me from the inside out. I don't want to hurt Reggie, ever, but a strong talk about boundaries is long overdue. For a long while, I thought I might be in love with Reggie. I spent my days fantasizing about the two of us being a couple and living happily ever after. He would meet me at the edge of our tent after a long day and sweep me up into a passionate kiss. I almost had myself convinced it was destiny. Then one day, I just stopped being able to picture it. The fantasy was the same, but the man had been replaced. No one in particular began to stand in for Reg, but where he used to be, a blank slate has appeared.

CONFESSIONS

"So, tell me everything I need to know about you," I say to Kieran. We are halfway through our first hour of operation No Re-Turned, as I have hilariously dubbed it, and I am getting bored. I pick up a dirt clod and mindfully chuck it over the edge of the hill.

"Sadly, there is not much to tell. I am an only child. My mom is dead-she didn't survive the plague. And, my father is a doctor," he replies.

"Woah, hold up! Your father is a doctor? Like a real doctor? He can use medicine and all that?" I ask, my mouth falling open in surprise. This is this most interesting piece of news I have ever heard, and here he is acting like it is no big deal.

"Yes, like a real, medicine using doctor. He actually worked on The Cure," he says, mindlessly drawing a circle in the dirt with a stick.

"Shut up! That is so freaking cool! Obviously, I knew real people had to have worked on The Cure, but I always figured they were being guarded in some secret facility somewhere," I joke.

"Some of them might be," he laughs, "but my dad always preferred to be in the camps with what he calls "the real heart of our country."

"So, that means your dad knows how to read. I'm so jealous! I have always wanted to learn how. When I was around five, I used to sneak into the elder meeting room and stare at the old documents for hours. I actually got pretty good at a few letters, but never enough to put whole words together," I confess, something about Kieran made me want to open up and tell all of my secrets.

"Well, if we are being entirely honest here... I can read," he admits, casting a nervous glance at me.

My mouth really gapes open in an exaggerated and surprised fashion with this revelation, and I just stare at Kieran in wonder. He can read! That means he might be able to help me learn how, but I don't know if I trust him enough to suggest it. I mean, he is practically a stranger.

"What, no sarcastic or funny comeback?" he asks, a small thread of worry beginning to spread across his face.

"Sorry, I am just a little shocked. Okay, a lot shocked," I say, returning my eyes to the town below. I can't get sidetracked from our main reason for being out here.

"Totally understandable. You are the first person I have ever told that to, so I didn't know what the reaction would be. I guess shock is better than running away, or any of the other horrible things I imagined," he says. I can sense the unease in his voice, so I do my best to look at him normally. He self-consciously diverts his eyes to the ground.

Trying to ease his mind, I ask playfully, "Like what? What unimaginable horrors did your mind conjure up?"

"Let's see, ratting me out to my dad. Who would kill me for breaking the rules by the way. He is a staunch rule follower. No exceptions. Or, galloping through the village yelling, Reader. We've got a reader here. Or, worst of all...thinking I was a freak and not letting me be your friend," he says, running a hand nervously through his thick hair.

I can hear the hurt in his voice when he says the last part. Kieran is not as tough as he is pretending to be, and something about that makes me like him even more. "Whelp, sorry to disappoint you. I hate rule followers, so ratting you out is not going to happen. My voice is hoarse from all of the yelling down the hill earlier, so no Paul Revere reenactment, and you are starting to grow on me, so you are stuck being my friend," I reply, gently bumping shoulders with him.

A gorgeous smile spreads across his perfect cheeks, and he seems to relax. "Thanks," he says.

The simplicity of his words does not take away from the meaning I can hear behind them; Kieran has never had friends before, and he is grateful for the opportunity.

"What was your old village like?" I ask, trying to keep the conversation going.

"Which one? We tend to jump around a lot," he answers, a sadness creeping back into his eyes.

"How about we start with your favorite," I reply.

He seems to perk up a little with that suggestion. "Hmmm, let me think about that for a second," he says, pausing, "I guess it would be Diego."

"You have been all the way to the southwest?" I ask, awestruck again. "No one I know has ever come from anywhere farther than the villages in the Midwest."

"We have been much farther than that. In fact, we have been outside of The Big Continent," he says. There is no hint of bragging evident in his tone, only a desire to be honest and relay the facts. "I guess in that way I am very lucky. In all, we have been to fifty different settlements, and to each of the ten regions."

"All ten? Holy cow! That is amazing. I've always wanted to travel outside of the southeast region, but it isn't allowed for us *normal* people," I sigh.

He reaches over and squeezes my shoulder gently, "There's still time." He winks as he says this, doing two things at once, reinforcing that he is giving me a hard time, and making my stomach do flips. This guy is really getting to me. Admittedly, he is the first new teenager to come into our village, and he is spectacular to behold, but that isn't it. I feel a pull toward him, much like the one I had felt with Brighton. Grrr, just thinking about Brighton makes my blood boil, and I toss another large clod of dirt down the hill. "Woah! What did that grass ever do to you?" he jokes.

"I was just thinking about someone," I reply.

"Anyone I know?" he asks.

"Nobody special," I say, pulling another chunk of earth free.

"Okay, then, back to the traveling then. You could always break the rules. In fact, you don't seem to be much of a strict rule follower anyway."

"Oh, I'm not. Doesn't matter though. I had my seventeenth birthday yesterday," I reveal.

"Mine is next week," he replies.

"Congratulations!" I chime.

"For what?" he says.

"Officially being the youngest in our group," I answer, clapping my hands for effect.

He suddenly stands up and places his fisted hand awkwardly in front of his face, "I'd like to thank the little people for allowing me the opportunity to garner this great honor. Without you and all of your constant problems in your villages, I would never have been granted the chance to travel yet again. Thus, I would have missed out on being the youngest of the next batch to turn in Alon," he jokes.

I can't help but laugh at the spectacle he is putting on, but I want to remain serious and ask him a few more questions. "Not to be completely nosey," I start as he sits back down beside me, a silly grin still permeating his face, "but is it like this everywhere?" I ask.

"Like what exactly?"

"You know, crowded, not enough food to go around, tense," I offer.

"Actually, you guys have it pretty good here. Most of the other places I have gone are much smaller and have way less resources. At least, you have the water to fall back on. In some areas, out west, it is so dry and hot the people sometimes succumb to dehydration," Kieran answers.

"Do they die?"

"Sometimes," he says.

"But how do The Healers allow that to happen? Aren't they supposed to help?"

"Zayda, The Healers aren't exactly who you think they are," he responds. Then, he quickly changes the subject. "So, what is up with you and Reggie?"

"You noticed that," I say with a sigh. "I'm not one hundred percent sure. We have been best friends since we were babies, but lately I get the feeling he wants more than that," I reply.

"Oh, he wants more than that. Trust me, I'm a guy, and I know when a dude is into a girl. He is *very* into you," he chuckles.

Rolling my eyes, I snort, "Great! Just what I need." Kieran just laughs and then focuses his full attention on the town below.

We chat periodically over the next few hours, but the subject does not drift back toward anything serious until around dawn. The sun is rising quickly over the horizon, bathing everything in a glorious pink hue, and we have only a few minutes left before the rest of the village awakens. We have just gotten up to head back to the main part of camp, and I decide to go for it before I lose my nerve. "Do you think you can teach me?" I ask.

"Teach you what?"

"To read?" I say.

"Zayda...we could both get into a lot of trouble for that."

My face drops. That is not the answer I was hoping for. "Okay. It was a stupid idea anyway," I grumble.

His face growing serious, indicating he senses how important this is to me, Kieran adds, "I'll think about it."

Squealing in excitement, I wrap my arms around his neck and plant a kiss on his cheek. "Thank you, thank you, thank you," I beam, my arms still clinging to him.

"Settle down," he says through my hair, "I haven't said yes."

"Not yet, but you will. I can be very convincing," I joke.

"Uh hum," a gravelly voice clears their throat behind us. Letting loose of Kieran's neck, I look toward the noise and see Reggie glaring at us both. I have no idea how long he has been standing there watching, but the murder in his eyes is quite clear. "I came to let you both know that a group of Healers is in camp. They said they are on official business, and I thought you would want to know. I guess I picked a bad time," Reggie sneers.

I have no choice but to ignore Reggie's reaction and pretend he hasn't just witnessed our embrace. He would not understand my desire to learn to read, and right now, we have more pressing issues at hand. "How many are there?" I ask.

"Looked like around twenty," he replies, a bit of the harshness fading from his voice. Reggie has a temper, but I can't remember him ever being angry with me for longer than ten minutes.

"Twenty?" Kieran asks for clarification.

"At least," Reggie responds.

"Did they say what they wanted?" I ask.

"No, but they said everyone needs to be in The Elder Hall in five minutes. I guess they will tell us what is up then," he says.

"Everyone? That sounds more than official. Did you get any hint as to why they were here?" Kieran asks.

"None. I'm sure it is nothing major," Reggie states. He sounds confident, but deep down, he must know this is not an ordinary occurrence. I know that. The once extinguished fire is back, and it is burning hotter than ever.

Trying to play it cool, I say, "Well, there is only one way to find out. Let's go."

***

We all walk together to the hall, and it is awkward as heck. I'm in the middle of both boys, and all of us are equally nervous, but Reggie seems angry still. Kieran seems to be better at keeping his emotions in check, whereas, Reggie can't stop shooting daggers in his direction. Get a grip. It's not like you caught us making out. And even if you did, you don't own me. I wish I could say those things out loud, but the situation is already tense enough. Thankfully, the hall isn't too far away, and we reach it in just a few minutes.

"Man, this place is crowded," I huff, as I push my way through the tight space, "I don't think we have all ever been in here at the same time before."

"Not that I can recall," Reggie adds. "Where is everyone else?" He is scanning the room looking for the rest of our group as he speaks, "The last full meeting was just for fifteen and ups. It looks like even the littlest littles are here."

"There they are over in the back corner," I say, pointing toward Posy and the gang huddled together in the rear by the exit. I am glad they found a space there because large crowds, tight spaces, and I do not mix well.

"Got you a place near an escape hatch in case you freak out," Camden teases.

"Thanks," I reply, planting myself with my back firmly pressed as far against the wall as possible.

Everyone looks as nervous as I feel, except for Posy; she looks worse. Her chocolate colored eyes dart around nervously, and her black hair clings to her damp forehead. "Are you okay?" I ask her, concern marring my voice. She just nods and continues looking around frantically. Nudging him softly in the ribs and pointing at Posy, "What is up with her?" I ask Kyle.

"Beats me. She started acting funny the minute we left you two last night. I heard her walking around her tent talking to herself around four this morning, so I went over to check on her. When I got there, she refused to open the door and screamed for me to leave her alone. I didn't wait around much longer after that, but she went right back to talking to herself after she told me to scram," Kyle states.

"Huh…" I start to respond, but our conversation is cut off by one of The Healers beginning to speak.

He stands about six and a half feet tall, is around two-hundred and fifty pounds of solid muscle, and has an overall 'don't mess with me' aura surrounding him. "We have come here to discuss a few matters with you all. My name is Major Mason. You can refer to me as either 'sir' or 'Major Mason'. The Council of the Southeast has asked us to fill you good people in on a situation of possible danger heading your way," allowing his words to sink in, he pauses for dramatic effect and looks around the hall for a few seconds. "A few months ago, the virus that causes The Turning mutated. Those mutations, which speed up the incubation of the virus, were not discovered until much later, and by that time, two days ago, a few individuals had completed the transition and escaped their villages. The nearest compound to be impacted is just a few hours walk from here, and we suspect, The Turned from there must already be close to Alon," he says.

The crowd begins to panic and the noise level grows too loud for Major Mason to continue talking. He appears to be allowing the people a few minutes to process what he is telling them before returning to his task. I cannot fully grasp what he is saying, and the chaos is making my brain jumbled.

Yelling over the chaos and waving his hands to get everyone's attention, "As I was saying, the danger is already closing in on you. I know you are scared, but I need you to hear everything I am saying to you, so please settle down and get quiet," he says. After just a few more mumbles, the crowd again is ready to listen. "Thank you. You are now aware of problem one. Now, on to problem two. Along with the decreased incubation period, the mutation has also made the virus communicable. For those of you who do not know what that means, I will explain. The virus is no longer just a danger for our young citizens. Anyone who is bitten by one of The Turned can now become infected," he finishes.

The room explodes into a frenzy. Women scream and grab their littles, holding them tightly against their bosoms. Men start pushing and fighting each other. It is pandemonium. Hoping to avoid the crossfire, my friends and I just flatten ourselves as close to the wall as possible. I can't believe the scene playing out before me. Our village is coming unglued.

Major Mason and his crew try unsuccessfully to calm the crowd, and eventually it looks like all hope for a productive meeting is extinguished. Until, rat-a-tat... rat-a-tat... rat-a-tat. Major Mason begins firing his machine gun into the air above the crowd. I must admit, despite making my heart jump out of my throat, it works. Everyone, including myself, drop to the ground and cover our heads.

"Shut up and listen!" Major Mason shouts angrily, "I will not waste another minute of my time trying to explain things and help you, if you act like that again. Do I make myself clear?" Stunned, we all remain silently glued to the floor. "I said, Do. I. Make. Myself, Clear?" he asks again.

A brave young soul near him has the guts to force out a small, 'Yes, sir,' and Major Mason relaxes somewhat again. "Okay, good. Now please stand up. Quietly!" He waits a few seconds before continuing, "Good," he says as we all comply, "I am going to open the floor up for questioning. Does anyone have one?"

A few hands toward the front where the elders are gathered shoot up. "You, with the glasses and baby," Major Mason says.

"Major Mason...sir...what are we supposed to do for protection? We do not have any weapons here," the woman asks, clutching her baby tighter after she speaks.

"We are working on a plan. There are two options currently being floated, but we have not decided on the best course of action," he answers. The crowd does not seem to like that answer, but they hold their responses down to a low groan this time. "Next, you, in the back," Major Mason says, pointing at me.

When did my hand go up? I can't recall making the decision to raise it. My brain is swirling with confusion, and I struggle to recall what I could possibly have wanted to ask this massive man. Finally, clarity hits me. "What happened to the members of the other village?" I ask, sighing internally because I fear I already know the answer.

A sly smile spreads across his face when he locks stares with me, sending shivers cascading down my spine. Major Mason just holds my glance for a moment before responding. "They were either killed or turned," he states, without a hint of feeling in his voice. Thankfully, Reggie and Kieran are there to catch me when my knees buckle, and I nearly faint.

"What is wrong with her?" Kieran asks Reggie quietly.

Reggie just sadly gazes down at me and whispers, "That's where her parents were just relocated."

"Oh," Kieran replies, guilt washing over his face.

I remain in a fog of despair for the next few minutes, barely able to keep up with the barrage of questions and answers being exchanged. From what I am able to piece together, we are screwed, and The Healers don't care. After the news I was just given, I don't care about any of it. My parents, who had raised me with love and kindness, were either dead or turned. I now have another reason to hate The Healers, not as if I need another reason to hate them, they have destroyed everything I ever loved.

Major Mason's rat-a-tat brings me out of my stupor. Apparently, the crowd was becoming unruly again, and I had tuned it out. "Now, I have answered all of the questions I can. Please allow me to introduce someone familiar with this location to elaborate further. June, the floor is yours," he says.

"What the actual eff?" I say, as a low murmur begins to build in the hall.

"Posy, why is your mom with The Healers?" Viola asks innocently, as if she is not quite believing her own eyes.

We all turn to face Posy and wait for an answer. Immediately, I notice she is not as shocked as the rest of us. She is staring directly at her mom, tears cascading down her face. Her body has started to tremble with the force she is exerting to hold back her sobs.

"I'm so sorry, guys. They told me if I did it she could come back," Posy confesses.

"Did what?" Camden asks, his face contorted into a mask of confusion.

"I just missed her so much. I didn't feel like I had a choice," Posy says.

"Pose, you aren't making any sense. What have you done?" I ask.

In answer to my question, June begins to speak, "Many of you are probably stunned to see me wearing this uniform. When I left here many years ago, I was just a villager such as yourselves. Now, I stand before you a soldier for the cause. Because of the dedication of one of your own, I have come to know some very important information. Posy, please step forward, my dear."

"Posy, what have you done?" I ask in horror. My chest feels like it is being crushed by a giant fist, and I struggle to catch my breath.

"I'm so sorry," is all she can say.

Meandering through the tight crowd, Posy focuses her eyes directly on her mother. Her slight shoulders continue to shake with the immense efforts to control her tears. Only once, does she turn around and look at the rest of us, and even then, she can't manage to settle on me. When she reaches her mom, the two of them embrace for a brief moment. The resemblance between the two women is remarkable; both are small framed and petite, ebony locks fall loosely to the small of their backs, and their warm, brown, chocolate eyes are both shaped like the most delicate and perfect almond.

"Thank you for joining me," June says, "People of Alon, you owe my daughter Posy a great debt. She has saved you from an unseen threat. Several months ago, during the winter harvest, Posy approached a visiting Healer and divulged to him that one among you has been venturing out and breaking the rules."

As she says this, I can feel the steel glare of Major Mason settle on me. The sly smile is back, and for extra emphasis he adds a wink. Holy crap! They are talking about me. How could Posy do this to me? A million reasons run through my head, but none of them make sense-until I see the way she is lovingly admiring her mother. She said she didn't even know about me going out before. Did she lie, or are they making all of this up? There is no way Posy would have done this to me on her own. She loves me too much. "Those bastards must have blackmailed her," I mumble under my breath.

"Our way of life and safety is delicately tethered to our willingness to follow the rules. We cannot allow such flagrant violations to be ignored. The Council has already taken the first step to neutralize the threat by relocating the offender's parents," June continues. Her words slowly begin to resonate with the other villagers, and they begin to piece together who she is referring to. One-by-one, I can feel their icy stares begin to settle on me. "The next step is to take Zayda into custody, so she can no longer pose a danger to our way of life," June finishes.

The roar from the crowd is even louder this time, and Major Mason does nothing to quell it. From the look on his face, I can clearly see the enjoyment he is receiving from their reactions. My heart aches to see the hate-filled glares of my village family. We have been together since my birth, and to know they now despise me is too much to bare. Not to mention, the agony from the gaping hole in my heart where Posy used to be. The choral echoes of "Lock her up" and "Get her" are reverberating all around me as the roomful of people converge toward my location. If Major Mason and his

Officers don't get to me in time, the others are going to tear me apart.

"Zayda," Reggie whispers, "You have to get out of here. Although I can hear him and know he is correct, my body remains frozen in place. "Zay! Snap out of it. If you don't leave, they are going to take you prisoner," he barks quietly.

Major Mason and the twenty or so Officers are already halfway across the room and will be here in just a few moments. "You're right, Reggie. What should I do?" I plead.

"Quick, out the back door," Kieran says.

"We will hold them off as long as we can," Camden adds.

"But, I can't go without you guys. I won't make it out there alone," I cry.

Gently cupping my face in his hands, "I will come for you as soon as I can. Don't worry," Reggie says.

"Okay," I reply with tears welling in my eyes. The others have moved out of the way and are forming a blockade behind me, so I can have access to the door. I can see the light from outside spilling in from the small crack in the frame. Focusing only on that beacon, I block out the encroaching footsteps and continued jeers, and run for the exit. My head pounds with the force of my body slamming into the wood frame, as I repeatedly attempt to open the tight door. It isn't budging at all, and I am quickly running out of time.

"I can't get the door open," I yell to my friends.

"Try again," Viola shouts as the first of the Officers make it to their location. I can hear the grunts and groans from the exchange between the two groups, but I don't dare chance a look back.

Ignoring the pain, I throw myself at the door one last time. The sound of cracking wood booms into the room as the frame finally gives a bit. Behind me, the increasing fury of scuffling bodies can be heard over everything else. Several loud thuds erupt as people fall to the floor. With sweat running down my forehead, I ram the door one last time and tumble into the safety of daylight.

LONERS

I run as fast as I can when I bust through the door, but the sun is a harsh contrast to the dimly lit hall I had just been in and my eyes are watering profusely. Plus, my haste is making me clumsy, and I keep tripping over my own feet. I know I must get down the hill into The Old City before they catch me, however, knowing this and doing it are not the same thing. Running and thinking too much is making me sloppy. As I run past the ashy remains of last night's fire, I try to clear my mind. It does not work, and I continue to fight off thoughts of what The Healers will do if they catch me. Not to mention, the crushing reality that my best friend in the entire world betrayed me in the worst possible way. All of those years we spent together, confiding in one another, spilling our darkest secrets were just erased in one moment.

Thankfully, the villagers are still back at the hall and I do not encounter anyone on my way. They would surely slow me down-or worse. Sliding slightly, catching myself with my right hand and scraping it on the rough ground, I begin to descend the hill, careful not to travel too fast and trip myself up. It is much easier in the daylight, but still a challenge. Halfway down, I snag my boot on a rock and fall on my stomach. As the air is forced from my lungs, I can hear the officer's shouts begin to emerge from the meeting place. Panicking and breathless, I claw at the ground and crawl the remainder of the way down. The voices are getting closer, but are still far enough away that I think I will make it. I look up toward The Old City, and relief washes over me; it is much closer than I remembered it to be. The differences I see in this part of the world, up close, during the day, are somewhat disorienting.

Finally, at the bottom of the hill, I pull myself upright and run with full speed into the square. I drop to my knees on the ground and hide behind the lush greenery. My face is well hidden, and I can see the masses slowly exiting the building in a stupor. The gang must have really fought hard to buy me my small head start, and I will owe them big for the rest of my short life. Surprisingly, the Officers are not following me down the hill. I don't understand why they would just let me go. I can see them walking from tent to tent and checking inside. Did they think I was hiding out somewhere in the village? "There is no way you are going to get that lucky." I say, collapsing to the ground and putting my head on my knees to rest.

While resting, I ponder my current situation. For the first time ever, I am truly alone, and it is terrifying. Sure, I have been outside of the village on my small quests, but I have always had the sanctity of my home to fall back on. Not this time. I would never be able to return there; The Healers have made sure of that. Instead, I will have to find a new place to live and new people to coexist with. No big deal. I'll just walk into the nearest village and claim a tent. I laugh sarcastically at this thought. Considering the recent news of The Turned outbreak there, that is also off the table. I truly have no idea what I am going to do in the long term.

For now, I have to focus on one thing at a time. With any luck, Reggie will come looking for me tonight, and then I will have help. He only knows his way to the area around the cathedral, so I stand up and begin making my way there. I need to find a hiding spot in one of the nearby, second-story apartments, so I can see him when he arrives. My favorite building has always been the large red one diagonal from the front of the church, and it will offer the best vantage point to see any approaching people.

Hurriedly, I make my way toward the structure, careful to hide from anyone who might be looking down from the village. The walk from the middle of the square to the building is only a short distance, but to be veiled as much as possible, I circle around the back left of the cathedral and go down an alley. My mother has told me stories about pirates taking this same path back in the late eighteenth and early nineteenth centuries. According to her, it is the quickest and safest route from the river to the center of town. I hope she is right.

Wandering around The Old City, on my way to my hiding place for the day, I take in the beauty of the architecture. I know the Officers will be out looking for me soon, and the last thing I want is to be found, but I cannot help but drink in everything around me. It is strange seeing the town during the day. Before, I have only explored in the dark, and many of the structures around me appear foreign in the new light. Of course, I remember my usual route, but it still feels alien. The buildings loom much taller than I remember; their brick facades and cast iron ornaments guarding the abandoned streets below. My soul desperately wants to pause and memorize each and every flower and vine cascading down from the rooftops, their colors serving as a reminder we are all just one piece of nature's puzzle, but I don't dare risk being exposed longer than I have to.

One particular building, a soft brown color, with a beautiful angel painted onto the side, touches something deep inside me, and I crumble to the ground in a heap. Allowing myself to fully feel the magnitude of loss, I openly grieve for my family-blood and chosen. Screaming into the sky, I release all the emotions I have been holding onto so tightly. "Why? Why did you have to take them all away from me? You couldn't just stop with mom. Or dad. No! You had to steal Posy too. I hate you!" I know it is risky, but I lie on the hot, brick pavement and stare into the sky for a few moments and just let everything out. My tears flow heavily down my face, but I make no motion to wipe them away. It does not matter. No one will see me here, and even if they do, I do not care.

Eventually, I am cried out and rise to continue. My eyes are swollen and puffy, and my head burns with the beginnings of a headache. However, I feel a little better. Nothing has changed in the time I had my meltdown, but releasing the pain into the air has made me lighter in many ways. I push all feelings deep down inside me where they can't cause me anymore harm, and walk toward my future.

***

Within a few minutes, I have made it to my pre-selected hiding spot. I stand on the street, concealed by the edge of the building, and look at my temporary home. The red paint on the upper level has faded from many years of hot sunlight, but the lower floor still maintains much of its original, vibrant, burgundy hue. Green trim lines all the doors and windows from one end to the other, and magnificent iron trim wraps its arms around the balcony the entire two blocks the building occupies. I can only imagine the splendor it beheld before The Turning made it a ghost. Finding a broken window on the ground floor, I squeeze myself inside and prepare to begin my stakeout.

Once inside, safe from the prospect of being spotted by someone, I relax a little bit. I can't help but imagine and picture the place during its prime. The stories my mom spun to me are dancing around inside my mind. I sit on the nearest silver stool and allow myself to get lost in daydreams about the past.

Men and women in brightly colored clothing sit scandalously close, their eyes interlocked, speaking in long dead dialects. As beautiful jazz music wafts through the air on imaginary wings, bringing with it the promise of good times to come and good times already passed, the couples are happily engaged in the act of dating. The man behind the bar works tirelessly to mix up the requested refreshments, and a lovely lady quickly scoops the filled orders up and whisks them off to their intended recipients. Occasionally, a passerby will wander in to escape the encumbering heat of the summer afternoon and break apart the magical world for a moment, but it does not last long and all melts back into the ease of The Old City. Soon, everyone will be full of liquid courage and will begin to sway in synch to the songs. Life seems to stretch on forever and yet the moments flash so quickly.

"Who the hell are you?" an unfamiliar voice says behind me, jolting me out of my haze.

I turn quickly to see two girls standing huddled together in the archway between the main room and one of the side rooms. The pair are filthy and bloody, and I can see the apprehension in both of their demeanors. The older girl, petite with strawberry-blonde hair and dazzling blue eyes, has her arms wrapped protectively around the shoulders of the younger girl, who has identical blue eyes but much paler, yellow hair. The two look way too much alike to not be related. "I am Zayda," I answer. I hold my hands out to them to show they are bare and to indicate I do not intend to harm them.

"Where did you come from?" the smaller girl asks. She looks to be around nine or ten, but seems somehow stronger than the other girl.

"I am from a nearby village," I answer, not wanting to give away too much information to these strangers.

"How close?" the older one barks.

"Close enough." I bark back, lowering my hands.

"That isn't really an answer," the older one replies.

"Why should I be the only one giving out information?" I ask.

"Because you came into our hiding spot," the little girl states, putting her small hands on her tiny hips in an attempt to be sassy.

"Well, I didn't realize you would be in here," I say, walking a few steps toward them. Deciding to get the upper hand, I begin to ask some of my own questions, "Who are *you* guys? And Where did *you* come from?"

"None of your business," the older girl says, protectively putting her arms around the smaller girl.

"Well, then I guess you won't get any information out of me either," I reply, crossing my arms over my chest in protest.

The smaller girl, reaching up on her tip toes, whispers a little too loudly in the other girl's ear, "Be nice. We don't have anywhere to go. She might be able to take us with her."

"We don't know if we *want* to go with her. Now be quiet, so I can figure things out," the older girl says. She raises her eyebrows as she scrutinizes me more closely. "Why have you been crying? Your face is all puffy."

"That is absolutely none of your business," I reply sharply.

"Well...excuse me for caring," she replies.

We all just stand there and stare at each other for a few seconds, none of us willing to give up anything to the others. Sensing this was not going to get us anywhere, and realizing I might actually enjoy some company until Reggie shows up,

I say, "Look, I don't mean to come off as rude, but you are the only people I have ever met in the wild. It isn't an everyday occurrence, and we all know why."

"Yea, I get that. You are the first person we have seen for days," she says, lowering her guard a little. After a few moments of pondering, she huffs and continues, "I'm Marla, and this is my little sister Julie. We are from Audubon, a day's walk from here."

"What did you say?" I ask, my heart racing with anticipation. If they made it out, then maybe my parents did also.

"Audubon," Julie replies sheepishly, "We...we...had to leave."

"Why are you staring at us like that?" Marla asks, irritation growing in her voice. She grabs Julie around the waist like she is preparing to bolt with her.

"Sorry, it's just that, I was told everyone from that village had been killed or...," I stop, not wanting to make the girls upset, and also not wanting to admit it could be true.

"Turned," Marla says, finishing my sentence.

"Yeah...turned. Is it true?" I whisper. Just by interpreting the looks on their faces, I know the answer before I ask, but I desperately need to hear the words aloud from someone other than Major Mason. "Could anyone else have survived?"

Marla moves her arm around Julie's tiny shoulders and pulls her closer, "Yes, it is true. Or, at least almost true.

Sadly, Marla and I are the only ones to escape alive, but some were still transitioning back at camp. It took less than a few minutes for most to turn. However, some were still changing when we ran."

I try to keep the sadness off my face, but I guess from Julie's response I do a pretty terrible job. "Why do you look so sad, Zayda?" her tiny voice asks.

These two have been through enough without me losing my cool right now. I can't imagine the horror of watching everyone you know and love be slaughtered and then reanimate. I decide not to cause them any additional pain, so I do the first thing that comes to my mind and lie. "I'm just sad that all of those people are lost."

"It was awful. When Jimmy turned, nobody expected it. He wasn't supposed to fully transition until next month. We were completely blindsided," Marla states. She seems in control of her emotions, and I appreciate that, however, Julie's trembling lip suggests she is on the verge of tears. I will not be able to keep myself in check if the little one breaks down. Heck, I am barely doing it already.

"Julie, do you want to go find somewhere to rest? Marla and I can talk about all of this scary stuff while you get some sleep," I suggest. Julie just looks from me to Marla several times, and then nods her small head. "Okay, let's go find somewhere comfy."

Downstairs in the building, we only find more tables and chairs from the old restaurant, so we venture up to see if there are sleeping quarters. The oak stairs creak and groan under the weight of our feet, and I'm positive that we are the first to traverse them in many years. Walking up the narrow flight does not take long, but my muscles are exhausted from fleeing the village. I am spent by the time we reach the landing. Looking around, I see at least seven doors on each side of the hallway. Knowing I need to find a room that looks out over the cathedral and where Julie also will feel comfortable, I focus my attention on the doors in the front of the building. Despite being more at ease than Julie, Marla seems more than happy to let someone else be in charge for a few minutes. Admittedly, I always feel better when I am leading, so the current arrangement is fine with me.

When we reach the first door, I turn the cold handle, only to discover it is locked. Julie lets out a sad cry of exhaustion behind me, so I turn toward her and give her my best cheer up smile. "Don't worry. We will find an open one. I promise," I say. She wipes her filthy hand across her blood-stained forehead and nods her head at me. I can't help but notice that her hair is matted with gore, so I reach down and gently pull a large chunk of flesh out of her bangs.

"Thank you," Julie says meekly, "I'm all messy." She then reaches up and interlocks her small fingers with mine. The sweetness of the act causes a lump to form in my throat, and I find myself once again fighting my emotions.

"You look beautiful," I say, while ruffling her hair. She just beams another toothless grin my way and starts humming a song. I can't believe how resilient Julie appears to be. I hope the rest of us can mimic her behavior. Surveying her sister, I notice she is looking at me with a combination of appreciation and wonder. I smile at her in acknowledgement. As we continue to check the remaining doors, Marla returns the smile and mouths the words 'thank you' to me. I just nod back and keep turning the handles.

Finally, we approach the last door from the end. The tarnished numbers hanging above the jam are crooked and falling off, and I doubt anyone has even tried to cross this threshold in over a decade. Praying it opens, I cross my fingers and hold my breath. With a loud groan, the heavy wood slowly creaks open, exposing a large room. I am relieved when we walk into a fully furnished room with a large, old fashioned bed in the middle of it. The sheets and blanket are covered in a giant layer of dust, but once we peel them off and shake them it is a suitable place for Julie to sleep. She happily climbs in, and after Marla rubs her hair and sings her a song, she is snoring away. I have settled myself on the floor by the window, crouching down so only the top of my head and eyes are peeking out. The sun is beginning to set, casting oblong shadows on the front of the church. My view is better than I had originally hoped, and I can see most of the square as well as the entire cathedral. If Reggie shows up, I will see him for sure.

Gently crawling out of her position in the bed next to Julie, Marla asks, "What are you watching for?"

"Oh, you know, just looking," I lie again.

"I hate to break it to you, but you are an *awful* liar," Marla replies, rolling her eyes and sitting down on the floor next to me.

Laughing lightly, "Haven't had much practice," I say.

"That I actually believe," she replies, an actual smile spreading across her face for the first time since we met.

"Will we wake her if we talk?" I ask, motioning at Julie with my head, genuinely concerned we might bother her.

"Not a chance. Once she is out, she sleeps like the dead. I wish I could block out the world for a few hours, just for one night, and sleep like Julie," Marla replies.

"How did you guys find this place?" I ask.

"Wasn't too hard. A new couple recently got transferred to our village, and they talked about here all the time. I knew if I followed the river I would eventually find it," Marla answers.

The mention of my parents makes my throat clench and my eyes burn, so I hastily turn my head and begin studying the road down below. "If you followed the river, then why aren't you up at the camp?" I ask.

I look back at Marla and size her up. Her face is fashioned into a scowl as she tells me her thoughts on the world, and her eyes are far off somewhere else. "We were right outside of it, but then all of The Healers and Officers showed up. I know it may be against The Rules to say so, but I hate those guys. I've always hated them. Even when I was a little like Julie, I could tell there was something sinister behind all their fake smiles," she replies. Usually I am skeptical of new people, and I have no good reason to trust Marla any more than anyone else, except I do. I really do. After what Posy had just done to me, I should be guarded against everyone, but there is just something in her voice that tells me she was being honest.

"Me too," I say. Marla nods in agreement. I continue, "They are responsible for everything bad in the world. Especially, everything bad that has ever happened to me."

"What bad things have happened to you?"

"Uh...those people who told you about here...They were my parents. The Healers made them leave our village because of me. They lied and said it was because your village needed the help. After today, I know that is not why," I confess, guilt washing over me for causing my parents' death.

"What happened today?"

"Let's not worry about that right now," I reply, turning my attention back to the window. I know I should tell her, but I can't bring myself to speak the words aloud; at least not just yet.

"Seriously, who or what are you looking for? Are Julie and I in danger here with you?" Marla asks, recognizing my reluctance, but not letting the subject drop.

"Maybe," I reply honestly. I turn to face her and decide if I want to risk becoming a basket case by divulging the horrible details of the past few hours. The understanding in her eyes causes me soften my stance a bit, and I contemplate opening up to her completely.

"Well, that's just great. If we are going to go down fighting for you, then you should at least be honest with me first," she says, smiling and convincing me to spill my guts.

"Touché'," I respond, before launching into the story.

***

We spend the next fifteen minutes or so with me filling her in on all the recent events. Marla is a great listener and just sits quietly, gasping and nodding in the appropriate places as I do my best to explain it all without screaming at the top of my lungs or crying my eyes out. I must admit, saying it out loud angers me even more, but telling someone else also offers much needed relief. I begin to feel a little lighter, and slowly my head clears. Small tendrils of a plan to get back at them start to wind their way into my brain, and by the time I am finished, I am thoroughly convinced of one thing; The Healers are not going to get away with ruining my life.

After I have finished my story, I decide it is safe to ask more about the incident. "What was it like?" I ask quietly, glancing at Julie's sleeping form on the bed. True to Marla's word, she is still zonked out.

"What was what like?

"The Turning?" I reply.

"Terrible. Jimmy had been sitting extra quiet at breakfast, but no one really noticed because he had started to withdraw more and more lately. We've all seen it a dozen times before; people just stop talking right before the change. I have always thought it was the human part of their brain preparing for the big shutdown," she says, putting the words big shutdown in air quotes.

"I know exactly what you mean," I say, thinking about Kyle's behavior lately.

She brushes her hand absently through her thinning hair and continues, "Halfway through the meal, he stood up and began staring off into space I was sitting directly across from him, and I swear the light just went out of his eyes. His pupils dilated and covered his iris like a dark cloud over the sun. When they went back to normal, they were completely yellow. I mean the entire eye. No more black dot in the middle. It was crazy! It was then, I saw that Jimmy was totally gone. Lost to the change. The first person to get attacked was Fern. She is...was...a little around six. I will never be able to get the sound of her screams out of my mind. He tore her throat open and spit it onto the ground in a sinewy heap. After that, she twitched on the floor for a few minutes before passing over. Jimmy had found his next victim already by the time she came back. Those of us who weren't in shock, realized what that meant, and started running. But, it all happened too fast for most to get out." Her small frame has started to shake with her words, and I know she is finally going to break. I abandon my spot by the window and go over to put my arms around her shoulders. She has been through an awful ordeal and needs comfort. At least, I can offer her that, if nothing else.

"I'm really sorry you had to see that," I say, trying my best to sooth her. Regrettably, I've never really done this before, so it is not coming as naturally to me as I was hoping it would. My arms are awkwardly draped, and the tone of my voice is off a bit, but she seems to be responding positively anyway.

Lost in sobs, her words are barely audible, "s 'okay," she responds.

I spend the next few minutes holding her and stroking her hair gently as she weeps. Eventually, she falls asleep with her head resting in my lap. Although we are around the same age, I suddenly feel very protective of this girl and her sister.

I internally vow that I will do whatever I can to keep them safe.

***

"Hey, I think I see someone down there," Marla whispers excitedly. After her much needed nap, she and I have been taking turns watching out for Reggie while the other rests for a few minutes.

"Where?"

"On the edge of the square," she replies.

Squinting my eyes, I can kind of make out a silhouette, but it is too obscured to tell who it is for sure. "I can't tell if it is him."

"Well, we should wait a minute until they step into the moonlight more. I bet you could make him out then," she happily adds, shifting her weight so she has a better view.

"True. The moon is still full, so there will be plenty of light," I say, casting my gaze back toward the levee to see if I can see anyone else. Reggie is good at sneaking around, but that doesn't mean he wasn't seen. I want to make sure, if he is the one down below, that he has not been followed.

"Do you see anyone else?" Marla asks, tracking my eyes.

"No. I don't think so."

Poking my arm and drawing my eyes back to the edge of the square, "Look, they are stepping out of the shadows," Marla says.

The figure down below begins running across the small street and dives directly into the cover of the cathedral where we had all hidden the night before, but not before I get a solid glimpse of their strong, lean body and shaggy hair. No doubt about it, Reggie has made good on his promise.

LOOSE ENDS

After I bring Reggie inside and up to our room, Marla gives us both a more in-depth rundown of what happened in Audubon. I do my best to remain quiet while she speaks, but so many of the things she says are either shocking or repulsive. Reggie, who has never had a very strong stomach for blood and gore, finds himself sitting in the corner with his head between his knees. His face is a ghastly shade of pale white. I pray he does not start vomiting because I will be right behind him.

"One by one, the bitten reanimated and Turned. I've never seen so much blood in my life. It was like someone had sprayed the mess hall with a hose filled with red water. It didn't take long before half of the village was infected. Some bodies were too badly damaged to come back, but that seemed to be the ones who sustained massive trauma to the head. I didn't notice this at first because the scene was so chaotic, but after the first five or more who were bashed in pretty good stayed down, it became more obvious. The first one I saw not getting back up was Madge-the resident nurse. Julie and I had retreated to a corner, out of sight, and Madge was taken down by a pack of littles. They tore into her skull like it was the inside of a melon and consumed most of her brains. She twitched a little but didn't ever get back up. After a few minutes, even the twitching stopped. The strength those small children possessed was, for lack of a better word, impressive. It seems like that may be an additional side effect of The Turning we didn't know about," Marla says.

"Wow!" Reggie says. He is finally recovering a bit from his bout of nausea but still looks quite green.

He has been sitting up watching Marla with keen interest; his face changing from utter horror to something closer to intrigue. I suspect he is less interested in the story than he is in Marla. For reasons I cannot completely explain, this bothers me. "What do you think that means, Reggie?" I ask him, intentionally drawing his gaze back to me.

The familiar adoration returns to his face, and he says, "Maybe we can stop them somehow. If they don't turn after extensive damage to the brain, then perhaps damage to the brain can stop them once they have transitioned. I don't know, just a thought. That might be crazy."

"I don't think that sounds crazy at all. I've heard stories of people encountering Turned in the wild and escaping by bashing them on the head," Marla states.

Excited for the possibility to meet another rebel like myself, I ask, "Who do you know that has been into the wild?"

"A few boys in the village closest to us. I met them a couple of times during a training trip. Our elders liked to have us learn as much about farming as possible, and these guys seemed to have the best irrigation system in place," Marla replies. She seems very proud to be able to offer this information. I get the sense she is a people pleaser, much like I used to be before Robinson died and I began to hate every single thing about the world.

"Did you travel to this village?" I ask.

"Yes, around a half dozen times."

"Could you find it again?" I say.

"Probably. If I went during the day."

"Zayda, do you think it is safe to go out there?" Reggie asks, rising to pace the room nervously.

"I don't know, but we can't stay here forever. The Officers will start combing these buildings soon, and we do *not* want to be here when they do. I'm surprised they haven't yet. What was happening when you left?" I ask.

"They were making plans to evacuate the village. I heard a few of them talking about needing to go by nightfall tomorrow. They will be taking all of Alon to The Sacred City as soon as transportation arrives. Apparently, the horde is closer than they originally thought," Reggie replies.

"Marla, how many of those things do you think there are?" I ask.

"Hard to say for sure. Our village had gotten smaller lately due to relocation and an unusually high number of teenagers Turning. Combine that with the casualties, and you are probably looking at two hundred," she says casually.

"Two hundred!" Reggie and I say at the same time. Reggie picks up his pacing and begins walking around the room in manic circles.

"Everyone will be slaughtered. We don't even have weapons up on the levee, and twenty Officers is not enough to protect five hundred people. I hope they make it out before...," I can't even finish the sentence.

"It will be okay," Reggie says, pausing his latest lap around the room and placing his hand on the small of my back. His touch sends shivers down my spine like it never did before. What is happening to me? One minute of him making moon-eyes at another girl, and I'm turning into a giggling school girl. Pathetic. Get a grip, Zayda.

"The kids at the other village know how to make weapons. They offered to show me how once, but I was too afraid of getting caught to let them. I bet if we ask them, they will come and help us fight," Marla says, taking notice of

Reggie's hand. Not liking the interaction between us, she shoots daggers in my direction. I squirm a bit to knock his hand loose. Now is not the time to have tension between the three of us. Sensing my intention, Marla relaxes her death stare. "Once we have the others, we head to The Sacred City?" she says.

"I think that is our only choice," I respond. "We can't beat The Healers, if we don't go to them; they would never be caught dead in the wilderness."

"That's a long way away. What if we run into the horde?" Julie's small, shaky voice asks from behind us. I had almost forgotten about the little sleeping on the bed. She is sitting in the middle of the mattress, her hair sticking out wildly on top of her head, absently wiping the remnants of sleep out of her eyes. "Will they tear us apart like mommy?

Rising to go sit next to her sister and comfort her, Marla says, "No, Julie bug. I won't let them hurt you. Don't worry."

Marla hadn't mentioned before that her mom was one of the people lost in her village. If it were as gruesome as Julie suggested, I don't blame her. No one should have to see their parent ripped apart. I was suddenly, and I must admit very selfishly, grateful I hadn't been transferred with mom and dad.

"Plus," I add, "You have me to help protect you now too." Julie smiles a big smile, exposing her missing tooth in the front. I don't have a little sister, but right now looking at

Julie, I know what it would feel like to do anything to protect one. In just a few short hours, Julie has claimed a piece of my heart. Moving to sit on the other side of the little girl, I say to Reggie and Marla, "We should rest before the sun comes up. When do you want to leave?"

"I think the sooner the better," Marla replies.

"I agree, but there is one small thing we need to think about," Reggie says, while making another lap.

"What? And can you please stop pacing? You are making me dizzy." I say. My eyes are still sore from all the crying, and watching him move around like a crazy person is making me sick to my stomach.

"The others. I know they will come looking for us. What if they go out wandering alone and can't defend themselves? I don't want them to get hurt," Reggie says, flopping down on the bed in front of us. He has that serious look in his eyes that I have only seen one other time before. I can see how torn he is about this, and I feel stupid for not thinking of it myself. He's right, the others will come looking for us.

"What other choice do we have?" Marla asks.

"I will go get them," I answer. Both Marla and Reggie look at me with shock. "Going back into the village is probably a suicide mission, but I can't let anyone get hurt because of me. I can get in and out without being detected. I've done it countless times before. If I go now, we will be back before dawn."

"I don't know, Zayda. Maybe I should do it. The Healers aren't out to get me," Reggie replies.

"Come on, Reg, you know you are terrible at sneaking around when you are really nervous. Marla and I saw you creeping in the square a full five minutes before you came out," I say.

He locks eyes with me and responds, "I know, but I don't want anything to happen to you. You are my best friend, and...I... I want to keep you safe. I don't know what I would do without you, Zay."

"Thanks, Reg," I say, while leaning toward him and patting his shoulder. "I appreciate you looking out for me, but we both know I am the only one who can get in without being caught."

"It's a crazy idea!" he yells.

"I know that, but it's my fault they are even in this mess. I have to get them out."

"Fine. But, we will walk you to the edge of the square," Reggie says, relenting to not fight me on the matter anymore. Despite his great intentions, there is no conceivable way he will make it back in-let alone out again-without them seeing him. Deep down I think he knows that.

"Julie and Marla, maybe you should stay here. I don't want to put too many people at risk. The Healers don't even know about you guys. They probably assume everyone from your camp is gone. The less they know the better," I say, rising to go.

"I agree. If it were just me, I would go with you, but Julie is already exhausted. We will wait downstairs for you to get back, and then we can all head out toward the other village," Marla replies.

"Good, it's settled then. Reggie will be in the perfect position to look out for us all. If you see anything wrong, Reg, come back here and hide until I return," I state.

The look on Reggie's face suggests that is not an option, but as the two of us leave, he responds with, "Sure thing, boss."

***

Surprisingly, Reggie doesn't put up a fight at the edge of the square. I am prepared for some resistance about me going up alone, but he just nods as I walk away. I can't help but think about him while I make my back up to the village. We have been through so much together, and he is such an important part of my life. Knowing we will not live to be adults, I have never allowed myself to contemplate a future. Now, however, facing a more imminent danger, my mind is wandering into unchartered territory. I have never looked at Reggie in any way other than as a friend, but the small, nagging voice in my head can't get over the way he had looked at Marla. The word jealous keeps popping into my brain. Why would I be jealous? I don't want him. Do I? Grrr... "This is probably not the best time for you to be having some sort of revelation, Zayda. Get a grip. So what if he is into Marla? She is a cute girl, and he is a cute guy. It's not like they are going to get married or something," I say aloud, attempting to convince myself that I don't really care. For some reason, the more I think about it, the angrier I get. Reggie is supposed to be in love with me, not someone else. "Pull it together! He was just looking at her, and you have more important things to worry about right now."

Shaking my head, I successfully clear away any remaining sparks of thought about Reggie and refocus my brain on the task at hand-finding my friends. From my vantage point on the edge of the village, my chin and chest pressed firmly to the cold, damp ground to avoid detection, the camp appears calm and quiet. I can see a few Officers clustered around the fire in the middle of the village, but besides that no movement can be found. Fortunately, our group all lives relatively closely to each other on the edge of the tents, so I don't have far to go.

"Okay, get the twins first, and then Kyle. Should be easy as pie," I mutter under my breath, rolling my eyes at the ridiculous situation I am putting myself into. I was lucky enough to escape The Healers and Officers the first time; this is insane. What about Kieran? Does he come with us? He wasn't really a part of the group yet, but for some reason the thought of leaving him behind makes me anxious. If there is time, then I'll worry about him. My heart aches with the sudden revelation that Posy will not be included in this rescue mission. Despite all she has done, I still love her, and it is going to take me a long time to stop thinking about her like a sister. My eyes begin to sting with fresh tears as I fight against the desire to mourn the fresh loss of my friend. "No time for that, Zayda. You have to focus," I say, wiping my eyes on my sleeve.

Slinking on the ground as low as possible, I make better time than I originally anticipated and am at the twins' tent in only a few minutes. Inside, I can hear the soft whisper of night-time breathing. Everything appears to be normal, which somehow makes me even more nervous. I shudder thinking about being caught here. Major Mason wanted my head on a platter before I escaped and made him look like a fool, so now he must be ready to shoot first and ask questions later.

"Here goes nothing," I whisper, while gently easing the door open. For some reason, talking out loud has always calmed my nerves, so despite the obvious danger in it, I continue to mumble to myself while I carry out my plan.

Inside, the area is pitch black. The soft glow of the full moon cannot penetrate the heavy tarp ceiling, and all the candles have been extinguished for the night. The day had been hot and sticky causing the tent to fill with the familiar smell of dampness and mildew; that combined with the darkness, make the overall sensation inside the tent like that of a coffin, and I feel claustrophobic. Thankfully, I have spent many days running around the confines of their home, know my way around very well, and will not have to spend much time in here.

"Viola and Camden sleep in the rooms to the front of the tent, so get in and grab them without disturbing their parents," I mutter.

Using my hands to feel my way along the wall, the coarseness of it a stark reminder of the harshness of our lives, I head toward their rooms. A few times, I stub my toe on the newly arranged furniture sticking out in the center of the room. "Guess they've been redecorating. Would have been nice to know before I broke all of my digits," I growl lowly. Maybe I haven't been spending as much time with my friends as I thought I had. It has just been getting increasingly harder to pretend everything is normal, and hanging out was another luxury I felt we couldn't afford anymore. Still, it would be nice to have a better idea where the chairs are scattered. "Keep making noise, you idiot," I say as I smash my knee into yet another obstacle.

"Who is there?" a voice says to my right.

Shit, I think, pinning myself flat against the nearest wall and holding my breath. I didn't hear the voice well enough to know who it is, and I do not want to have to explain myself to Mr. or Mrs. Banks. They have always been nice enough to me, but they are goody goodies when it comes to following orders. Heck, almost all the village is for that matter. They would sound the alarm for sure if they knew I was back.

"I said, who is there?" the voice repeats.

Reflexively, I take a small breath. The motion is larger than I anticipate, and immediately after I exhale I am shrouded in white light.

"Zayda! Is that you?" the voice asks.

Holding my hand over my eyes to shield them from the brightness, I say, "Yes. It's me. I came back for my friend."

"Friend? Am I not included then?" the voice questions and then busts out laughing.

"Cam?" I ask, relief washing over my body.

"Duh! Who did you think it was?" Camden replies.

"I didn't know exactly. One of your parents, I guess. Can you please lower the flashlight?"

"Sorry," Camden says, lowering the light, "Boy are you lucky it wasn't. The world has gone apeshit since you got away. I think they would turn you in just to get some peace around here. All day long, we have been being grilled by the Officers. 'Where would Zayda go? Have you ever been outside of camp with her? Does she have any weapons? Would she come back? Blah...blah...blah... It has been exhausting."

"Sounds awful! Sorry you all are caught up in this mess. I honestly didn't think they would find out about my...uh...indiscretions, and I certainly didn't think they would freak out like they did. It's not like I killed someone," I reply.

"Don't be sorry. We knew the chance we were taking too. None of this would be happening if it weren't for Posy," Camden says. The bitterness in his voice is easy to pick up.

My body tenses with the mention of her name. "Have you seen or talked to her?"

"Only for a minute. She tried to come up and explain herself while we were being held for questioning, but no one really responded to her. I think the shock of the situation, along with being super pissed off, made us all apprehensive. Even when she was apologizing and defending her actions, she did not seem sincere. Her entire demeanor was robotic and stiff. It was as if she were reciting a speech someone else had written for her. Somehow, she doesn't seem like the same Posy anymore. It's like she has been replaced with a...a...," Camden says.

"...A zombie," Viola says, emerging from her bedroom and finishing Camden's sentence for him.

"Yes, exactly," he replies to his sister.

"I thought the same thing. Her eyes were glassed over and her voice was off. I don't know what The Healers are up to, but I'm willing to bet Posy is a major part of it," Viola says.

"Do you think Posy is safe?" I ask out of true concern for my old friend.

"Safer than the rest of us. Definitely safer than you. Are you crazy coming back here?" Viola chastises.

She actually sounds concerned for me, and I wonder if I have misjudged her. "I have some news," I say, not sure how to break everything I have found out to them.

"Okay...Are you going to tell us, or just wait until we guess?" Viola asks, obviously annoyed.

"Yeah, sorry. I met some people, and they are going to help us, but I just don't know how to tell you everything right now. I think it would be best if we get Kyle first and then talk when we get to The Old City," I reply.

Viola and Camden both exchange a knowing glance. "You didn't tell her yet?" Viola asks, momentarily forgetting what I just said.

"No, we haven't had time."

"Tell me what?" I ask, my nerves once again beginning to burn in my stomach.

"Kyle's gone," Camden states.

"Gone? What do you mean gone?"

"Mandatory quarantine. Anyone with over half of the symptoms has to be under armed guard until further notice," Viola says.

"Where are they keeping him?" I ask. My plan is suddenly becoming more complicated, and I don't have any grand ideas on how to simplify matters.

"In the meeting hall. I hate to tell you, but you do not have a chance to get him out of there. They have at least ten Officers with guns watching the building at all times," Camden says, shifting his weight as if the heaviness of his words is crushing him.

"Plus, he looked pretty bad before they took him away. I caught him staring at my neck twice today during questioning. And I don't mean admiring the curve of my neck. He was daydreaming about tearing my jugular out. I could see it on his face," Viola states. She doesn't say it with malice, but rather with conviction. There is no doubt in her voice or tone that Kyle is now dangerous.

However, I am not buying it. "Oh, come on! He still has months left."

"He did. Before the mutation. Did you forget about that?" Viola asks.

"Of course not, but Kyle? He would never hurt any of us," I naively say.

"Times have changed, Zay, and Kyle has too. He needs to stay with the Officers," Camden says gently.

Regrettably, I resign to accept Kyle's captivity-for now. "I guess you are right. I just hate the thought of him being locked up like an animal," I say.

"We all do, but it is too dangerous for him to be out. You heard what happened at Audubon. If Kyle turns early, the entire village will be put at risk," Camden replies. I just nod my head in agreement, sadness cloaking my soul in a dark cloud. Within the past day, I have had to wrap my head around losing my parents, being a fugitive from my village, and being betrayed by my best friend. Deep down I know they are right, but I have lost so much recently, and adding Kyle to the list was not something I had been prepared for.

"So, what now?" Viola asks.

"My grand scheme was to come back and get all of you, so we could meet up with the people I told you about. The girl, Marla, knows how to get to another nearby village. She says the teenagers there know how to build weapons and can help us fight," I say.

Rolling her eyes to express her disdain, "Oh yeah, these new people who are going to help," Viola says.

"Fight who?" Camden asks, uncertainty marring his handsome face.

"First the horde, then The Healers," I state.

"Woah! Wait a minute. You want to fight the horde? We don't have any idea how to fight. Are you trying to get us all killed?" Camden asks.

"Seriously? Zayda, I think you've actually lost your mind," Viola adds.

"I know it sounds crazy, but if we don't stop them we will be in jeopardy forever. You guys have heard the old stories about what life was like before The Healers took away The Turned. We won't survive if we don't take them out," I respond.

"Or, we could just stay here with the Officers and let them keep us safe," Viola says. I can see the regret on her face the second the words were out of her mouth, but it is too late to take them back.

"Yes, *you* two can, but I don't have that luxury anymore," I say, flatly. I can't tell if Camden is on board with leaving or not, but Viola appears to be adamantly opposed to the idea. "We are running out of time, and I can't force you to do something you are against. If you don't want to come with me, then stay here. It's okay. I understand." I really did understand. I was asking them to give up their entire lives to help me win an unwinnable war.

"Give us a minute to talk about it. *Please*," Camden requests.

"Sure. I'll wait outside behind the tent. The sun will be coming up soon, and I must go. If I don't see either of you in the next five minutes, I will consider that your answer," I say, walking toward the door. They both nodded in acknowledgement as I leave the tent. "I can't do this without you guys," I call back before shutting myself outside once again.

***

Huddling in the dark, my body crouched behind their tent as I try to blend into the shadows, I reflect on our conversation. The twins are right to be worried. There is no guarantee we will even make it to the other village without dying, and even if we do, the future beyond that looks bleak. Suddenly, I feel guilty for being selfish enough to ask my friends to abandon their lives and give up their safety for me. Reggie has come voluntarily, and for that I am grateful, but Viola and Camden are being coerced into joining me. Part of me hopes I will never see them again. At least then, I won't have to worry about being the cause of their deaths.

"You are really something, Zayda," I say, putting my head in my hands and feeling sorry for myself.

"I agree," a male voice says as a body rounds the side of the tent, causing me to jump and back away on my bottom. Trying to find purchase, my fingernails dig deeply into the soft dirt, and a small scream escapes my mouth.

"Woah! It's me, Kieran. I didn't mean to scare you," the shadowy figure says.

"Kieran? What are you doing out here? And why are you always jumping out of the dark at me?" I ask, my voice shaking with fear.

"I couldn't sleep, so I decided to take a walk," he answers, moving closer to me and helping me to my feet. "I've been worried about you since you left earlier. I overheard a few of the Officers talking about what would happen if they found you, and I started freaking out."

Kieran's sincerity catches me off guard, and I struggle to immediately find an appropriate response. Instead of speaking, I just look at him and contemplate my next move. Without Kyle, we can use the extra manpower, but bringing Kieran will cause tension with Reggie. Will the benefits outweigh the negatives? There really is only one way to find out. "I came back to ask the twins to come with me. We are forming an alliance of sorts to resist The Healers," I say.

"Wow! Do you think that's a good idea?" Kieran asks. He isn't judging me, just asking out of general fear for my wellbeing. His heartfelt concern makes me happy I decided to ask him to come.

"I wasn't left with much of a choice. Once they branded me a hazard and tried to arrest me, I had to adapt and come up with a way to save my life," I respond.

With a smile spreading wide across his face, Kieran says, "Where do I sign up? I've never really been a fan of authority anyway."

"If you're serious, I'm getting ready to leave as soon as they come out. Well, if they come out. I left them inside discussing it. Camden seemed ready to commit, but Viola was a bit apprehensive. I can't blame her. This is a big deal, and I can't guarantee we will not get caught or worse. There is a chance you could die. Are you sure you want to do this?" I say. Kieran just continues to smile. Why is he so damned cute, even now? I can't shake the feeling that him joining us will be devastating for Reggie and my friendship, but I desperately want to spend more time with him.

"Zayda, you and I both know that our days are numbered. The way I see it, I have two choices. Follow the Officers, like a dumb sheep, to some imagined 'safe place', or go down fighting for someone I believe in," Kieran states. The smile has faded from his face and in its place, is a look that can only be interpreted as determination.

"You barely know me," I respond.

"I know enough to want to spend as much of my remaining time as possible with you," he says, purposefully moving forward and placing his soft hands on the sides of my face, "and if that means I have to be a rebel, then a rebel I will be."

Something comes over me and I lose myself in the moment. I lean toward Kieran, surrendering my lips to his. The eagerness of him returning the motion causes us both to become breathless. For a few moments, all the world's problems are erased. His hands gently caress the small of my back where my long, white hair falls, sending shivers down my spine. Awkwardly but with determination, I move my fingers up to entwine them in his dark curls. None of this is familiar, and it is obvious we are both figuring it out as we go. However, it feels so right and so normal. The amount of need and yearning I sense makes me a little afraid. I have always imagined my first kiss, but the fantasy was nothing like this. Instead of fireworks and butterflies, I feel comfort and safety. With these thoughts running through my mind, I almost forget where we are.

"Uh hum. Get a room guys," Viola says teasingly as she suddenly emerges beside us.

Kieran and I abruptly pull away from each other, dropping our hands to our sides. My cheeks burn with embarrassment from being caught making out. His, on the other hand, smolder with what I assume is desire. He continues to stare into my eyes for a few seconds longer before looking at our audience. "Good to see you two," he says, the tone of his voice suggesting he is not entirely pleased with their sudden presence.

"Wish I could say the same," Camden replies coldly. He is staring at us with his brow furrowed and lips pulled taut. Camden will never admit it, but I think he is secretly hoping Reggie and I will hook up.

"Sorry. I didn't expect you for a few more minutes," I apologize.

"Obviously," Viola snickers and wags her eyebrows at us.

"Well, we are here now, so what is the grand plan to get out of the village?" Camden asks, the glower vanishing from his face.

"I don't have a grand plan. I just assumed we would sneak out like before," I reply.

"Unfortunately, during your face sucking session, the Officers all started patrolling. Did you not notice them?" Camden questions. He looks irritated once more.

"Uh, I guess not," I say looking around for the first time. Camden is right, Officers are everywhere. I can't believe we haven't been spotted yet. The only thing that makes sense is they didn't suspect the couple making out behind the tent to be the girl on the run and her new accomplice. Of course, they didn't, no one would expect me to be that stupid. Except, apparently I am. Panic begins to rise inside me, and I struggle to think clearly and come up with a way out of this mess. "I don't know how we are going to get out of here without someone recognizing me."

"What if we create a diversion?" Kieran suggests, moving to stand in front of me and block my form from anyone walking by.

"What kind of diversion?" Viola asks, mirroring Kieran's movement.

"I don't know. Something to draw them all to one spot, so we can take off. Like an explosion? Maybe?" Kieran says.

"And how are we supposed to do that?" Camden asks, irritation still heavy in his voice. Sending his red shaggy bangs into his eyes, he shakes his head to emphasize his annoyance.

"Oh, I might have something stashed in my tent," Kieran says with a wink.

"What the what? How did you get an explosive? I'm pretty sure those are totally against the rules," Viola states.

"Let's just say I'm a collector," Kieran replies. He then turns and jogs off into the distance toward his tent. Once, he turns around and gives us an excited thumbs up.

The three of us remaining just stand and look at each other in utter confusion. After several moments, Camden is the first to speak. "What a dork! What can you possibly see in that kid? And...Where the hell would he *collect* an explosive?" he asks.

"I. Have. No. Idea," I respond, emphasizing each word to make sure they know it applies to all questions asked.

"Looks like your boyfriend has some secrets," Viola teases.

"He's not my boy...oh, forget it," I say. After what just happened between Kieran and me, I have no idea what he is, but this is not the right time to get into a discussion about it.

"Whatever you say," Viola replies, wagging her eyebrows again.

"Will you please stop making that ridiculous face at me?"

"Not until you stop doing naughty things in the dark," she responds, wagging them at me even more this time.

"And *he's* the dork," I reply.

"Not my words, but I will have to agree with my bro on that one," she says.

"Whatever. Can we please just let it go for now?" I ask.

"For now," Viola says. I can see by her face that she fully intends to bring this back up again the first chance she gets. I just hope it isn't in front of Reggie. Even if he has been making moon-eyes at Marla, he will not be pleased to hear about me having my first kiss with Kieran. Speaking of Kieran, I can see him running back to us now. He is carrying a small orb in his right hand.

Out of breath, "Got it," Kieran whispers as he stops in front of us.

"Jesus! You are fast," Camden says.

"I kind of already had it out. You know...just in case," Kieran says, glancing knowingly in my direction.

"Well, I for one am glad you were prepared. How does this thing work?" Viola asks.

"I'm not entirely sure. There is a paper strapped to it with directions on it. I'll read that and find out," Kieran replies.

Camden and Viola both gasped audibly. "You can read?" Camden exclaims.

"Oops. Guess the cat's out of the bag," Kieran says, nonchalantly shrugging his broad shoulders and reading the paper.

Viola looks at me, her eyes narrowing, "You knew about this?"

"It might have come up," I say, lowering my eyes and absently digging the toe of my boot into the dirt.

"Don't you think that is something you could have shared with the rest of us?" she chides.

"Sorry, it's not like we've had time to sit around and chat about life and stuff lately. I've kind of been run out of town and all. Or, did you forget about that tidbit?" I retort. Viola just stands quietly, a look of shame spreading across her face.

"Okay, I've got it figured out," Kieran says. I am thankful for him interrupting our uncomfortable silence. He is standing with the explosive balancing on his right palm, and his pointer finger on his left hand sticking into a piece of metal on top of the small ball. "I'm supposed to pull this out while holding down this lever, and then toss the ball toward my target. What is my target?" he asks.

"How big of an explosion does it make?" I ask.

"I'm not really sure, but it couldn't be too big based on the size of this thing. It isn't much bigger than an orange," Kieran replies.

"Wait, you've never seen one go off before?" Camden asks.

"No, but I've heard stories about people using them in the old days."

"Fantastic. Did you guys hear that? He's heard stories," Camden says, slapping his palm on his forehead.

"Well, to be on the safe side, we should throw it somewhere there aren't a lot of people. We don't want any innocents to get hurt," I offer.

"You wouldn't be too worried about those 'innocent people' if you had heard how they were talking about you all day," Viola states.

"That bad?" I ask, not sure I really want to know the answer.

"You are officially enemy number one. The words traitor and noose might have been tossed around a few times," Camden adds.

"Ugh. Still, it doesn't matter if they hate me, I can't let my feelings get hurt and effect my judgement. We will throw it by the river. At this time of the morning, no one should be there," I say.

"You're the boss," Kieran chimes.

He is still wearing the ridiculous look on his face from when we were kissing earlier. I just shake my head at him and try not to look annoyed. He really does mean well, and if this works, he is saving my butt-big time. "I guess then all that is left is to decide who will throw it," I say.

"Not it," Viola snaps, "you guys have seen me throw before. I'll end up dropping it on my foot and blowing my big toe off."

"True," Camden replies "I could do it. I have a pretty good aim."

"Wait, it's my bomb. I think I should get to do it," Kieran protests.

"But, if you get caught, then your dad will be pissed at you. Plus, you will end up on The Healer's hit list like me. I think I should be the one," I say.

"Why should you take all of the risk?" Kieran asks.

"Because, like Viola already said, everyone already hates me. You guys have a chance to come out of this unscathed. No one is trying to catch you and lock you up," I reply.

"No, but the minute we leave here with you we are just as guilty as you are," Camden says. Taking note of all our faces, he looks calmly around our small group. "Despite all the jokes, this is a big deal. No matter who throws the bomb, we are all going to be altering the rest of our lives."

"Thanks, Debbie Downer. Geesh. We get it. Life of peril. Officers chasing us. Possible having Turned chomping on our faces. No home to come back to...blah...blah...blah," Viola jokes, playfully poking her brother on the arm.

"Okay, it's settled then, we are all fully committed," Camden says to Viola.

"Duh. I thought that was decided the minute we came out here," Viola replies.

"If I'm all in, then I'm all in. I'll throw the explosive," Camden announces.

We all nod our heads in acknowledgement. The look on Kieran's face implies he understands that Camden feels he needs to do this. I can understand why he feels he has to; it is his way of making sure he can't back out. Nothing like a little trial by fire, so to speak, to make you an official outlaw. I sometimes forget that other people are not as quick to break the rules as I am, and Camden is the prime example of a law-abiding citizen. He has always been a good kid, and this dive into the abyss is probably going to be the hardest on him.

Grabbing the explosive from Kieran's hand, Camden runs off toward the river, taking us all by surprise, and yells, "No time like the present! See you down the hill!" With that, we all scatter and pray for everything to work out.

PIECES

"He should be here by now," Viola says for the twentieth time. She has been pacing along the space by the window, wringing her hands nervously, for the past hour or more.

"I'm sure he will be here soon," I say, for also the twentieth time. Truthfully, I am beginning to worry about Camden also. We heard the bomb go off a few moments after he ran for the river, but we didn't have the luxury of waiting behind to see the plan carried out. At least the main objective of us getting away had been achieved. Screams could be heard from every direction as Officers scrambled to find the source of the blast; with all the chaos, Kieran, Viola, and I slipped away unnoticed.

"Camden is a resourceful guy. He will be okay. I'm sure he is just trying to keep them from following him," Reggie says. I am happy to hear him say something. Since we returned, he hasn't uttered more than a few syllables to any of us. My guess is he is more than a little unhappy with Kieran's presence being exchanged for Camden's, that and the news about Kyle. Not that I'm some kind of genius, mind-reader or anything, but the look of disgust that flashed on Reggie's face when Kieran walked into the square behind me was hard to miss. Even Marla seemed to notice the contempt. When we got back here, she walked over to stand next to Reggie, but quickly relocated to a seemingly safer position beside Julie. If Kieran's mere existence caused this violent of a reaction, I can only imagine what Reggie will do if he finds out about the kiss.

"Thanks, Reg," Viola says. She seems to relax a bit with his words, or maybe it is just the reaction to the small amount of tension being removed from the room. We have all been feeling it.

"I hate to bring this up, but if we don't head out soon, we won't make it to the village before nightfall. I don't mean to sound insensitive, but maybe we could leave some clues behind for him to follow us there," Marla states.

"We are not leaving without my brother!" Viola spits. The way she says it is more like a slap than words, and Marla visibly cringes with the force.

Retreating farther into her corner, Marla sheepishly says, "I didn't mean anything by it. I'm sorry. I won't bring it up again."

Walking over to Viola and placing my hand gently on her shoulder, I say, "She's right, Vi. We can't risk staying here much longer. The Officers will realize you all are gone and come after us; if they haven't already." She just silently shakes her head no and begins to sob. "Please. Camden would not want you to put yourself at risk for him. Reggie is right, he is a resourceful kid and will find us."

"Just give her some space to think," Kieran suggests. He has crossed over to stand right by us and is reaching out to hold my hand. I don't even have to look up to feel the daggers Reggie is shooting in our direction. Casually, pretending to warm them, I begin to rub my hands together. "Cold?" he asks, trying to save face.

"Yes. I get this way when I'm nervous," I lie.

"Since when?" Reggie huffs.

"Since always," I snort.

"News to me, and I do know you better than *anyone* else," Reggie replies, looking directly in Kieran's direction and adding extra emphasis to the word anyone.

"I think you meant to say longer," Kieran says with a chuckle and walking back to his original spot on the barstool across the room.

"Enough! Things are already tense around here without you two acting like a couple of babies," I yell.

"Whatever," both boys say at the same time. Even the shared response can't splinter the blockade between them. Reggie retreats to the far corner between this room and the next, and continues his visual assault on Kieran. Kieran just smirks at Reggie like he has won some kind of prize. At this moment, I hate them both.

"About time," Marla mumbles, twirling a piece of hair around her finger. I sense her feelings might be being hurt by the way Reggie is behaving. Something tells me, she had thought Reggie liked her too, and now she isn't sure.

Wanting to make her feel better, I say, "Boys! They can be real jerks sometimes, don't ya' think?"

"Mind your own business," she replies, a tear threatening to spill out of her eye.

Still trying, I say, "I'm just trying to help."

"Well, I don't need your help, so back off!"

"Fine," I say.

"Fine," she says.

Her words, though minimal, irritate the crap out of me and send my brain on an internal tirade. Why is everyone so emotional right now? You can't even be nice to someone without them biting your head off. Maybe, I would be better off going out there alone. I don't need this aggravation. I mean, who does she think she is? It's not like I'm begging

Reggie to pay attention to me. Okay, maybe a little, but it's not my fault he has anger issues and thinks we are an item. As if things aren't stressful enough without the drama, she has to start being a jerk too. Giving them my best dirty look, I stomp off into the other room to continue my tantrum.

***

About twenty minutes later, when all our hopes have almost faded, and I have gotten over my fit, Julie gleefully exclaims, "I see something. Over there, by the bushes. I think it's a person."

We all run over to the window to peer out and catch a glimpse of what Julie has seen. The sun is shining brightly overhead, but despite that, my eyes cannot find the figure she spotted. "Where did you see it? Can you point for me?" I ask the little girl.

Raising her small finger, she points to a large, overgrown hedge halfway inside of the square. "Right there. It was moving pretty fast, but I'm sure I saw something. See, there it is again," Julie cries.

"I think I see it too," Viola says, a glimmer of optimism spreading on her face.

"Wait, there's another one," Julie says.

Panic rises inside me. Camden should not be coming with anyone else. "Are you sure, Jules?" I ask.

"Positively absolutely," she proudly replies. It is obvious the young girl is pleased with being the first person to make this discovery.

"Should we hide?" Marla asks.

"I don't know yet. Unless they had a scout follow us, they won't know what building we are in. I think we should be okay. For now," I respond.

"Camden won't know either. I don't think you told him where we were heading before he ran off," Viola points out.

"Crap! You're right. Everything was happening so fast," I say.

"I can go get him," Reggie offers.

The prospect of Reggie going outside and getting captured by an officer makes me queasy. "That isn't a good idea. What if it isn't Camden, but rather two Officers? We can't afford to lose someone else," I say.

As my words register, Viola's face falls. "You don't know it isn't Camden. He could have gotten out. He did get out! If he is being followed by someone, he needs our help," she says.

"I understand where you are coming from, Vi, but I can't put any of you in more danger. You wouldn't even be here if it weren't for my stupid plan. I'll go," I reply.

"You would do that for him?" Viola asks, a look of relief washing over her.

"Of course, Camden is my friend too," I say.

"Well, you aren't going out there alone," Reggie states as he gets up and begins moving toward the door.

I am all set to argue with him, but the look he is giving me suggests it would be a moot point. "Alright. Let's go," I surrender.

"Be careful," Kieran says. He has been standing by watching the exchange quietly.

Knowing Kieran probably wants to go with me too, but not needing any additional turmoil, I just nod at him and offer a small smile. Kieran is a great guy, and I have yet to figure out my feelings for him. However, Reggie is too important to me to continuously hurt him over someone who is, for all accounts, a stranger. I wish things weren't so crazy right now, so I could take five minutes to analyze my life, but sadly that is not in the cards. "You ready?" I ask Reggie.

"For you, always," Reggie replies, casting yet another sour glance at Kieran.

"Oh, for crying out loud," I mumble before grabbing the handle and stepping outside.

***

Outside, alone for the first time in days, the current strain on our relationship seems to hover heavily in the air like a dense fog. I want desperately to tell Reggie he doesn't have anything to worry about, that I am not falling for Kieran, that things between he and I will remain the same forever, but I would be lying.

"Can I ask you a question?" Reggie says, breaking the smothering silence.

"Absolutely," I reply, trying to sound as casual as possible and failing miserably.

"Why did you bring him back with you? I mean, I know we need help fighting, but why him?" Reggie asks.

Sympathy courses through my veins when I see the tears threatening to overflow his emerald eyes. "He kinda just showed up, and then everything escalated so quickly. Plus, he *is* responsible for hatching the plan that allowed us to make it back here. I know you don't like him, but we really do need all the help we can get," I answer honestly.

Reggie sucks in a deep breath before responding, "Do you like him?"

Now it is my turn to take a deep breath. "Honestly," I say, pausing to carefully consider my next words, "My entire world has been turned upside down. Lately, most days I don't have two minutes to think hard on anything. There is no easy answer to that question, so I'm just going to say maybe. But...I also love you, Reg. You have been one of my best friends, have always been there for me, and I know you always will."

"What if being your friend isn't enough for me anymore?" he asks, running his hand nervously through his thick, mousy brown hair. A hint of apprehension threatening to break the damn behind his eyes, "I don't think I can sit by and watch you fall for someone else."

"I don't know that answer either," is all I can manage to say. I know it is not enough, not nearly enough, but it is all I have to offer.

"Oh," is all he replies.

Pausing at the edge of the square, I look deeply into his eyes and search for something, anything, to say to ease his pain. Nothing comes. If only, there was more time to sit and think. If only, we were not running for our lives. If only, we were not on another mission. If only... "Can we talk about this later? We need to focus," I reply, desperately wishing I did not have to do this to him.

"Yes, but only because we need to find Camden. Don't think you can avoid this subject forever," Reggie replies.

"I know you better than to ever think you would let a topic drop," I say teasingly, "Now, be quiet so whoever is in there doesn't hear us."

Crouching down, we slink past the iron gate and position ourselves behind the nearest cluster of plants. Dark green foliage, stretching over eight feet tall and three feet deep, masks us from the duo approaching on the trail. Signaling we should both look to the left, Reggie points two fingers from his eyes to the trail where the sound of rapidly approaching footsteps can be heard. It is impossible to tell if the nearest steps are being pursued by the other, but one thing is clear—they are going to be upon us any second. Many years of synchronicity kick into gear as Reggie and I, without communication, lean forward in preparation to launch ourselves at the encroaching bodies.

"One, two, three," I mouth, counting off my fingers at the same time.

Just as the two cross directly in front of us, Reggie shouts, "Go," and we throw the full force of our weight into the figures.

Rolling on the ground, arms and legs entwined with my unknown, masked enemy, I struggle to gain the upper hand. As my feet find purchase in their solid flesh, I can hear groans and screams reverberating through the air. Reggie and his target also fight for dominance, and more thuds echo ours in the daytime air. Several times, I land on top, only to be overtaken again and pinned to the ground. Whoever this is, they are definitely stronger than me. My head bounces off the hard pavement with each spin we take, and blood pools inside my mouth from where I bite the inside of my cheek. All the while, my assailant continues to overtake me. "Get off of me, you stupid bastard," I yell.

"You attacked me," a gravelly voice says, smacking my head down on the ground again. It is hard to make out through the thick material covering his mouth, but my

wrestling partner most assuredly sounds like a large man.
"Why did you jump me?" he continues.

"Why are you here?" I choke out, my head smacking the
ground again. Speaking is becoming more difficult with each
blow; my vision is swirling and clouded over from the
trauma.

"Zayda?" another voice calls out from nearby, "Get off
her! She's with me." Even through the thuds and smacks, I
can hear the familiar cadence of Camden's words.

"What? This crazy lady is the one who is going to lead the
rebellion?" the man asks.

"If you don't kill her first. Now, stop banging her head on
the ground," Camden shouts.

"Sorry, she just scared the shit out of me. Not to
mention, *she* jumped *me*," the man replies, rising off my
chest.

Choking and coughing, I continue to lie flat on the
ground for a few more moments. I repeatedly blink my eyes
to try and clear my still unsettled vision. My body aches from
the fight, and I can already feel the bruises and swelling
spreading throughout my limbs. "Who the hell are you?" I
manage to mumble to the broad shouldered, husky man with
the crew cut standing over me.

"This is Officer Jones. He helped me fight off several
other Officers and escape after the explosion," Camden
answers for the man.

"Why would you do that?" Reggie asks Officer Jones.

"Because he hates The Healers as much as we do," Camden answers again.

"Can he speak for himself?" Reggie says, irritation showing in his voice.

"Yes, I can speak for myself. I just don't usually talk to people who just tried to kill me," Officer Jones replies, pulling his mask down and exposing his square and muscular jaw.

"Well, when we saw you both coming through the square, we didn't know who you were. And then *you* tried to kill me," I sneer.

Officer Jones looks sheepish and embarrassed, "Yeah, sorry for that. Had I known you were a woman, I would not have tried to bash your brains in," he states, actual remorse shining through in his tone.

"Gee, thanks. Glad to know you weren't taking it easy on me because I'm a chick," I say. I know I should not let it bother me, but comments like that really tick me off. I do not need a man to take it easy on me. I can't help but shoot daggers at Officer Jones.

"Hey! No need for the evil eye. That's not what I meant. Just that...," Officer Jones pauses, I assume he is trying to come up with the best response. "I don't know exactly. Just that...Oh forget it. I'm Nathan," he says, offering his enormous hand for me to shake, "I think we might have gotten off on the wrong foot here."

"Zayda," I say, shaking his hand and sizing him up. Nathan appears to be around twenty-five, which makes him just a little older than the youngest to grow up post-Cure. "Thanks for helping Cam," I add, trying to chill out.

"No joke," Camden chimes in, "without Nathan, I would have been toast. The blast knocked me on my butt and twisted my knee something awful. By the time I stopped seeing stars, the other Officers were almost on me. Our new friend here helped me up, and got me the heck out of there."

"Pretty lucky for Camden that you were at the right place at the right time," Reggie says, his face a blank slate, but I can tell he is suspicious of Nathan's intent. To be honest, I question it also. No one got as high in the ranks as officer by hating The Healers.

"It sure is. I wasn't even scheduled to be on patrol this morning, but Harrison fell and hurt his ankle last night." Something about his words seem to hint at an alternate meaning, but I do not yet know what that is. He seems like he is highly skilled in the art of camouflage. Looking left to address Camden directly, the intensity on his face increasing one hundred percent, his brow drawing down, and a seriousness only a soldier could possess overtaking his cadence, Nathan says, "I am not alone."

Perplexed, I close the small gap between Nathan and me, trying to read his body language and decipher what his words mean. "Not alone? As in, there are other Officers down here with us? Or, not alone in another way?" I ask.

"I'm not sure I can trust you all enough to say," Nathan answers.

"Then why say anything at all?" Reggie asks. His translucently pale skin begins to flush with color, and even the others seem to sense his rising irritation this time. Deep down, I know Reggie is being pushed to his breaking point; that combined with the accelerated physical changes I can see happening more by each hour, make him dangerous. He still has at least six months until his full Turning is to occur, however, deep down, I know it will be sooner-much sooner.

"Because I wasn't thinking clearly. Look, I want to help you all, but I'm going to need some time to think before I fully commit. Too much is at risk," Nathan responds.

The soldier appears, for the first time, to be being completely genuine. His last words weigh heavily upon me. Too much at risk? What does that mean? Have we underestimated the gravity and scope of the situation? My mind reels with all the questions. "Fair enough. Maybe after you meet the rest of the group, and see we have nothing to hide, you will feel more at ease," I say.

"Camden hasn't had much time to fill me in on the details. How many more are there?" Nathan asks.

"Not many, but we hope to find more," I reply.

"How?" Nathan asked.

Smiling, I answer, "Now, it's my turn to keep a few secrets."

ALLIANCE

Back at home base, as the others have decided to call it, the drastic change in the atmosphere is immediately noticeable when we walk in. Viola is no longer pacing and fretting about Camden's return, instead she is braiding Julie's hair; the small girl is holding a tattered teddy bear in her arms. Judging from the look on her face, she does not care about the condition of the toy. As Viola gently picks up small pieces of Julie's fine hair and weaves it into a delicate pattern, the two of them chat away like life-long friends. Julie's eyes light up when she sees me and tells me about the other cool toys she found in one of the adjacent rooms. Marla is in the main hall and has somehow managed to scavenge up some food; she is looming over her spoils smiling. It is all spread out on the bar like a regal feast. Kieran is gone, but the girls assure me he is on a small mission and will return any time. The scene almost appears normal, but I know better than to assume anything is ever going to be normal again.

"What's with the party?" I ask.

"We saw you all in the square and knew everything was okay. I wanted to throw us a celebration before we leave," Marla replies.

"Took you long enough to get back," Viola says, standing to hug her brother. "You had me worried, brother."

"Sorry, sis. I tried to get back as fast as I could," Camden replies, limping toward Viola.

"What did you do? Are you hurt?" Viola asks in a panic.

"Just a little bump from when the bomb went off. No big deal," he replies, grabbing her into a giant hug.

After Viola and Camden hug and cry in relief, I introduce Camden and Nathan to our new friends. Camden and Marla seem to really get along well and are joking and laughing like old friends. Marla's laugh is very pleasant and light, casting the entire room in a brilliant hue. Everyone seems to relax with each trilling chorus of merriment, and I realize then and there that she is going to be monumentally important to us all. The world has been so dark and gloomy lately, so a beacon of hope is more than welcome.

Casually observing us from one of the barstools, Nathan appears to still be skeptical of us all and is staying to himself. Periodically, and by that, I mean every two minutes, I cast a wary glance his way to try and figure him out. Each time, he is doing the exact same thing-nothing. I have no more reason to mistrust Nathan than Marla or Julie, except for the whole ex-officer thing, so I don't know why I am being so overly cautious. Intuition? Probably more like paranoia. Deciding that the sooner he and I get to know each other, the better each of our situations will be, I go to talk to him. As I approach him, he looks up at me nervously and shifts his weight on the stool. I don't blame him for being skeptical and worried; he has just given up his entire life. In that way, we are very much alike. I think I should give Nathan some slack. Trying to break the tension and make him feel more at ease, I start the conversation on the light side. "How long have you been an officer?" I ask.

"Since The Cure...uh...started not just curing anymore," he replies. There is an underlying sadness to his words, and I wonder what this man has been through.

It may be pushing too hard, but I ask, "Why did you join them if you hate them so much?" This is a question I have longed to ask one of them for so long, and now that I have the opportunity, I am not sure I am prepared to accept the answer.

He sucks in a big breath before answering, "In the beginning, I truly believed in the work they did. I mean, who wouldn't want to save the world and be a hero? I had two older brothers, so I knew the threat that existed if we didn't stop The Turned. My dad and I enlisted on the first day the sign went up," Nathan states.

His response surprises me. There is no big revelation in it, but that is what causes me pause. All along, I just assumed anyone who decided to be an Officer, did so because they were a horrific monster. Apparently, they are just normal guys who want to keep us safe. I feel immense pity for Nathan in this moment, and I deeply want to understand him better. "When did you stop believing in the cause?" I ask.

"About a year ago, something seemed off with the new orders we were getting. Each day, the requests became more bizarre," Nathan says. Like he is releasing a heavy burden that has been squashing him into the ground, his posture seems to relax and he sits up straighter with each statement he makes. He looks at me with sad eyes and continues, "We aren't only going after monsters anymore. "

"I don't understand," I reply.

"The Council is trying to take over the world and enslave you all. Phase one started last year," he says, with a hint of reservation. Nathan pauses, and looks around the room, he seems to be considering very deeply whether he should continue. With a sigh, he does, "Phases two and three began yesterday."

"How many phases are there?" I ask, terrified to hear the answer.

"Four," is all he manages to choke out. Tears brim his round eyes as he reflects on things I am yet to know.

Fearing that I am pushing him too hard too fast, I stop asking questions and just put my hand on top of his for comfort. The last few minutes of conversation with Nathan have done two things: make me trust him completely, and make me even more determined to destroy The Healers and everything they represent. Their plans are not yet totally known to me, and honestly, I doubt Nathan knows all of them, but from what I have witnessed lately, they must be apocalyptic.

"You guys okay over here?" Kieran asks, appearing for the first time since our return. Extreme concern mixed with a deeper, hidden feeling mask his face. Based on his posture, I am sure he has heard at least part of our conversation.

"When did you get back?" I ask, quickly changing the subject, so I can try to figure out what Kieran is hiding.

"Not long ago," he replies, narrowing his eyes at me suspiciously and giving me a half smile. Everything about him seems alien right now. The Kieran that I have come to know is not present anywhere on this stranger's face, and I can tell he is being deliberately evasive in his responses.

"Julie said you went out to get something. Where is it?" I ask, trying to play it off like I am excited to see his surprise.

"I couldn't find what I was looking for," he replies, again giving me the feeling he is lying.

"What was it? Maybe I can help you look," I offer, attempting to back him into a corner.

"Now, if I told you, it wouldn't be a surprise anymore," he says winking, his real smile spreading lightheartedly across his face. And just like that, the old Kieran is back. "Who is this?" he asks.

"I got so caught up in prying you for answers about the *surprise* that I forgot you haven't met Nathan yet," I say, still going along with his façade. He does not look convinced by my act, but plays it off much better this time. Not wanting to tip him off that I am suspicious, I walk over to him and intertwine my fingers with his. "Kieran, this is Nathan, the officer who helped Camden escape. Nathan, this is Kieran, the last of our group. He and his father just relocated to our camp a few days ago," I add. With the word 'relocated', Nathan's shoulders stiffen and he appears to get extremely uncomfortable.

"Nice to meet you, and thanks for your help," Kieran says, reaching his hand out for Nathan to shake.

Unsteadily, Nathan shakes Kieran's hand. I can see how nervous he is and see him visibly trembling. "Nice to meet you too," Nathan manages to mumble. Hopping off his stool, he begins to walk away from us. Long gone is the confident stride he demonstrated on the journey back here. "I've been up all night, and I'm exhausted. Gonna' find a place to rest for a few hours before we head out," he says. On his way out the door, he turns to me and says with urgency, "We really need to finish our conversation before we go. Come find me in a little while."

"Okay. Why don't you have Marla walk you up to the room we have been using. Then, I will know exactly where you are," I reply. Hoping he understands the underlying tone of my message, I give him a nod.

"Will do," Nathan replies.

"Food's on," Marla shouts with excitement.

"Hey, Marla, I know you just finished making all of this food, but would you be able to show Nathan the upstairs bedroom so he can rest?" I ask.

"Sure, no problem," Marla replies. She walks over to Nathan and loops her arm through his. "Shall we?"

"Why thank you ma'am," he replies.

"Tell me everything there is to know about you," Marla says as the two of them begin walking away.

"Oh, there isn't much to say. I am...," Nathan says. His voice fades to an inaudible level as they approach the bottom of the stairs.

Turning back to Kieran, as normally as possible, I say, "So, you hungry? Somehow, she managed to find all this food and put together a phenomenal spread for us.

"I can always eat," he replies, his eyes still tracking Nathan's exit.

"Then, let's get our grub on. I'm starving," I say, nudging him playfully in the ribs. The feeling that something is wrong will not dissipate, but I push it aside and focus on our need to formulate a plan. Kieran has given me no reason to mistrust him. In fact, he has been a remarkable ally during this ordeal. Plus, I am really starving, and the food looks amazing.

***

Looking around at my old friends and my new ones, I can't help but reflect on how much I consider them family. One benefit of the current world we live in is alliances can be forged in the most unlikely of places. If you would have told me a week ago, that I would be on the lam with this ragtag group, I would have laughed in your face. Still, here we all are.

The feast Marla has prepared looks amazing. She has managed to acquire a multitude of canned and pickled items such as: pie fillings, exotic fruits, sausages, eggs, green beans, okra, red beans, and even some crawfish. Our diet up in the village consisted of mostly oats, dried beef sticks, river fish, and the occasional fresh fruit, so this is a welcome treat. My mouth is watering just imagining the different sensations hitting my tongue.

"What did Nathan tell you, Zay?" Kieran asks, shaking me out of my food fantasy.

He is currently fully back to being just Kieran, but I am not willing to forget so quickly what happened before. "Not much. He mainly just talked about why he joined the cause," I answer, grabbing an egg and popping the entire thing into my mouth; the salty, vinegar taste is heavenly. I glance at Kieran to see if he is satisfied with my response. Despite being curt, it is an honest answer.

Casually chomping on a green bean stalk, Kieran turns to Camden, "How about you? Did he give you any insight into what might be going on? I figure the more we know before heading out the better."

My heart lunges into my throat. Camden hadn't seen the way Kieran acted, so he has no reason to be evasive. What if Nathan has told him the same things as me? I silently pray for him to hold back, and cast him a pleading look with my eyes. Camden knows me better than Kieran, so I will have to hope he picks up on my subtle clue. "We didn't really have too much time to talk," Camden replies, momentarily casting a knowing glance my direction. "All I gathered was that he was tired of being an officer, saw an out, and he split," he adds, licking the sugary pie filling off his fingers.

"I've never heard of anyone doing that before," Viola says, the juice from the canned peaches running down her chin.

"I'm sure it would not be something they would want to advertise," Reggie states. He is watching me intently. Maybe I was wrong about no one catching Camden and my exchange. Of course, if someone would have noticed, Reg would be the one. It didn't matter though, I would have confided in him eventually anyway. As far as I am concerned, he is my most trusted ally at this point.

"True. It doesn't paint them in the best of light, nor does it maintain their 'all powerful' persona," Viola adds, grabbing another pickled sausage from the jar.

"One thing I do know, Nathan said there were others like him," I state, watching Kieran's reactions like a hawk. Nothing. He doesn't even bat an eye at my statement.

"How many?" Kieran asks, his voice not betraying his cool demeanor.

"How many what?" Marla asks, returning to the room and joining the conversation.

"Other Officers helping Nathan... and...He didn't say for sure, but any extra bodies are a good thing," I reply. Never before have I uttered a truer statement. We need all the help we can get. "I'm going to take him some food in a minute, so I will see what I can find out then," I add.

"I meant to ask you, Marla, where did you find all of this stuff?" Kieran says. Anyone else would have thought it just a curious question, but I find it to be another indictment of his character. He suddenly seems incredibly inquisitive.

"I found a storage room in the back. It was locked with a giant bar, but I managed to get it off. Most of the cans were dusty, and they have probably been in there since the beginning, but everything tastes okay to me. You guys think so too?" Marla says, a proud smile on her face.

"Yummy for sure," Julie cheers. Marla's meal is probably the most food the young girl has had in days. Heck, as thin as she is, years might be more like it.

"We should put some cans in our bags, so we don't have to scavenge along the way. Speaking of which, we really should get going in the next half hour or so," Camden states. He appears rested and nearly recovered from almost being blown to bits and captured. Pausing to shovel more food into his mouth, he surveys us all meaningfully. "I'm certain they will come looking for us soon, and we aren't too far off the beaten path here," he adds.

"Marla, can you find your way to the other camp if we avoid the water? I know you and Julie came in that way, but it is far too risky now. There will be Officers crawling all over the levee by now, and it offers a perfect view of the river walk," I say.

"Yes, once we get outside of The Old City, I can find some of the markers I left along the way," Marla replies.

"You left markers?" Reggie asks a hint of admiration touching his voice.

"Well, yeah. We didn't know what we would find when we got here, and I wanted to make sure we wouldn't get stuck in a jam," Marla says, beaming at Reggie. It appears her sour feelings from earlier have faded, and she is back to being a fan of Reg. She is not very good at masking her emotions, and her developing crush is blatantly displayed on her face. I take a few moments to really look at her. She is not conventionally pretty, honestly a bit plain, but there is something below the surface that erases all of that. I can't name it exactly, but my instincts say it is her resolve and intellect. Reggie must be picking up on that too because he appears to be getting more smitten with each glance her way. Funny thing is, with Kieran back-even if he is acting strangely-I don't mind as much.

"How long do you think it will take us to get there?" Viola asks.

"I told Zayda earlier that it would be a good day's walk, but I think now that we've had some food and built up energy," Marla pauses and grabs a piece of okra and shoves it into her mouth. Through garbled chewing, she continues, "plus, we won't have to stop and forage. I think we could be there in much less time now. That is, barring any obstacles along the way."

Her logic is solid, and I am ready to put as much distance between us and The Healers as possible. "Okay, so here's the plan then, I'm going to take some food to Nathan and check to see when he will be ready to go. Viola, look around for anything we can use for protection. Reggie and Marla, grab as much food and water as we can comfortably carry. Kieran and Camden, keep a close watch and make sure no one has come down from Alon. We will meet back in this room in twenty minutes," I say.

"What about me?" Julie's small voice questions.

"I saved the best job for you, Jules," I say, smiling at the sweet little in front of me. For being so young and having just gone through a terrible ordeal, this girl is tough as nails. I am impressed with her resilience. Reaching down to touch her tiny shoulder, I continue, "You have to sit on the stairs while I talk to Nathan, so you can warn me if anything goes wrong. Do you think you can do that?"

"You bet!"

"Awesome. Let's go," I say, grabbing some food with one hand and wrapping my other around hers. "Lead the way."

On the way out of the room, I cast a glance back at everyone, focusing discretely on Kieran. He is trying to hide it, but I can see a tinge of anger on his face. Guess he didn't expect me to take a guard. *Don't underestimate me*, I think, as we ascend the stairs.

***

Sitting criss cross on the bed next to Nathan, as he eats the food I just brought him, my eyes are open wide in shock as I let what he has just confessed to me sink in. "I can't believe this! I was part of their plan all along?" I say.

"Yes, you were part of Phase Two. And, I guess, technically Phase One. What was the name of your friend that ratted you guys out? Posy?" Nathan asks. Still too shocked to say much, I just nod my head. "She was probably scouted out and flipped over a year back. Surprisingly, The Healers were easily able to get one mole in each village. Then they, the mole, reported back on anyone who was breaking the rules," he adds.

"But how did they know I would break them?" I ask, puzzled by how well their scheme has worked.

"Someone always does. It has been happening since the beginning, but you would never have known. The Healers have a way of making rule breakers disappear. Can you remember any almost Turned who just up and got relocated with very little time left?" Nathan asks.

"Just one. Last year, there was a kid named Randy. I didn't know him very well because he was super quiet and always kept to himself. He got relocated to a different region two months before his final transition. His parents were besides themselves when it happened. Why?" I ask, stupidly not connecting the dots yet.

"He wasn't relocated. He was removed," he replies.

Pondering what he has just said, I remain quiet for a few seconds. I have never heard the term removed used in such a manner before. It sounds like Nathan is suggesting Randy was killed, but then why not just say that? "What exactly does 'removed' mean?" I ask.

"Only the higher ups know for sure, but we all have our theories. Mine is that they are taken off somewhere to be held captive until they Turn, and then they are killed. Many others think they are killed right way. Some, think they aren't killed at all," Nathan responds.

"Not really any great options there. Why would they keep them alive, and why didn't they remove me?" I ask.

"Because of Phase Two," he states, not offering much more information.

"Are you going to elaborate? What the hell is Phase Two?" I ask, rising from the bed and pacing, growing increasingly more agitated by his evasiveness.

"Phase Two is effectively creating uneasiness and discord in the villages to make them trust The Healers more. By making your people all hate you, they created a common enemy and forged a greater alliance to them. You were always supposed to escape," Nathan says. He seems incredibly uneasy with this particular aspect of the conversation.

"Why would they let me escape?" I ask. My brain has been trying to formulate a list of reasons why, but nothing at all makes sense.

"I don't know. We weren't given that information. Only the highest officials know all the specifics of any Phase," he replies.

"Okay, then can you tell me why they would keep The Turned alive? That seems dangerous and stupid."

"There have been murmurings of a Turned army for a few years now, but I don't give it much credence. No Healers, despite their inherent madness, would be crazy enough to think they can control one Turned, let alone hundreds," Nathan says.

Allowing the image of an army of Turned to soak into my mind, I flop back down and think. I've only seen a Turned from far away, and it was terrifying. I can't imagine how horrifying they are up close, let alone in a large group. "I think you are right about that part. The concept is way too out there, even for The Healers. Earlier, you started to tell me about the other Phases and plan. Can you fill me in on the rest now?" I say.

"Phase Three just started a few days back when they released the mutation," Nathan starts to say.

Interrupting him, "What? The Healers are the reason for the Turning speeding up? Why would they do that?" I yell.

"I don't know why, but that is the reason I had to get out. I can't be involved with them destroying people's lives, and using them as pawns in a game," he responds.

I want so much to ask him more questions, but Julie runs into the room before I have the chance. "Someone is coming up the stairs," she says breathlessly, her cheeks red from her hasty entrance.

"Great job, Jules. You were an excellent lookout. Do you know who it is?" I ask.

"No, but they are getting close," she replies.

"Okay, stay here with Nathan, and I'll go check it out."

Julie nods her head and climbs up on the bed to sit closer to the officer. Hurriedly, I make my way down the hall and hide behind a large, black desk. I don't want whoever is coming up to see me before I can access their intentions. It is probably just one of my friends coming to check on us, but it could be Kieran, and I want to see which Kieran it is.

The humidity in the corridor, combined with the lack of airflow from all the doors being locked closed, causes me to gag and cough on the stagnate smell of mold that permeates my nostrils. Holding my breath and trying to keep from making noise, so I don't alert the person coming up the stairs, makes my eyes water and cloud over. I am very limited on how far I can see. I can clearly hear the heavy footsteps, along with an underlying sound I cannot yet place, of the intruder echoing off the narrow passageway as they continue to move closer to me, but no part of their body is visible yet. Periodically, I wipe my eyes with the back of my hands and peer out to see if I can catch a glimpse of whoever is coming.

After what feels like hours, a dark tuft of patchy hair appears midway up the stairs. Stretching my neck to get a better look, I am able to begin to make out the figure. Slowly, more of the person comes into view; their forehead-pale and veiny; their eyes-yellow and frantic; their nose and lips-covered in oozing sores and fresh gore, their torso-thin and emaciated-it is one of The Turned. A growl erupts from inside of it as it sees me for the first time. "Nathan!" I shout, jumping to my feet and running for the open bedroom. "It's one of them!"

The long hallway seems to elongate in front of me as I make my way sluggishly toward the doorway. My every motion feels like I am swimming upstream against a heavy current, and I don't think I will make it to my destination before the monster catches me. Shuffling feet and low, feral snarls are the only noises I hear besides my own labored breathing. Chancing a look only once, I swivel my head to see where the monster is, and am shocked to see it has already cleared the top of the stairs and is staggering and twitching down the hall behind me. Terror fills me. I have never seen a Turned this close before, and I am not prepared for the reaction my body is having: my heart pounds feverishly in my chest, filling my ears with the loud throbbing of my own blood; sweat pours down my face like a fountain, again obscuring my vision; my legs shake and tremble with each frantic step, making me clumsy and awkward. If this is a test of my grit, I am failing miserably.

"Hurry!" Julie shouts. "He's getting closer." The young girl's face is twisted with fear, but otherwise she is doing much better than I am-reminding me that this is not her first time seeing one of The Turned this close.

Panting and gasping, I launch myself into the room and quickly spin around to watch in alarm as the creature continues to advance. Julie runs to me and presses her small body into my arms. As Nathan quickly takes my place in the hallway, Julie sobs and shakes soundlessly in my arms. I do my best to console her, but fail. I am too much of a mess to be of much comfort to anyone else. A few more steps and the beast will be on us. With the confidence only a soldier can manage, Nathan spreads his feet apart, raises his gun, aims, and fires one single shot. The creature falls to the ground in a heap; a large bullet hole smoking in the middle of its forehead.

"Are you okay?" Nathan asks, bending to help Julie and me up from the floor.

It is clear The Turned is dead, but that does little to calm me down. Quivering, I take his hand and rise. "I...I...think so," I reply.

"First time seeing one up close is always the hardest," Nathan says, trying to comfort me.

Nodding my head, less in agreement and more in general acknowledgement, I say, "Hope it's a long time before I have to test that theory." Deep down, I know there is little chance of that happening.

"What the hell was that?" Reggie yells. He is sprinting up the stairs, taking them in pairs to hurry the climb.

Following closely on Reggie's heels, "Was that a gunshot? Julie, where are you?" Marla asks frantically.

"I'm right here, and I'm okay," Julie responds, her voice still a bit shaky from crying.

"Holy shit!" Reggie says, clearing the flight of stairs and whirling down the hallway. His face goes white when he sees the body lying in the middle of the floor; a pool of black has started to seep out of the hole in its skull, and is growing larger by the second.

"How did *that* get in here?" Marla asks in shock. She stops running the minute she sees what has happened. I can see her looking back and forth from The Turned to Julie, presumably sorting between her instincts of nurture and flight. So far, flight appears to be winning.

"We didn't see anything outside," Camden apologetically states. He, Kieran, and Viola have just topped the stairs and are now huddled behind the others, fear riddling their faces.

"Doesn't matter. All that does, is they never…ever…travel alone. We have to get out of here now," Nathan states.

As if on cue, a large crash erupts from downstairs. "Sounds like more," I whisper, suddenly afraid to speak out loud.

"In the bar," Viola says, pointing at the floor to indicate the location of the sound.

"Is there another staircase?" Reggie asks.

"I don't know. We didn't really have time to look around," I reply.

"There is. Outside on the balcony," Nathan points out. He has started to slowly retreat into the room, so the rest of us follow. Viola lets out a small squeak as she passes over The Turned. Another crash responds below. Putting his finger to his lips, "Shhhhh," Nathan says. Viola holds her hand up, finger and thumb in a circle, acknowledging his warning. One- by-one, we tiptoe into the room. When the last person to enter, Kieran, makes his way inside, we gently close the door to mask our voices.

"One of us needs to go first and check to make sure it is secure," I say, moving to the open, ceiling-high window. Nathan is right, there is a ladder leading down from the balcony, but years of rust and neglect may have compromised its integrity. I can see several spots where the black paint has worn off completely, exposing an array of red, gold, and brown-indicating different levels of decomposition.

"I'll go. I think I'm the smallest, and I'm a great climber," Marla offers.

"She is a great climber. Best in the village," Julie proudly corroborates.

We all survey her, deciding if she truly is the best one for the task or not. I feel like her small arms and low upper body strength may make her vulnerable to falling, but she is definitely the smallest of the group besides Julie-who is absolutely not going out there first. A sudden influx of groaning and shuffling nearby in the hallway makes our choice urgent and abruptly much easier. "Time seems to be up for debating. If you are comfortable with being first, go for it," I say.

"No sweat," Marla replies, her long but thin, reddish hair flowing in the breeze as she ducks to go out the access window to the balcony. We all follow her lead and join her on the warped wood. There is plenty of room for us all to spread out, but I have concerns about the weight limit on the old structure. The sooner we get people down, the better. "Here goes nothing," Marla calmly states. She makes her way to the ladder, grabs the top rung, swings her body around facing the building, and begins her slow decent.

"How does it feel?" Nathan asks. He is pacing nervously back and forth, periodically peering down and shaking his head. I suspect he is afraid of heights, but do not mention it. No need to freak him out more.

"Feels pretty sturdy," Marla replies, already more than halfway down and picking up her pace. "A few of the rungs are a little loose, but nothing to be concerned about," she adds.

Bang!

"What was that?" Viola asks, fear making her voice squeaky and loud.

As if in response, another bang sounds, this time much closer. "I think they are trying to get in the door," Kieran says. Bravely, he ducks back into the room, puts his head against the door and listens intently. Scratches and thuds reverberate on the other side of the flimsy old door. First only a few, then a chorus of dozens. Suddenly, the door bucks with the force being applied to it from the gathering mass of Turned. Kieran, his eyes going wide, quickly spins around and runs for us. "There are a lot of them, and they know we are in here. We have to go. Now!"

"I'm down," Marla yells from the street below.

In all, it only took her about one minute to climb down the thirty or so feet, but some of us may be slower. "We are going to have to speed this process up. When the first person is halfway down, the next will start. Julie, you first," I say, taking her hand and leading her to the edge, "Marla will be waiting for you at the bottom."

"I'm scared," Julie says, looking at me with wide eyes.

"I know, but we have to get down there, or the monsters will get us. I will stand right here and watch you go. Keep looking at my face while you climb," I reply, lifting her up and placing her on the top rung.

"Promise you won't leave?" Julie asks.

"Promise," I reply, crossing my finger over my heart. Julie nods and begins to climb. For such a young girl, she moves remarkably fast. "You are doing great. Keep looking at me," I say. She smiles her toothless grin and nods again, her blonde hair whipping wildly about her head as she descends. Seemingly, each rung she climbs down is met with a louder bang on the door. "We aren't all going to make it down before they break that door," I say to the remaining people on the balcony while maintaining eye contact with Julie. I can't tell if they are agreeing with me or not because no one makes a sound. "Someone needs to look for another way," I yell.

"There is another ladder on the adjacent room's balcony, but I don't know how to get past the break in the floors," Camden says.

"How far is it?" I ask.

"About five feet, maybe a little more," he replies.

"I can jump that," Nathan offers.

"Someone else can go down now. Julie is halfway," I state. "You are still doing great, Julie. Someone is going to come down with you now, so I have to move out of the way. Just look at their back while you climb." Julie nods her small head in acknowledgement and continues her steady descent.

"I can't jump. Can I go next?" Viola asks.

"Yes, go," Reggie says.

"Okay, Julie, Viola is coming down now," I say.

"Okay," her small voice responds, sounding miles away.

Another series of loud bangs, along with the sound of splintering wood burst from the bedroom. "We only have a few more minutes, guys. Two more of us can go down here, but the rest will have to use the other. Decide who, and get over there," I say, helping Viola onto the ladder.

"Okay, who can clear that jump with me?" Nathan asks.

"I don't know if I can with this bum knee," Camden says.

"That's okay, I can do it," Reggie offers.

"I'm not sure. I've never really practiced jumping distances before. What if I fall?" Kieran asks, sincere worry in his voice.

"I can do it. Trade me places," I say.

"No way," Kieran responds.

"Yes way. Don't think for a minute that because I am a girl I can't do it," I hiss.

"That's not what I meant," Kieran replies.

"For crying out loud! Can you please fight about this later?" Camden growls, more splintering wood sounds from behind us, nicely supporting his point.

Shaking his head in defeat, Kieran says, "Okay, but please be careful."

"Duh! I'm always careful," I joke, "Now hurry up."

"I'll make the jump first," Nathan says, rubbing his hands over his short hair to psyche himself up, "I've been doing this stuff for a long time. Plus, that way I can help catch you two if you have trouble." Reggie and I both nod our heads in agreement. Nathan is for sure the best choice to go first.

Thankfully, the railing that separates the two rooms is loose, and Nathan can just pull it out of the wall, giving us a clear path. Behind me, the world is a tornado of noise; the frantic sounds of my friends, making their way down, swirling together with the hungry groans of The Turned. I try to block it all out and focus on my group, but the rising crescendo makes it nearly impossible. My hands, damp with sweat, instinctively cover my ears, momentarily muting the unfolding chaos. Nathan is saying something to me, but I can't read his lips, and I am hesitant to launch myself back into reality so soon. Frustration furrowing his brow, Nathan frantically waves his hands at me. "What?" I respond, irritation coloring my voice.

"I said, move back, so I can get a running start," Nathan replies.

Doing as he says, I take five, large steps back, bringing me even with the window. Immediately, I regret this. My senses are vigorously assaulted by the clawing and pounding of The Turned, making me dizzy and nauseous. Chancing a glance toward the first group, I see that all but Kieran has begun the downward climb. "How much farther do they have before you can start?" I ask him.

"Camden just got on," he replies, his limbs quaking with trepidation, "I should be good in about a minute."

"Great!" I say, "We will meet you all behind the church. Take care of each other."

"You too," he says, returning his gaze to track Camden's progress.

"Who's next?" Nathan yells. While I had been distracted by my conversation, he already cleared the jump.

Standing beside me on my right, wringing his hands in an urgent manner, Reggie looks paler than normal, and his now yellowing eyes are frantically darting from my position to the door, which is vastly more splintered than just moments ago, "Zayda, you go next. I want to make sure you are safe before I jump."

The crunching sound of more wood shattering drifts out of the window. I am warring with my desire to save myself and protect Reggie. I feel so responsible for him being in this position, and I will willingly give my life to save his. Plus, I want to wait until Kieran has started his way down before I am across. Perched directly between both boys, my past and potential future gawking at me with concern in their eyes, I succumb to emotion; fresh moisture freely flows from my eyes. "No, you go. My actions got us into this mess. I'll be right behind you," I say to Reggie.

"I've let you get by with being the hero multiple times over the past two days, but I have to draw the line here. Either you go, or no one goes," Reggie says, firmly planting his feet on the ground for emphasis.

"I can't leave you both behind," I say.

Reggie's face contorts into utter disgust, "Both? You mean you are refusing to save yourself because of him? Why? You don't even know the guy."

"Come on guys!" Nathan yells from the other balcony. He is standing close to the edge waiting to catch the next person if necessary.

"Reg, he is important to me. Please try to understand that," I say.

"Whatever, Zayda. We don't have time for this right now. Once your precious *boyfriend* gets on the ladder, jump," Reggie says, the venom with which he says boyfriend makes me flinch.

"Camden is past the halfway point. I'm going now," Kieran says while climbing onto the ladder. At first, I think he is going to make it down without issue, but that quickly changes. His hands are trembling so badly, that he loses his grip with his right hand and slips off the top rung. "Help! I don't think I can hold on," he yells. Hoping to stabilize him,

Reggie and I rush over to the side and each grab onto of one of Kieran's hands. Wet with nervous perspiration, my hands are slick and unable to gain purchase. Each time I take hold of his fingers, they slip right out of mine and Kieran flails in the air wildly. Reggie seems to be having better luck, and thankfully he has a firm grasp on Kieran's other arm; otherwise, he would have fallen. "Pull me up!" Kieran cries. Wiping my hands on my pants to dry them, I try one last time to hook our hands together. I stretch my arm and shoulder as far as I can, my stomach-digging into the side of the building where I am leaning the majority of my upper body over-cries out in agony. Closing the last few inches of space, our fingertips almost touching, I thrust my hand into his. Success! Pulling with all our might, Reggie and I painfully and slowly lift Kieran over the edge-one small inch at a time.

"Pull harder, Zay," Reggie huffs. His face is red and strained, the effects a stark contrast to his pallor. I can see the tendons bulging on the sides of his temples as he uses all his might to hoist Kieran's dead mass over the last ledge.

"I'm pulling as hard as I can," I say; my life of hard labor in the garden had not properly prepared me for the strain of lifting an almost grown man. Before this moment, I had truly misjudged my own resilience, and I feel humbled to realize the limitations of my own body. "He's much heavier than I imagined."

"Brace your feet against the top of the ladder to gain traction," Reggie says.

Doing as he suggests, I straighten my legs out underneath me and slide into a sitting position, my knees locking in place to offer more support. Reggie is right; it helps, and we are able to lift Kieran up the remaining distance. Finding himself on solid ground again, Kieran rolls onto his back and clutches his chest, "Thanks, that was a close call," he says, his breath ragged and coming in rapid increments. Reggie and I collapse beside him, also winded and exhausted.

"Hey guys!" Nathan yells.

None of us have the strength to return his cry.

"Hey guys! Guys! Look!"

Finding a small remnant of energy, I look his way. He is staring, his eyes frenzied, at the room behind us. I roll onto my stomach and survey the space. "Shit!" I yell. "Get up! Reggie, Kieran, get up now! They are almost through!" I jump up to my feet and gape in horror at the blood-soaked arm jetting out of the large crevasse in the wood. "We have to get off this balcony!" I say, just as another arm manages to squeeze itself into the widening breach. Reggie and Kieran see this too and both let out a small cry of distress. We all know we should move, but we continue to watch in morbid curiosity as pieces of the door fly into the air. Each piece of shrapnel hitting the wall is met with a corresponding growl from the horde. What once was a disjointed chorus of sporadic noises is now a humming symphony playing in perfect harmony; the group appears to be converging into one mass. *Crack!* I cringe as the final barrier breaks like a dam opening, and the first Turned bursts forth. "We don't have time for the ladder. Everyone, run for Nathan," I shriek. We all thrust ourselves up with maximum effort and run forward in a single file line. First, Kieran catapults himself over the void; he clears it easily and lands forcefully into the waiting arms of Nathan. Both men fly backwards and slam into the cast-iron railing on the opposite end of the balcony. Quickly righting himself, Nathan runs forward and prepares to catch the next person-Reggie. Much like Kieran, Reggie effortlessly executes the jump, however, his landing is much more graceful and Nathan only has to place his hands on Reggie's shoulders to stabilize him. I am still running at full speed while all of this is happening; the entire event unfolding over the course of just several seconds. My legs are burning with fatigue by the time I approach the edge and hurl myself into the air. Knowing it will not help my momentum, I still can't stop myself from flailing my legs wildly in the sky. Part of my brain thinks it will propel me forward, but the rational region knows better. I land on the edge, spinning my arms in circles to steady my balance, but still falter backward. One minute I am looking directly at Nathan's square face, and the next I am gazing up into the sapphire, blue sky. I'm falling! No amount of effort to right myself helps, and I continue to rapidly tumble. Judging from my height and the distance to the ground, I should hit in a matter of seconds. I close my eyes and brace for the impact. Only...it doesn't come. Chancing a glance, I open one eye and see Kieran smiling broadly back at me. His fingers are tightly gripping the front of my shirt.

"Thought, I'd pay you back," he says with a smirk and heaving me upright.

"Th..th...thanks," I reply, trembling as he releases me and I stand on my own. My eyes are still swimming, and my ears are thundering from the sudden blood flow from the tumble. Gently shaking my head, I try to clear away the disorientation. Reggie and Nathan are viewing the exchange from a few feet away, both look like they are dumbstruck from me almost taking a deadly stumble over the edge. Reggie, more so than Nathan, but they are both obviously shaken. "I guess we are even," I say, casting a shy smile at Kieran.

"Looks that way," he replies, returning the gesture. Something inside me falls for him even harder at that moment, and I realize I have a big crush on Kieran, maybe even more than a crush. He closes the gap between us, wraps his arms around my waist, and gently places a kiss on my lips. Even though I know Reggie is observing this action, I give in to the embrace and surrender myself to the feeling of serenity Kieran evokes in me yet again. With that kiss, my skepticism melts away, and I remember the shy boy confessing his secrets to me not long ago. I could stay in his arms forever.

However, our moment is cut short by scratching noises on the window of the other balcony. I push myself away from Kieran, my face is hot and burning from another shot of adrenaline and blood flow, and I hope it is not obvious to everyone else. Still, I do not have time to dwell on such trivial matters because a body erupts from the window, bringing with it shards of glass and sending bit of rotting flesh sailing through the air. We all turn and observe the scene emerging in front of us; a Turned has made it outside. He appears confused by the lack of company on the platform and spins around in a circle, a low groan reverberating and building from deep within his bowels. Unconsciously, I cry out and cover my ears to block out the menacing howl. Instantly, I regret this decision because it alerts The Turned to our location, and he begins slowly shuffling toward us. Soon, many more have joined him, and the terrace is full to bursting. I lean my head over the railing and yell down to the others, "Leave us. Run to the church. We will meet you there." Thankfully, they do not hesitate this time and begin fleeing.

Too many days neglected, combined with too many frenzied bodies, pushes the balcony to its limits, and the screws holding it into the façade of the building begin to pull free. The four of us just watch, pinned against the safety of our railing. Screeching and clawing, the first Turned to break out reaches for us and falls to the unforgiving stone, street below. We can hear the hard thud followed by the soft squish of his head smashing into the pavement. I chance a glance over to see if he is getting up, but he appears to have met his final death. Sickness and relief wash over me simultaneously as I see a glimmer of hope for us all. We can't escape down the ladder right now because the horde is too close to it, but if they fall, either one-by-one or in a mass group, we will have a chance. "He's dead," I say to my friends.

"Good riddance," Nathan says, spitting on the ground for effect. "I hope the lot of them are meeting him in Hell very soon." A stud snaps free from the building, in seeming agreement with his words, sending two more turned over the edge. Despite three of the monsters being disposed of, there are still dozens more to contend with.

Coming up with what I feel is a brilliant plan, I walk closer to the edge where the two platforms meet and extend my arm. As expected, the fervor released is unimaginable. The Turned in the front of the row gnash their teeth and grasp at the air in an attempt to capture me. In their haste to claim a meal, five more tumble to the ground below, and the next section eagerly takes their place.

"Brilliant!" Reggie says. The hint of triumph in his voice does not go unnoticed by me, and I feel proud to have thought of such a great idea.

The second row takes even less coercing before they meet their maker on the harsh streets of The Old City. All the while, the constant motion The Turned appear to maintain causes the structure to become even more unstable. If we wait them out for a few minutes longer, the entire group will undoubtedly cascade to the ground with the balcony. Still, I am enjoying the cat and mouse game, so I go back to the edge and taunt row three. They are not as easy to arouse, and many of them have excessive amounts of gore on their faces. Is it possible for them to get full? It is a dumb idea, dead things being full, but what if it is true. Maybe deep in the recesses of their brain, a few human traits remain. Even though exciting them is challenging, it is not impossible, and soon another four join their comrades on the lower level.

I am preparing to let someone else have fun, but something familiar catches my eye. Toward the back of the group, a petite Turned shuffles absently about. I think The Turned is a she, but it is hard to see fully because she is tiny and the others loom over her so much. I stretch my neck up to get a better look, and I can faintly see patches of hair; it is the color of freshly fallen snow. There are only two other people besides myself who I have ever seen with hair that color. As The Turned part ways, and she clearly comes into view, I see her. Black, dried blood is caked onto her once delicate mouth; open sores fester and ooze, breaking open on her face; and worst of all, her vacant, yellow eyes do not recognize me at all. A fierce growl erupts from her mouth. "Momma!" I shout, before all goes dark.

MOVING ON

I wake up dangling upside down, my head slapping rhythmically against the chiseled back of someone. The sun is shining brightly overhead, and I gauge from its position it is well after noon. Squinting to block out the harsh rays, I survey my surroundings. We are no longer in any part of The Old City that I recognize. In fact, I think we have left the city all together. It is difficult to discern from this angle, but I do not remember any heavily wooded areas near there. Casting my eyes downward, I can vaguely pick out seven sets of boots. That means, everyone made it out alive. I sigh audibly.

"Hey! I think she's finally awake," Julie's small voice chimes. She rushes over to plant her forehead firmly against mine, and flashes the cheesiest smile I have ever seen. "About time, sleepyhead," she says as she laughs hysterically.

"Hey, Jules," I reply. Despite being incredibly uncomfortable, I am unable to stop myself from laughing back at her. The walking motion stops, and my ride gently flips me over his shoulder and places me on my butt on the ground. Stretching my limbs to clear away the stiffness, I look up into the serious face of Nathan.

"You had us worried there for a while," he says, raising his arms over his head and interlocking his fingers to stretch out his muscles. "I was beginning to think you were going to sleep all of the way to the next village."

"How long was I out?"

"Well over an hour," he replies.

"An hour? Why didn't you guys wake me up?" I ask. The tiny blossoms of hysteria threatening to bloom in my voice. "I can't believe I passed out for an hour. What happened with all The Turned? Where is my mom?"

"Relax, Zay," Reggie says, plopping down beside me on the grass. He looks relieved yet apprehensive, and does not say anything for a very long time. His silence is maddening, and I want to grab him by the collar and choke some answers out of him. Instead, I sit calmly and wait. He must have good reason for weighing his words so carefully. Finally, he brushes the white hair out of my eyes and begins speaking, "when you passed out, you hit your head on the corner of the railing. If you reach up, slowly, you will feel the bump on the side of your head. Be careful though, it is probably still very tender." I do as he says and gingerly feel the side of my head. A knot the size of a goose egg jets out from right above my right temple. Flinching from the pain, I pull my fingers away and study my hand; I see that it is covered in a thick coat of blood. "That brings us to issue two. Your blood ignited a fire in The Turned. They were ravenous and could not contain themselves. Within just a few moments, their scrambling brought down the balcony," he continues.

Knowingly, I place my hand over his and ask, "Are they all gone?" He just places his hand back over mine and nods his head, tears welling up in his eyes. "Well, that's that then," I say, pulling my hand away and abruptly standing. The quickness of the motion starts my head reeling again, and Nathan has to catch me before I tumble to the ground.

"Woah! Hold on there, Zayda. You probably have a mild concussion. Don't move around too fast, or you will end up riding my back again, and no offense, but you are heavier than you look," Nathan says with a chuckle.

"Bite me!" I snap back.

"Ahh, not so witty comebacks. That is a good sign that our Zayda is almost back to normal," Camden says. He and Viola have also sat down to rest and are currently smiling at me like two idiots. I can't help but smile back. Regardless of how much she irritates me, the twins really are great friends, and I am grateful to have them here with me.

I grab a clod of grass and dirt and chuck it at them, "I'm witty," I say, feigning hurt feelings.

"Sure, and I'm nice," Viola shoots back.

We all laugh at her response. For some reason, I can't stop laughing. Her comment wasn't that funny, and it did provide some much-needed stress relief, but I honestly can't stop myself from cracking up. Several times, I try to reel it back in, only to have my cackle erupt again. I feel like my ribs are going to break from the force of it, and my breathing is getting spastic. However, I just keep laughing and laughing.

"She's cracking up," Marla says.

"I'm...not...cracking...up," I say in between chortles. I plop back down and roll onto my side, clutching my stomach to contain the eruption. Trying to stifle the laugh only makes it much worse. I am on the verge of insanity, and I have no way to reel myself back in.

"Zay, calm down," Kieran says. He has moved over to get a better view of my antics, but I can barely see him through the wall of water pooling in my eyes. It has been a long time, probably since Robinson was alive, that I have laughed this hard. "No, seriously. You are going to draw attention from the woods. We need to be quiet," he scolds.

"Ooohhh! We need to be quiet everyone. Kieran says so, and he is a big deal," I say through giggles. "We don't want to bring out the big bad meanies like my mom. They might come chomp on our faces," I snicker. The laughter is flowing even harder now, but the feeling of euphoria is being replaced by a much harsher one-grief. As rapidly as it came, my fit of laughter extinguishes and is replaced by a bout of sobs. I try to bury my face in my knees, but the snot streaming down into my mouth obscures my breathing. Knowing it is an ugly cry, I still let it flow, releasing days of pent up sadness and frustration in one moment. The others just watch and wait for me to get it out. Screaming toward the sky, I bellow, "Why? Why are you doing this to me? Can't you see that you've won? You did it! You broke me!"

With this outburst, my friends begin to converge on me, wrapping their arms around my body in a warm embrace; some stroke my hair, others rub my back, but only one whispers into my ear. "You are not broken. You are the strongest person I know, and you will beat them. If this had happened to any of the rest us, we would have given up long ago. But not you, you are better than that. Let it all out, and then help us kick some ass," Reggie says.

Sniffling and wiping both of my hands longways over my face, I begin to pull myself together. I stand up and tilt my chin to the sky, letting the air dry the rest of the moisture. Lowering my gaze to directly address my friends, I gather up all of my hatred and strength, "You're right. If I give up, they win, and they can't *ever* win. The Healers will pay dearly for every life they have ended. Every life they have ruined. And every promise they have broken. They will pay for making us monsters!" I say with renewed conviction. I have come too far, and lost too much, to quit now. Not to mention, this ragtag group is counting on me to lead them. Taking a breath, I say, "We can't conquer the evildoers in the world without a kick ass master plan. So, let's make one."

"Sweet! Zayda is back and ready to kick some Healer butt!" Marla shouts.

Julie gets excited and begins dancing around. "We're going to beat The Healers. We're going to beat The Healers. Zayda's back...Zayda's back, and we're going to beat The Healers," she chants.

"Okay, little bit, calm down," I say. Then I playfully grab her around the waist and spin her around in the air.

"Weeeeeee," she squeals. The two of us laugh as I continue to twirl her. Getting dizzy and remembering my possible concussion, I stop and place her carefully on the ground. "Noooo...again," she cries.

"Sorry, Jules, but I'm going to puke if I keep spinning like that. You don't want to get throw up in your hair, do you?" I joke.

"Ewwww, gross. Stay back," Julie laughs, while making a cross with her fingers to ward off evil.

"I promise I won't come near you. You'd be even safer if you went over by that tree and picked some of those pretty, purple flowers," I say, trying to get her to find something to occupy herself with while we all talk. She may be strong willed for her age, but that doesn't change the fact that she is just a little. The things we may have to do are going to be tough enough for us; she doesn't need to be burdened with them.

"I'll make you and Marla a princess crown," she says, skipping away toward the spot I pointed out. It is just far enough away for us to be able to talk privately, but not far enough where we will have to worry about something happening to her.

"I guess the first order of business is location. Where the heck are we?" I ask, sitting down in a matted down patch of grass that seems to cut through the brush. Having been knocked out for the trip, I seriously have no clue where we are, and I am feeling disoriented. Looking around, I can see an expansive forest stretching out in every direction; the trees growing together to create a lush, overhead canopy. Judging from the size of them, this is an old area. If there had ever been a footpath, it is now long gone and concealed by overgrown brush and grass, most of which is knee high at the least. Rotating to look back the we way came, I see the story is much the same, except, for a few areas where the trees appear to have been burnt-only skeletal shells stand in this part. The burnt trees produce the allusion of tall, boney men watching our every move. I shudder and look away.

"We have been following Marla's markers north for the past hour, and this trail, if you would even call it that, has been pretty constant. I don't know if the horde mashed the grass down, or if someone else has recently traveled through here. However, it has come in handy." Nathan says. For some reason, him pointing out the path makes my stomach queasy. It doesn't add up with the other elements of the forest. He must know this as well. "If Marla's memory is correct, we are only an eighth of the way to the next village. I fear, we will not be there before nightfall at this rate," Nathan continues, worry masking his face. "We lost a great deal of time dealing with the horde on the balcony."

"At least, we have already dealt with them," Viola says. She looks paler than normal, and I notice a blemish protruding from her usually flawless face. I try not to dwell on it too much. Heck, she could just be getting zits from all the perspiration and running. We all have breakouts from time to time. I repeat this in my head several times, but deep down, I know it is not true.

"Not all of them," Marla responds. "Like I told Zayda and Reggie when we first met, I saw over two hundred of my village turn before I fled. What did we see back there? Three, maybe four dozen? That means, there are over one hundred still ambling about these woods."

"Shit! I didn't even do the math earlier," Reggie says. He looks incredibly bothered by the news. We all should be.

"We can't stay the night out here with a bunch of turned running around. If they stumble upon us, we are as good as dead." Camden says.

"And, we need to find the other Officers," Nathan adds.

"True. Would they know to go this way?" I ask.

"Our plan was to go north, so yes. We should intersect them on this route," he replies. "We had a plan in place. I'll explain more on the way." Nathan doesn't' say so, but I don't think he wants to give Kieran too much information before we go. I think this is probably a good idea. At least until we figure out why he is acting so strangely.

"For now, we just keep on moving and hope for the best," I say. "If we walk quickly and don't stop to eat, we will be well north of here before nightfall. Hopefully, the horde stayed together and went the same direction. That would put them closer to Alon than us. We *should* be safe. When we get to the other village, we will make our weapons and find a boat to take to The Sacred City."

"Does anyone know how to drive a boat?" Marla asks.

"How hard can it be?" Camden says. "I'm sure between the seven of us we can figure it out."

"Eight," I correct.

"Well, I didn't exactly think Julie was going to operate a boat," He replies.

"True. Duh! Sorry. I think my brain might still be a little scrambled from earlier," I say.

"No worries. Are you going to be up for walking right away?" Camden asks.

"I think I will be alright. I just hope I don't slow us down too much," I reply.

"What if we didn't have to walk?" Kieran yells from a short distance away.

We all shift our gazes toward him and look with confusion. He points his finger to a slight clearing in the brush. I stand up and walk over to it, pull back the foliage, and reveal the yellow backside of an old bus. I don't know how any of us missed it before now, but it is like a miracle has been sent down from Heaven. Excited, I say, "Anyone know how to drive?"

"I do," Kieran says, smiling proudly, but also nervously. After he revealed he could read, the others grew extremely wary of him. Add driving to the list, and he might as well be one of The Healers in their minds.

"Well then, what are we waiting for? Kieran, start it up." I say. Allowing myself to feel some relief from the break we just caught, I sigh. But, deep down, the fire begins to stoke itself again. Kieran has way too many secrets.

***

Kieran is not the world's best driver, but considering the shape of the overgrown trail we are traveling down, he isn't the worst either. As if to confirm my statement, he roughly hits a divot in the road and sends me flying out of my seat. "Watch it up there," I yell. He just looks in the large mirror, shrugs his shoulders, and gives me a 'sorry' smile. Besides the periodic bounce out of the chair, it is nice to be riding and not walking.

I've been happily gazing out the window, my princess crown Julie made blowing in the wind, taking in the landscape. The breeze blowing through the open windows offers a small reprieve from the stifling temperature outside. We are all somewhat used to the harshness of summer in the southeast, but not without an adequate water supply. Already, my lips are cracking open and bleeding from slight dehydration. Hopefully, by tonight, we will be at the village and will be able to boil some water to fill our almost empty canteens. Had it not been for Marla finding that closet, we would not have any canteens to begin with. Before we left, she saw a box of them on the floor in the very back, and we used the bottled water to fill them all halfway. I must admit, a box of canteens and a storage room full of food seems like an odd find in a building that has been abandoned for decades, but I'm happy for the items nonetheless.

"Hey, Zay," Reggie whispers, leaning across the aisle and getting inches from my face.

"What?"

Darting his eyes around to make sure no one is listening, Reggie leans in even closer, but does not begin speaking. I can see him carefully surveying everyone to make sure we will not be overheard. Sensing his unease, I do the same and see that everyone but us is taking this opportunity to nap. Julie and Marla are cuddled together in one seat; the small girl's fingers absently twirling her sister's hair as they sleep. Once again, I am reminded of how much I care for them both already. Viola and Camden are sitting across from each other, both of their mouths agape with slobber running down their chins. Big dorks. I can hear Nathan snoring like a grizzly, but without standing up, I can't see which aisle he decided to settle in. Kieran, of course, is still driving. I stare in his direction for a few moments, taking note of any changes in body language that would indicate he is aware of our conversation. When I am confident he isn't, I respond, "What's going on? You are freaking me out?"

"What was up with Kieran before we got on the bus?"

"You're going to have to elaborate, Reg."

"With the tree?"

"I honestly have no idea what you are talking about."

"I snuck off to go to the bathroom before we left, and on my way back I saw him using a rock to make a mark on one of the trees. I couldn't get close enough to see what it was, but the whole situation seemed bizarre," Reggie says.

"Marking our location, so if we need to find it again," I offer, not even convincing myself.

Shaking his head, "I don't think so. We aren't going to be going back that way. Ever! If we make it out of The Sacred City alive, Alon is going to still be lost to us," he says.

"Then why?"

"I think he was sending a message to someone else," Reggie replies.

"But who?"

"Your guess is as good as mine. I'm telling you, *there is something off with him*," Reggie says, accidentally raising his voice.

"Off with who?" Kieran asks from the front of the bus.

Reggie and I both right ourselves and look in his direction. I have no clue what to say, so I just offer nothing. Thankfully, Reggie is fast on his toes and comes up with an acceptable response. "Brighton. Zayda and I were just talking about how oddly he behaved last time he was in Alon."

"I've met Council members from all of the regions, and they are all a bit off," Kieran laughs. He is alternating between watching the road and watching us in the large mirror above the dashboard. "Brighton is actually one of the more normal ones I have encountered. At least, he knows how to talk to people. Many of the others have been isolated from the common folk for so long, they have no idea what to say. It's like talking to a door most of the time," he adds.

"If that is normal for one of them, I would hate to meet the rest," I joke.

"Oh, *you* would for sure," Kieran says, something in his tone implies a hidden meaning. Reggie notices it also, and is currently shooting daggers at the back of Kieran's head. These two are going to come to blows soon, and I will be caught in the crossfire. However, I can't blame Reggie because I am really beginning to have doubts about Kieran's intentions also. His overall demeanor changes so rapidly anymore that I never know which Kieran I am talking to- sweet, kind, and gentle, or evasive, blunt, and scary. I've heard of people having personality disorders where they flip flop between pleasant and hateful, but I've never seen it in person. Maybe this is what's wrong with him.

Changing the subject, I say, "How many miles have we gone?"

"Around seventy-five."

"Fantastic. I think we will be there in no time then," I reply, faking my best 'we are still cool' voice. I turn my attention back to the window. Something seems off. "Hey, Kieran, have we already been by here before? Some of this looks really familiar."

"Maybe, I got a little confused a while back, and had to make a circle," he replies.

Confused? How could he be confused when he has never taken this path before? Something isn't adding up. "Are we back on the right track now?" I ask, keeping the suspicion out of my voice.

"I think so," is all he says.

Nathan, who is in the seat directly behind me, has woken up from our chatter. "What's all of the yelling about?"

"Sorry, didn't mean to disturb you," I say to him.

"No problem. I need to be up scouting for my comrades anyway. Our rendezvous point has got to be getting close," he replies, stretching his arms above his head.

"What should we be looking out for?"

"A large boulder surrounded by poppy flowers," Nathan says.

"What are poppy flowers?"

"Tall, flaming red flowers with purplish blue centers. They are hard to miss," he replies.

"They sound beautiful."

"Eh, I guess so. I'm more of a violets kinda guy," he replies, winking and laughing.

"Do you think they all made it out? You know, before the horde got there?" I ask.

"Probably. Last I heard, they were rounding up a bunch of busses just like this one to shuttle everyone. Pretty lucky for us that they left one behind," Nathan says, looking up front at Kieran. Evidentially, Reggie and I aren't the only ones who are suspicious of our ridiculously good luck. "*And that good ole' Kieran there can drive. I've never heard of anyone outside of The Council and The Healers being taught how. Not even the highest-ranking Officers can drive."

Feeling the need to defend Kieran and not fully understanding why, I say, "Maybe because his father is a doctor and worked on The Cure."

Nathan's body goes rigid. "Say that again," he says.

"What? His father is a doctor?"

"No, the other part."

"He worked on The Cure."

"That's what I thought you said. Listen, Zayda, we might be in danger. Kieran is..."

"Hey! Is that the boulder you were talking about?" Kieran yells from upfront, interrupting Nathan's sentence.

Nathan visually follows the direction Kieran's finger is pointing. "Yes, that's it," he replies. He stands up to exit the bus, but pauses when he gets directly beside me. Barely speaking, he leans down right by my ear and says, "Don't go anywhere alone with him." Then, he moves to the front of the bus. "I'm going to jump out and look for a sign that they are nearby. You should probably kill the engine to save fuel," he says to Kieran.

"Good thinking," Kieran says, stopping the bus and turning the ignition off. "Need any help out there?"

"Nope, I'm all good. Stay here in case something goes wrong and you guys need to take off," Nathan says, walking down the three stairs that lead to the bus door.

Kieran pulls the handle to open the door, and says with venom, "Be careful."

Nathan flinches, obviously not missing out on the thinly veiled threat those two words carry. "Back at ya'," he responds, returning the tone.

"Always," Kieran says, shutting the doors behind Nathan as he goes out.

***

Everyone is awake now, and we are watching Nathan from inside the bus, our faces pressed up against the glass like those little pickled sausages we ate back in The Old City. Julie is taking great joy in raising and lowering the window a million times, and Marla looks on the verge of smacking her. "Hey, Jules, why don't you go grab a can of fruit from the backpack and have a snack?" I say.

Julie jumps up and runs at full-speed to get her treat. "Fruit. Fruit. I love fruit," she sings as she rummages through the pack.

Relief washes over Marla, and she mouths the words "thank you" to me. I dip my head in acknowledgement.

Nathan is on his second circle around the rock, obviously not immediately finding what he is looking for. Suddenly, he stoops down and hurriedly begins combing through a thick patch of poppies with his bare hands. Standing up, his hand held high in the sky, a shiny metal object glimmering in the sunlight, he cheers, "They were here. Come out and help me search the nearby woods."

Exiting the bus, we all rush over to where Nathan is waiting; his smile is expressing the feelings his mouth has not yet said. Somehow, the childlike grin softens him. In this moment, I find myself really liking the officer, and looking forward to meeting others like him. Never, had I imagined people who worked for The Healers could be kind. "What did you find?" I ask.

"Smith's ID badge. Almost didn't find it; he hid it a little too well. That makes me nervous," Nathan says, "The only reason he would wedge it into the ground like he did was if he thought someone was following them. We should find them as quickly as possible and get moving again."

"Where would they go to hide?" Viola asks. She is wringing her hands together, and nervously darting her eyes around to survey the area. In fact, everyone besides Kieran is doing the same thing. I watch him closely for a moment, trying to read his face, but he is carefully guarding his reaction. Looking back at Nathan, I see he has been doing the same thing as me. When he makes eye contact with me, he mouths the word "enemy" and darts his eyes toward Kieran. "I know," I mouth back. The entire exchange only takes a second, and then we are back to pretending all is well.

"Our plan was always to go a few feet into the woods and wait for the primary defector to seek us out. The position of the ID badge is critical; it points to the side of the road they are on. So...we need to start searching over there," Nathan says, indicating the left side of the road. "If we go in groups, we can cover more ground."

"Perfect. Cam and Viola, naturally you will want to stick together. Reggie, Marla, and Jules, you will make a great trio. And, Kieran and Nathan, I guess that means the three of us are a team," I say to everyone. Nathan looks relieved that I hatched such a sneaky plan to keep us both by Kieran's side. Kieran on the other hand, appears enraged; all threads of civility are rapidly melting off his face. Desperately, I hope to be wrong about him.

"Group one, over by the edge of the poppy field. Group two, stay right here. My group, we will take the area to the right of the boulder. Everyone, interlock fingers with your group and then spread your arms as far as you can," Nathan says. We all comply, me in the middle of Kieran and Nathan. How do I keep finding myself between two men? "Okay, now drop your arms. This will serve as our perimeter. Walk forward with your group and stay together. Meet back here in ten minutes. If you get separated from your team, stay put and whistle twice every ten seconds. I will be able to track you. If you find the other Officers, whistle three times in rapid succession every thirty seconds until we all find you," he finishes.

"I won't ever doubt you're a soldier again," Reggie jokes. "You are almost as good at barking orders as Zayda."

"*No one* is as good at barking orders as Zay," Viola says. She is grinning like a crazy person, and I know she is trying to lighten the mood. I feel like since we were thrust into this insane situation, she and I have bonded on a whole new level. In a small way, she is filling the void where Posy should be.

"Shut it, Vi," I say in return, laughing and giving her a wink.

"Will do, boss lady. Shutting it," she says.

With that we all begin walking toward our respective parts of the woods. The nervousness in my gut will not subside, and I know it has as much to do with Kieran's possible betrayal as it does heading toward the unknown in the forest. He seemed so genuine and kind when we first met back in the village, and even during the first few hours in The Old City, but now, with the addition of Nathan to our group, an emerging hostility is palpable in the air around him. As we enter the edge of the trees, pushing branches out of our way to clear a path where none exists, I decide to pry Kieran for some answers. Having Nathan here with me, gives me courage to push the limits. "So, who taught you how to drive?"

Kieran gives me a sideways glance, sizing me up to determine my motivation for asking him this. "Some guy in one of the Northwest villages, I think he was a retired Council member. My dad and I were relocated there for almost a year, and the old man and I kinda just hit it off," he says. There appears to be a degree of truth to his words, but also a hint of deception.

"I've never heard of a Council member retiring to a village," Nathan says.

Come to think of it, neither have I. Most of them are rewarded for their service to The Healers by being given a large house in The Sacred City. "Me either," I add.

"Surprise! You guys don't know everything," Kieran barks.

"I never claimed to know everything, but I can smell BS when I hear it," Nathan says.

Stopping dead in his tracks, "Are you calling me a liar," Kieran asks, taking a few steps toward Nathan, the two of them now standing nearly nose to nose.

"What if I am, tough guy?" Nathan says, squaring up and erecting himself to his full height.

"Then we might have a problem." Kieran replies, cracking his knuckles.

"Oh, we already have a problem."

"Yeah, and what is that?"

"Woah, guys, cool it!" I say, wedging myself between them. Guess I wasn't the one who was going to be pushing Kieran's buttons after all. Nathan has rocketed past subtlety and flown straight to full-on accusation. If I don't stop them, they are going to rip each other's heads off. "We don't have time for you to prove how tough you are."

"Then tell your friend here to back down," Kieran says through gritted teeth and glaring at Nathan over my shoulder.

"Both of you need to back down," I say, but neither of them budge. "NOW! I'm not kidding. Is this worth us being found?"

Kieran and Nathan's postures both soften, and they each take a step back. Neither speaks, but it is clear the issue has been dropped. At least, for now. They start walking again, silently glaring at one another. Irritated, I take off ahead of them. The brush is becoming thinner the farther back we go, which is good because my arms are already covered in countless small scratches. Thankfully, our government issued boots have thick soles because the landscape below is full of sharp rocks that would easily pierce a normal shoe. However, the deeper we go, the easier time I have walking. I notice some of the branches are broken and snapped off, indicating we aren't the first to pass through this spot. I hope it was Nathan's friends and not a group of Turned. I shudder with the thought, but quickly cast it out of my mind. Despite the reason we are here, I am enjoying the scenery, and my mood begins to improve. For the first time since we entered the woods, I can hear birds singing; it is glorious. I've always loved the melody of songbirds, but rarely got to hear it back home. The most common bird in Alon is a seagull, and they have a hideous caw. Combine the symphony with the small beams of sun periodically breaching the dense canvas above, and I am almost euphoric.

"What are you smiling about?" Kieran asks, a twinkle in his eye. In that instant, he returns to the boy I know from before all this craziness started, and I forget I'm supposed to be suspicious of him.

"The birds," I reply. As we walk under another break in the leaves, I tilt my face up and spread my arms out like a bird soaring through the sky.

"They do sound pretty," he replies. I chance a look at him and see he is mirroring my actions. The sun allows some of his natural highlights to show, and I see that his hair is not as dark as I once thought. Small flecks of red and gold tug at his temples.

"Amazing. It is so peaceful out here. It's easy to forget about all of the madness out there," I say.

"I try not to forget," he says. Again, I peer at him and see that his expression has changed drastically; the sadness is almost tangible. I am reminded there is much I do not know about this boy.

Not knowing what to say, I let the moment pass. We have been out here for around five minutes already and have yet to see any concrete signs of the Officers. I am starting to think they did not come this way. "Can we stop for a minute?" I ask, bending to the ground. "My boot is untied. I need to fix it before I trip and kill myself."

"Sure, no problem," Nathan says. "We probably need to decide which direction we want to go before we turn around. They wouldn't be past this point. I suggest we go right a few yards and then head back in. That way we can cover extra ground."

"That sounds like a solid idea," Kieran replies. A hint of the aggression he exhibited earlier is still there, but overall his tone is much less hostile.

"Okay," I say, standing up. "I'm all tied and ready to roll." A drop of liquid falls from the sky and lands on the back of my head. "Crap, do you guys feel that? I think it is starting to rain."

"I don't feel anything," Nathan says.

"Me either," Kieran adds.

A series of drips answer their responses. "Well, I feel it. It is either rain or one of those birds is peeing on my head," I say. Reaching up to feel my head to make sure I'm not imagining things, I run my palm through my hair. When I pull it away to look, it is covered in blood. Too shocked to speak, I just hold out my hand for them to see.

"What the hell?" Nathan says.

We all three incline our chins and stare up at the sky. High up in the branches, I see them. The mangled bodies of the other Officers; their throats have been slit, and their eyes gouged out. My scream echoes through the forest.

A minute later, when I am finally, not hearing my lingering yell coming back to me, I say, "Oh my God. Who could have done this?" Nathan is bent over a nearby bush vomiting his guts out, and Kieran is sitting on the ground with his head resting between his knees. Neither man has a very strong continence, and neither answers my question. They don't need to, we all know who did this-The Healers. Realizing this, I say in a panic, "We have to go. We have to get the others and get out of here. The Healers could be watching us. Do you hear me? We. Have. To. Go." A bloodcurdling shriek from the distance is the only answer I receive.

CHAOS

Sprinting at full speed, the three of us hurl ourselves through the forest, no longer caring about the branches tearing at our flesh. As I painstakingly try to weigh the many possible reasons for the scream, my mind races as fast as my feet. The only thing I know for sure is it was a female voice. "Can you tell where it came from?" I ask Nathan, my words coming out in ragged huffs.

"Just up ahead. I think," he replies, equally winded.

Another scream erupts. It is the same voice, but the scream sounds much more wounded this time. My heart thumps viciously in my ears as I try to close the gap between us and the others as quickly as possible. We are approaching a clearing, and I can see motion up ahead. "I think I see someone," I pant.

As we clear the final distance, I see the other groups have beaten us here. Quickly, I survey them. One. Two. Three. Wait? That can't be right? Where are the other two? Screeching to a halt directly behind them, I see they are all huddled around two masses on the ground. I can't see who it is, and my brain is failing to make any sense out of the scene in front of me. "Guys?" I stammer. No one reacts. The stillness of their bodies makes the hair on my arms stand up. "What is going on?" I say, pushing my way past them. My heart is not ready for what I see.

On the floor of the woods, covered in fresh blood, Julie's petite body lays convulsing. A large gash in her neck sends crimson ripples into the air, and her beautiful blond hair clings to her forehead in clumps. Cradling Julie's beautiful face in her lap, Marla frantically presses her shaking fingers on the wound; she does not look my way or even seem to notice I am there. I can tell by the child's pale color that Marla is doing this in vain, but I do not dare speak it aloud. "It's okay, baby. I've got you. You are going to be alright," Marla says, leaning down to kiss Julie on the head. As she struggles to get air, Julie's eyes dart around wildly; the fear in them makes me go weak in the knees. Her arms flail madly in the air, trying to grasp an invisible thread of hope. A single tear escapes and slides down the little's cheek. "No, baby, don't cry. I've got you. You don't have to be sad. I will protect you," Marla says softly. Despite her words, Marla knows she cannot save her sister, and her tears fall faster. "Remember that song momma used to sing to us?" Marla asks Julie as she begins to hum a familiar melody. "Hum hum hum hum hum" I recognize the tune as one my mother also used to sing; I think it is called Rock a Bye Baby. As she too recognizes the tune, Julie's eyes begin to settle down and her struggles cease. While stroking Julie's hair, Marla just continues to hum the lullaby to her dying sibling. We all stand there and watch helplessly as the light flees Julie's eyes.

It is only a few minutes later that Julie's body stiffens, and a fresh puddle of blood erupts from her mouth making her gag. Marla tries to roll her over on her side to expel the blood, but Julie begins violently seizing. Her frail frame shakes with enough force to knock Marla backwards. Julie convulses for a few minutes. Her spasms increase with each passing moment, and then it just stops. "Noooooo," Marla shouts. "Come back baby. Please don't leave me. Please. Come back." She then crumbles in a heap, shrouding the lifeless body of the little.

The Pitiful sounds emanating from Marla seep into my very soul. I spin to face my friends, "How?" I manage to get out. Viola raises her hand and points a few feet to my left. Swiveling my head, I follow her finger. There, with its head beaten in by a large rock, lies one of The Turned. There is a fresh bloodstain on what remains of its face. Dejected, I collapse to my knees beside Marla and Julie's intertwined figures on the ground, and wrap my arms around them both.

***

"We have to do it," I hear Nathan whisper. I am still holding onto Marla and Julie, but have lessened my grip a bit. The last few minutes feel like a nightmare, and I shake my head to clear away the cobwebs that have attached themselves to reality and casted everything in a fog. Part of me understands the words Nathan is speaking, and that part knows I need to snap out of my stupor now. The other part of me wants to curl up into a ball and sleep until everything returns to normal. "The change will happen soon," Nathan continues.

"Give them a bit more time," Viola says. The empathy in her voice is so obvious and foreign sounding for her that I look up. She stands, just a few feet away, clutching Camden's arm for support. Although her face is dry, I can see the redness rimming her eyes. The way she looks at Marla and Julie shoots fresh pangs of hurt throughout my entire body, and I lower my head onto Marla's back again. I will never be able to fix this, and I hate myself for letting it happen. I failed Julie just as much as her sister did. We both promised to keep her safe from the monsters, and we both lied.

Below us, I begin to feel a slight twitching motion. Marla feels it too, and we both straighten our backs and peer down at Julie's body. Her eyes remain closed, but beneath the surface a flutter is visible; I can't help but think it looks like she is dreaming.

"It's happening," Nathan states.

"What do we do?" Reggie asks.

"I've got to stop it," he replies.

Marla lunges to cover Julie, "Don't touch her," she growls. I just sit, too stunned to speak. This is the first time I have seen someone turn. My brain is warring between morbid fascination and utter disgust.

"Marla...you have to move out of the way, so I can help her," Nathan says.

"Help her? You mean kill her!"

"She's already dead."

"Shut up! She's not dead," Marla shouts, "See, look, her fingers are moving."

"She's becoming one of them," Nathan says.

"Liar!"

"I know this is hard, but she would not want to be like this," Reggie adds. His words seem to resonate a bit with her, and she sits up slightly. "Look at her, Marla, you can see the changes starting. Julie's gone. I'm so sorry." Marla doesn't respond, but seems to be taking his words to heart. Her eyes scan Julie from head to toe. Already, the color has completely faded from her face and the tendrils of blackish veins are beginning to worm their way through her skin. Taking in the transformation of her baby sister from little to monster, appears to be too much for Marla, and she just shakes her head violently.

"NO!" You are wrong!" Marla shouts again.

Grabbing her face in my hands, I force her to look directly at me. "They are right. You've seen this before. Don't let Julie become one of The Turned. She was too beautiful. Too kind. Too amazing. Help her stay that way," I say.

"But...I love her so much."

"I know you do. That's why you have to do this," I say. Realization sinking in, Marla just nods and scoots away from Julie's reanimating form.

Walking toward the girl, remorse filling both his voice and face to bursting, Nathan says, "I will make it as quick as possible, and you don't have to watch." Guilt washing over him as he reaches into his pocket and retrieves his pistol. Marla squeaks out one last, barely audible protest, and then clenches her eyes firmly as she covers her ears tightly with her palms. Just as Nathan raises the gun to fire the merciful shot, Julie's now yellow eyes pop open and a guttural growl erupts from her mouth. One shot, reverberating on a continuous loop throughout the woods, answers her.

Then, all is quiet again. No birds. No animals. No sobs. Only utter and complete silence mark the end of Julie's existence. Anguish over my futile attempt at protecting her makes my body feel like it is heavily laden with lead veins. The only feeling as strong as my sorrow is my hatred. Slowly, I allow those emotions to take over. Rage begins to rise inside me casting everything in a red hue. My limbs tremble with the rush of adrenaline that is accompanying the blossoming wrath I feel. Quivering, I stand and roar into the sky. There are no words, only the primal growls of the beast released from deep inside me.

Opening my eyes, I see the stunned faces of my friends; Marla has risen also and is looking at me with understanding. All traces of doubt have been erased from her voice and replaced with sheer determination when she says, "Let's make those assholes pay."

***

Our makeshift funeral only lasts a few moments. With no tools to dig a grave, we do our best to gather enough timber to cover Julie and then set it ablaze-a Viking funeral on land. We do not share stories of her life, nor do we make statements about how she is in a better place. Instead, we stand stoically, fingers interlocked and heads bowed, and let the blaze fully ignite our cause. When it is over, we begin making our way back to the bus. I can't help but focus on the empty space beside Marla. Remembering the group does not yet know, I say, "The other Officers are dead. We found them before…" I can't finish the sentence. They all know what I am going to say, so there is no point.

Kieran, who has remained silent throughout this entire ordeal, says, "It looked like they had recently been killed. I don't think we are safe here. If The Healers are in these woods, they surely heard the gunshot and will come looking for the source of it."

"My question is, how did The Healers know the others would be here?" Nathan asks. His question floats in the air for all to hear, but his eyes are directing it to Kieran; the suspicion is obvious to everyone. I can see Viola and Camden exchanging knowing glances. Reggie, already suspicious before, appears delighted to have another person sharing in his contempt and distrust of Kieran. Marla, still reeling from her sister's death, is shooting daggers in Kieran's direction.

"Why are you all looking at me like that? I've been with you the whole time," Kieran responds.

"Dude, you've been off since Nathan showed up. First, you disappear on some quest to find a surprise, and come back empty handed and acting sketchy. Then, you make some weird mark on the tree back where we found the bus. What the hell was that all about?" Reggie says.

"What marks?" Camden says, pausing to stop Kieran from walking forward.

"Get out of my way!" Kieran snarls.

"Not until you answer the question," Camden says. He continues to stand his ground and block Kieran from advancing.

"I don't owe you any explanation."

"Yes. You. Do," Nathan says, joining Camden to block Kieran's path. "My friends were just ambushed and murdered back there, and the only person in this group who is acting shady is you."

"Forget you!" Kieran yells. "I am not going to be accused of doing something that I didn't do. Zayda, will you please put a stop to this?" I hate myself for it, but I just remain silent. The others are right. "Seriously? You aren't going to say anything? Guess I was wrong about us," he replies.

"Guess you were, asshole," Reggie smirks. The way he says it makes me feel even worse about betraying Kieran.

"What did you just call me?"

"You heard me."

Kieran pushes past Nathan and Camden, moving them both out of the way with such ease it gives the illusion they are made of paper. Storming up to Reggie, he gets mere inches away from them touching noses. "Say it again."

"Asshole."

Rearing his arm back, Kieran punches Reggie right in the nose. Blood erupts from the wound, splattering across both boys' faces. Reggie stumbles a few steps back, reaches up and feels his crooked and bleeding nose, and then all hell breaks loose. Slamming his body into Kieran's, Reggie knocks them both to the ground. I scream, "Stop it," but neither of them is listening. The fury of limbs flying is impossible to follow, and I can't see who, if anyone, is getting injured in the melee. Mixed with the sickening sound of flesh hitting flesh, a barrage of curses and mumbles echo through the air.

"Kick his ass!" Nathan shouts.

"Choke the truth out of him!" Camden adds. Reggie's hands have settled on Kieran's throat, and he is happily obliging Cam's request. Kieran's face is a grotesque shade of red and his eyes are bulging out of his head. Worse still, Reggie's visage is illuminated in the glow of pure joy as he watches the life being squeezed out of Kieran.

"Stop!" I stammer again. "Please, just stop it!" I look around for someone to help me break them apart, but I can see I am alone in my desire to have this end quickly. Of course, Nathan and Camden are loving every minute of this, and both stand on the edge of their toes as if waiting for their chance to join the battle. Viola is watching with neither approval or condemnation, and the blankness in her eyes suggests she is still in shock from Julie's death. Marla is staring at the brawl, pure unadulterated hatred radiating from every pore of her body, each blow to Kieran seems to elicit more of a response from her, and her vitriol becomes more blatantly obvious. Shuddering, I can't help but think, if Marla were fighting Kieran, he would already be dead.

Desperate, I cry out again, "Kieran, Reggie, stop before you kill each other!"

"He deserves to die for what he has done," Reggie grumbles. His breathing is rapid and labored from the exertion, but his words are clear. Kieran is still struggling to breathe, but my words seem to spark a renewed surge of energy, and he bucks Reggie off him. Taken by surprise, Reggie falters and lies dumbstruck on his back. As the pair seem to regroup, all is briefly quiet.

Kieran is gasping and desperately trying to catch his breath; the beige tint is returning to his face slowly. "Are you okay?" I ask. Still choking, he does not answer aloud, but nods his head. Guilt washes over me, and I move to place my hand gently on the small of Kieran's back. My intent is to sooth him a bit, so he can breathe easier, but also to show I am sorry for not sticking up for him. Kieran stiffens as my hand brushes against him, and he turns to look at me. He reaches up and places his hand on my cheek. Leaning into the gesture, I say, "I'm sorry." Suddenly, I am lifted into the air and sat down a few feet away from Kieran.

"Don't you ever touch her again!" Reggie screams as he rushes Kieran and lands a solid left hook into his face. The blow, shattering Kieran's nose and making the two boys look like bloodied twins, hurls them back into another frenzy and they resume trying to kill each other. Rolling over on top of Kieran, Reggie momentarily gets the upper hand and pummels the fleshy pulp of his nemesis's face. "She will never be with you!" Reggie shouts. "I'll kill you before that ever happens." Reggie's words seem to deeply resonate with Kieran, and he furiously begins to push back. Surging with adrenaline, Kieran manages to kick Reggie off and retake the dominate position. "Get off me!" Reggie yells.

Holding Reggie by the shoulders, Kieran repeatedly slams Reggie's head into the ground. All humanity is gone from him; in its place, a monster emerges. Viciously, he continues the assault. Reggie's eyes roll back into his head with each thud, and a new flow of blood emerges from his mouth and nose. He no longer possesses the ability to fight back, and his arms have gone slack at his sides. Horror fills me as I see my friend lose more of himself with each pass. Even from my vantage point, I can see that Reggie will pass out very soon if this continues for too much longer. Urgently, I run toward Kieran, jump on his back, grab the neck of his shirt with one hand, and claw at his fingers with the other. I must break apart the animalistic fury he is being controlled by. My small body is no match for the all-consuming rage erupting from him, and I quickly wear myself out physically. I fall off his back and scramble to my knees. Placing myself directly in front of him, so he can see my face, I shout and beg, "Kieran, you are going to kill him! You have to stop! Please! Stop for me!" As he turns to me, Kieran's arms relax a bit, and he halts the attack. Slowly, he rolls off Reggie and sits beside him on the ground. Bloodied and broken, they both remain still for a few moments.

I can see Kieran thinking of what to say; his brows are furrowed in concentration. Blinking, he looks at me with tears in his eyes and says, "I never meant for any of this to happen."

"I know. You couldn't have..."

"No! Listen to me," Kieran says cutting me off, "I didn't expect to fall for you. Had I known how amazing you are, I would never have agreed..."

"Agreed to what?"

"It's so hard to explain. It all seemed so different before actual people were involved."

"You aren't making sense."

"Please forgive me!"

"Forgive you for what?"

"That," he says pointing behind me.

Swiveling my head around, I see them. Walking into the woods, five people wide and ten people deep, an army appears. The Healers have found us.

BETRAYED

My first instinct is to run, but as I spin around to do so, I see we are surrounded. At least two dozen Officers flank us on all sides. Even if we do run, they have weapons, and I'm sure they would be more than happy to use them. Instead of fleeing, I erect myself and stand as tall as I can, in hope of conveying confidence I do not actually possess. The others mimic my stance and move to join me in a unified front. We join hands, interlocking our fingers in a sign of solidarity.

"Oh, how quaint," Major Mason says. The legion of Officers part like a flock of birds encountering an obstacle in the sky, and he steps forward with his usual sly, half-smile. "Look at this merry band of misfits standing up to the big bad man," he mocks.

"Screw you!" I spit.

"Now, is that any way for a lady to talk?" he says, moving a few feet closer to us. His broad shoulders and hulking body quiver in time with his menacing laughter. "Took us a while to catch up to you. I bet you thought you were going to beat us and be the hero, didn't you?"

Narrowing my eyes, I respond, "There's still time."

Laughing even harder, "You just don't get it. Can't you see you have lost?" he says.

Keeping my composure intact, but trembling on the inside, "Many battles make up a war," I say.

"Give me a break!" he says, turning around and addressing the other Officers. "Do you hear this one? She thinks she is going to win the war. Her and her group of...how many are left now?" he says, turning back to us. Approaching and standing in front of the remaining members of my group, he begins counting and singling them out. "One. Marla. I think that's it, right? So sorry to see you without your little sister by your side. I can only imagine she didn't survive this journey. Such a shame you had to get mixed up with the likes of Zayda, or who knows...she might still be alive. Oh well, as they say, the past is the past." Marla's resolve breaks, and her anger melts away with his words. The stoic girl who was just here disappears, and she begins to weep again. "Oh, such a pity. I wasn't sure if I was right. My condolences, dear. I was truly hoping to be wrong. I mean, how tragic, escaping your village and The Turned, only to be killed a few days later. Tell me, do you feel relieved now that you no longer have to care for her? She must have been a pain being so little and helpless. I personally can't stand littles, especially six-year-old girls, but that's just me," he says, smirking at Marla. She has stopped crying and is glaring at Major Mason with pure hatred. There appears to be an internal struggle between anger and grief going on inside of Marla. "Fun! I see you have some spunk left in you after all. I'm going to love destroying it."

He takes a step to the left and stands in front of the twins. Now, who's next?" Two and Three. Camden and Viola. The funny man and the bitch. I've heard all about you back in the village. How you two were always running around with Zayda. Your parents are truly disappointed in your actions. I can honestly say, I don't blame them. I mean, I would be pretty pissed too, if I had to go to prison because of my kids. At least one of you could have stayed back to take the blame for them. It really is quite selfish. tsk...tsk...tsk," he says. Camden and Viola remain strong, but I can see both of their chins quivering slightly. They love their parents deeply, so this news must be like a blow to the gut. "What? No waterworks? I thought for sure you would cry, Camden. I doubted Viola's heartless self would plop out any tears, but you, you seem like a sensitive kind of guy. Huh? Can't believe I missed that one. Losing my touch," Major Mason says, shaking his head in fake disappointment, "Must be from the heat. I do my best thinking back in The Sacred City in the air conditioning. You'll love it there, except you won't be enjoying the AC like me in the dungeon with your folks," he finishes, laughing heartily as he steps away from them. Once he is no longer looking at them, I can see Camden begin to buckle. Viola senses it too and squeezes his hand tighter to warn him to be strong. Sucking in a deep breath, he rights himself again and just stares blankly ahead.

Bending to look down upon Reggie's bloody face, Major Mason continues, "Damn, number four. You look awful. What the hell happened to your face? You look like someone hit you with a brick. I bet that hurts something fierce. Some price to pay for the girl of your dreams, Reggie. Truthfully, I don't see it. I personally prefer brunettes, and she doesn't seem that special to me. Maybe you've seen more of her though. She hiding something special under those tattered clothes of hers? Must be for you to follow her all around this godforsaken place. I hope she still wants you after that mug heals all jacked up." Major Mason thinks this is particularly funny and doubles over laughing, slapping his knee exaggeratedly for effect. Reggie sits upright and spits blood on the Major's shoes. "Woah now! That is just unnecessary. Can't you take a little joke?" Reggie raises his grime coated right hand and lifts his middle finger. "Guess not," Major Mason laughs while moving over to Kieran.

"And here we have number five. Well, not technically. You look like shit too. I guess you and number four over there took turns using each other as punching bags. Once we get back home, we'll have to have your father fix you up," Major Mason says, putting his hand on Kieran's shoulder. "You have been a fantastic asset, Kieran. Sneaking back to camp to let us know where you all were headed, and then leaving a trail for us to find. Tipping us off to the Officers' desertion, so we could insert a plant. Brilliant! And let's not forget about the time you were driving and got *lost* to allow us to pass you up. You earned a gold star for sure with that one. I'm proud of you. Come on over here and join your comrades." He shakes Kieran's hand and then pushes him toward the group of Officers. Kieran complies, and lines up next to the other men, careful to keep his gaze diverted from us.

"Bet you guys feel pretty stupid right about now," Major Mason says to the rest of us. "Trusting a complete stranger with such important secrets. That is one of the dumbest things I have ever heard. Zayda..." he says, facing me again, "How does it feel to be betrayed twice? I bet finding out that Kieran here is a double agent was a real shocker. I can just imagine the look on your face," Major Mason makes a face mimicking what he thinks I must have looked like. I want to punch him in his bugged eyes and gaping mouth. "I mean, first that delightful little thing Posy-she's a real gem by the way, sells you out to us, and then your boyfriend turns out to be worse than her. Tough stuff." He pauses to see if he is getting the reaction he had hoped for. Unsatisfied, he continues, "By the way, she's fitting in great in The Sacred City. I'm sure you were curious about your bestie. Best part, she filled us in on all the good dirt on you, so we can anticipate all your tricks. Sorry, no surprises from you." He winks at me. "You'd be so proud of her. I bet she will be joining her mom on raids real soon. Chip off the old block, she is. We wouldn't have been able to do any of this without her. Remind me to let you two get reacquainted when we get there. I'm sure you will have lots to talk about."

Not missing a beat, I say, "Looking forward to it."

"Feisty! I like it," he says before turning his attention to Nathan. "Ah yes, last but not least, the defector. I guess you are technically number five now. I wish I had some witty things to say to you, but...I hate every single thing you stand for. Soldiers who think they are better than the cause. Soldiers who think they can change the way of The Healers. Soldiers who think they have the right to free will. You. Make. Me. Sick. Too bad you weren't here to see your friends in the trees over there beg for their lives. It was quite pathetic." Major Mason leans in and gets real close to Nathan's ear to whisper, "Can I let you in on a little secret? I'm the one who took out their eyes. Little souvenir if you will." He reaches into his fatigue pocket and pulls out an eyeball, the optic nerves still attached, and tosses it at Nathan. Flinching, Nathan bats it away. Major Mason erupts into violent laughter. "You should see your face right now! You are white as a ghost," he snorts, "Fitting, since you are about to be one." With that, Major Mason abruptly stops laughing, removes his pistol, and shoots Nathan directly between the eyes. Instinctively, I cry out and shield my head in my hands. Apparently, so do the others because they are still cowering when I chance a look up. A lifeless gaze staring from his eyes into the sky, Nathan's body lies limply on the ground. I choke back vomit in my mouth and quickly avert my gaze. "Okay, now that that is taken care of, let's get these guys on the bus. I promised Eli I'd deliver our guests before nightfall," Major Mason says, no remorse in his voice.

***

The bus is crowded and hot on the way to The Sacred City. No amount of wind can properly circulate the air in the densely-populated vehicle, and I am soaked in perspiration. Each of us is paired with an armed guard in our seat. Mine is a particularly burly man with atrocious body odor and poor personal space parameters; his arms and legs are firmly stuck to the right side of my body. I feel like I am going to suffocate well before we can get to our destination. The others are also glued to the windows trying to avoid the

Officers lurking next to them. Reggie is seated right behind me, and I can hear him groan softly every time we hit a bump; he is in immense pain from his fight with Kieran. Camden, separated from Viola for the first time in days, is being held all the way at the back. I can't see him now because when I try to look back my smelly friend elbows me hard in the ribs and says, "Eyes forward." Jerk! Viola is across the aisle from me, but she hasn't looked my way one time since we got on. I am positive she hates me now and blames me for everything. Honestly, I can't fault her. If I hadn't snuck away; if I hadn't convinced them to come with me; if I hadn't trusted Kieran; if I hadn't done a lot of things, none of this would have happened. I sigh in response to this thought. "Shut up!" my guard bellows. Hugging the wall more, I peek up a few rows at Marla. Her tears have not started flowing again since Major Mason's little pep talk back in the woods. Judging from her posture, she is still deeply grieving. Guilt bores into my soul when I think of the empty space under Marla's arm where Julie should be, and I feel like I'm drowning.

I absently run my sweaty fingers over the flower crown Julie made me. My heart still aches tremendously for the loss of the girl, and I am struggling to keep from breaking down. To distract myself from my feelings of culpability, I return my mind to imagining the multitude of ways I can exact revenge on Kieran. So far, I have come up with cutting out his tongue and feeding it to him, setting his hair on fire, and poking his eardrums out with a sharp stick. Ugh! None of those things would erase the stupidity I feel for having been played. How could I have been so stupid? Am I that desperate for love, or am I just that damaged from life? The saddest part, I still somewhat believed him when he told me he wouldn't have done this if he would have known me first. How could I believe anything he says? I know how, I'm an idiot. Still, there was something about the way he looked at me that made me feel the familiar tingle in my stomach that he always elicited. As much as I hate him right now, I still cling to the hope he isn't lying. I must be the biggest idiot on the face of the planet.

As if sensing me thinking about him, Kieran glances over his left shoulder, peers back at me from his seat up near the front, and blows me a kiss. The butterflies return, and I can feel my face flush. I feel so stupid for allowing myself to have a response to him, but it's not my fault if my body reacts to him. Is it? Wringing my hands in my lap, I try to stop my racing heart. Continuing to stare at me, he points to his head with one finger and mouths the words, "I'm. In. Yours." I cringe at the truth and malice behind the words, and he laughs at my reaction. He then smiles like I have never seen him smile before. It is terrifying. All humanity drains from his blood, crusted face, his eyes go cold and blank, and the edges of his mouth draw up into an animalistic snarl-exposing all his teeth and most of his gums.

Major Mason laughs heartily when he sees my reaction, and slaps Kieran playfully on the back. "You are quite the devil. Still messing with her, even after you've won. I think you are a boy after my own heart," he laughs.

Kieran just turns to him and joins in his roaring laughter. I'm not sure if it is his intention, but Kieran successfully and permanently extinguishes any remaining flutters in my stomach with his attempt at mind games. Rapidly, I twist my head and avert my eyes out the window, but I can still hear his maniacal cackling. Shivering, I close my eyes and push all happy thoughts of Kieran out of my mind forever.

NOTHING'S SACRED

I must have fallen asleep because the next thing I know the day has faded into the soft, purple glow of twilight, and we are pulling up to an enormous, metal gate adorned with colorful etchings that are difficult to make out. On both sides of the monstrous gate, stretching as far as the eyes can see, an iron fence, at least eighteen feet tall, shuts The Sacred City off from the outside world. We slowly roll closer. As we do, I can begin to see the etchings more clearly, and I gasp. Hundreds of images of The Turned being killed in various and sadistic ways adorn the shining steel surface. One Turned is being beheaded, grizzly, yellow and white tendons string from its detaching appendage; another is being lifted into the air by a blue, steel spike that has been rammed through its eye and out the top of its skull; a boot is smashing in the craniums of a pair of Turned in one scene, the contents oozing out a crimson puddle around their bodies. My stomach lurches in protest as I struggle to divert my gaze. Marla vomits on the floor in front of her, confirming my speculation that I was not the only one glued to the images.

"Welcome home!" Major Mason says, standing up and facing us as the gates begin to swing open. Behind him, the crack slowly widens, revealing bits and pieces of the hidden world of The Council and Healers. Rumors have surrounded the city for years, but no commoner has ever gone beyond its walls and came out to tell the tale. As far as I know, the only people besides The Healers and Council to ever come and go freely are The Officers.

Despite my fear of what is to come, I find myself curiously craning my neck to soak in as much of the newly emerging landscape as possible. Gigantic buildings, towering over the ground below, extend skyward in masses; each one, illuminated with an unnatural, yellow glow generating from its very core. The effect creates the deceptive illusion of hundreds of knowing eyes peering down upon us. "Electricity," I say under my breath. So, at least one of the rumors is true. Hundreds upon hundreds of Officers and commoners alike scurry about like rats seeking food in the dark. Never before, have I beheld so many people in one place at a time. There has to be more than a thousand souls inhabiting the land behind the walls. As we proceed in, I can see raggedy street merchants, dressed in rags worse than mine, peddling their goods. Fruit, fabric, jewelry, meat, and various other forbidden wares are handed out without scrutiny from any of the nearby Officers. A stark contrast to the traders, men and women alike walk around in brightly colored and seemingly brand new garments; tall, intricate hats decorate their heads. Looking down at my dirty and time-worn clothing, I regard the difference between my attire and theirs. Even the horses pulling the carts passing by are far better dressed than my friends and me.

"No wonder they won't let anyone in here," Viola says with a huff.

"Quite the spectacle, isn't it?" Major Mason says, a hint of disgust in his voice. "Take the main road, so our guests can see The Sacred City in all of its glory," he says to the bus driver.

"Sure thing, boss," the driver responds. He then turns left and follows a large street that runs parallel to the river. With the light's unnatural glow reflecting off the surface of the water, it is easy to forget I am staring at the same river as the one that flows by Alon. No hints of the murky mud gleam up from the gentle waves lapping against the bank, instead, only yellowish whitecaps touch the shore.

Breaking my eyes away from the entrancing sea, I take in the buildings to the right. Large electric lanterns hang off the fronts of them all, and several more freestanding lanterns line the streets on both sides. This is the brightest place on the planet. Intermingled with several smaller structures, more colossal towers shoot up into the now black, night sky, and still even more people walk freely along the streets. My earlier estimates of the population were way off, and I mentally adjust the tally to ten thousand plus. We round a corner and come to rest in front of an oddly shaped edifice; it looks like a large turret has been placed directly in the middle of a gigantic, five-story home that has been split in half. To the building's left, I see a massive, circular structure made entirely out of grey, stone bricks; torches with real fire hang along the perimeter suspending long, eerie shadows in the air. Faintly, I can hear a crowd chanting behind the sinister façade. "This is our stop," Major Mason says to us. Stepping down onto the first stair to exit the bus, "Get your butts moving," he barks.

Roughly, we are pulled to our feet by our respective Officers and pushed toward the front of the bus. All the bodies aboard take a few minutes to exit, leaving me with more than enough time to fret over our fate as I await my turn. Rule breakers are not a common problem in our village, so I genuinely have no idea what to expect from The Council. Maybe they will let us go with a warning. Sure, that's a likely scenario. I can see the headline, *Four members of the village of Alon have been set free after being found guilty of setting off a bomb in town, exercising blatant disregard for The Rules, and helping an AWOL Officer plan to take down The Healers.* Doesn't sound very likely

"Hurry up!" Officer B.O. says, aggressively pushing me square in the middle of my back, his huge knuckles penetrating my spine.

"Ouch! I'm going. You don't have to be a jerk about it."

"Just get going, and watch your mouth. I have more important things to do than babysit you all night," he growls, pushing me again.

"Fine! Just stop pushing me."

Exiting the bus onto the smooth and even pavement, I can't help but notice how much cleaner and newer everything looks here. Even the older buildings have a fresh coat of paint on them. Observing the same thing, Reggie says, "Looks like The Sacred City has a bit more down time to worry about upkeep than the rest of the world. Must be nice to not have to worry about surviving, so you can make sure your, large, well-lit headquarter is pretty and fresh." The sarcasm in his voice is not missed by anyone in our vicinity, and they all look directly at him.

"Maybe you'll get lucky and your punishment will be them letting you paint for the rest of your miserable life," a nearby officer says, chuckling.

"Fat chance! These guys are going to The Pit for sure," another officer returns.

"What's The Pit?" Marla asks meekly. The anger and fire in her seems to be subsiding at an alarming rate. I hope she does not break completely.

"Now, if I tell you that, I'll ruin the surprise," Major Mason says. He has his usual grin plastered on his square face, and again I want to punch him in his smug mouth. "Soldiers, you are dismissed to go to your next post. I can take it from here. Kieran, you can go with them. Jones, take him to meet up with his father over at the lab." Kieran quickly turns away from us. I am thankful that he does not look my way again.

"Bastard," Reggie mumbles. He stares with malice at the back of Kieran's head. "Don't think this is over."

"Can it, tough guy," Major Mason says. Reggie does not say another word, but the look of hatred does not leave his face until Kieran is almost out of view. Extending his arm in a sweeping motion to usher us inside, Major Mason continues, "Prepare to meet all four members of The Council of the Southeast."

***

Inside, the building is just as well kept and pristine. The main entry room is painted a soft blue all the way up to the rounded ceiling some twenty-five feet above. Dancing playfully along the underside of the dome, angels and cherubs shoot arrows at one another, and a bearded man on a cross looks longingly with his sad eyes toward a glowing light. Magnificent, crystal chandeliers dangle proudly from the ceiling in several different points, the clear orbs attached glowing brightly and illuminating the room. This must be how the electricity gets into the room. My mother mentioned these to me before, and I think the word is light bulb, but I cannot be for certain. Several more 'light bulbs' line the walls attached to shiny, brass torches without fire. Large, tropical plants with pale, yellow fruit hulk in each corner of the room, and hundreds of other vegetation with variously colored blooms litter the immense space. A cool breeze, much like fall's gentle kiss, wafts through the air instantly chilling my sweat.

As we all enter, a tall, striking woman with neatly pinned hair rises from behind a dark, mahogany desk to greet Major Mason. "Sir, they are expecting you in The Hall of the Greats. Please follow me." He simply nods and we follow behind her.

The walk to meet with The Council takes us down a long, narrow corridor. It may be just my nerves, but as we progress, I feel as though the walls are closing in on us; the hallway is unnaturally slim and the ceiling much too tall for such a tiny space. Intensifying the effect, there is a lack of any décor hanging on the harsh, yellow sides. Even with our meager means back in Alon, we had a few portraits or relics decorating the interior of our tents; this lack of comfort seems intentional. Our guide's sharp, high heels clack loudly on the hard, marble floor with every one of her long strides, further increasing the overall feeling of severity. Chancing a glance back, I see two, thick, wooden doors have been closed to seal off our exit. I guess with everything else to look at in the entrance, I overlooked them before. One thing is for sure, no matter what happens from here on out, there is only one way out of here, and that is forward.

After what feels like hours, we arrive at a set of metal doors, much like the gate that closes off The Sacred City to the outside world, these doors have etchings of The Turned on them. Not wanting to revisit the graphic and gory depictions, I focus my attention on the faces of my friends. Reggie, badly swollen and bruised now, looks straight ahead with no emotion at all, Viola and Camden, forcible separated again, lock eyes with each other and use their bond for strength, and Marla is still looking down at the floor in silence contemplation. We are a pathetic looking group; dirty, hair disheveled, streaks down our faces where tears have fallen and then dried, clothing in tatters, various stages of The Turning appearing on our bodies. Wait? That's strange, all my friends have obvious symptoms of the acceleration, but I feel nothing. Holding out my arms and turning them over several times, I inspect them thoroughly.

There is not one single lesion or vein, nor pallor. I lift my hands up to my eyes. No brittle nails. Running my hands through my hair, I feel the same fullness as before. Squinting, I scrutinize my reflection in the metal doors; my eyes are also unchanged. How can this be? I should have at least two of the ailments by now. I am cut off from my thoughts by the loud knocking of Major Mason on the doors. Laboriously unhurried, they creak open with a loud groan, slowly revealing The Hall of the Greats.

***

Row upon row of red, padded seats in a semi-circular pattern fill the outer portion of the hall and spread downward toward a large, gold desk with four, enormous, black chairs with barely visible, shadowy occupants-The Council of the Southeast. We are standing at the top looking down, and I estimate there are approximately two thousand, vacant seats in all. The room is massive in scope and presence, and carries with it a feeling of deep oppression. Dark, purple curtains hang on every inch of the walls, making the room feel much smaller than it really is. Although it is still lit by the fake fire of electricity, the room is barely cast in a glow and it is difficult to see clearly all the way down to the bottom. Unlike the rest of the building, this room is not cooled to the outside air and the humidity looms like a thick, wool blanket on a hot night. I sharply inhale a deep breath, trying to calm my rampant nerves and find some friendly oxygen for my suddenly, laboring lungs.

"Enter!" a large voice booms from down below. I squint my eyes to try to make out who spoke, but cannot see well enough.

"You heard him, move it," Major Mason growls.

Methodically, we make our way down the slick ramp to the desk and The Council. My heart is pounding feverishly in my throat. My knees are weak with worry, making me slower than normal. Still, I do my best to hold my head high and charge toward my fate with grace and dignity. Behind me, I can hear the others slowly shuffling their feet in time with mine. Besides a few ragged intakes of air and our movement, the hall is completely silent. The closer I draw to the bottom, the more clearly I can make out the people sitting there. Even though there is an even number, it is obviously set up to convey a seat of superiority. In the middle, sits Eli, with his shining, silver hair pulled into a taut ponytail; his piercing, amethyst gaze is boring holes into my soul as he stares directly at me. Next to Eli, on his right, sits a strikingly beautiful woman-about thirty years old-with hair the color of fire and eyes as green as the salt sea. Despite her stunning features, something about her scares me more than Eli does. She too is staring directly at me; I shudder and quickly divert my eyes to the next seat. Perched with his hands folded neatly under his chin and his fingers resting on his lips, sits another man about the same age as the woman. There are no extraordinary or notable features for him. He has small, brown eyes, brown hair, and is of average weight and build; yet, he too conveys a degree of malice with just his scowl. I do not dwell on him any longer than necessary and hurriedly regard the final seat. Before my gaze even falls upon him, I can feel his on me. It seems like an eternity since the last time I saw him, and he is every bit as stunning as I recall. Even in the dim glow, I can see the mesmerizing, purple luminescence of his eyes, and my heart skips a beat. Despite, his presence at the desk, he does not emit the same, authoritarian vibe the others do; his hands are folded neatly in his lap, his regard of us is natural and non-threatening, and a slight softness tugs at the corners of his loosely pressed lips.

"Holy crap! Who is that?" Marla whispers to me, finally coming out of her stupor a bit.

"That's Brighton Nash," I say.

"He's dreamy. I mean, he's probably going to sentence us to death, but still," she says. I do not respond, but every inch of my body knows exactly what Marla is referring to. Brighton Nash is a man unlike any other.

When we are a few feet away from he and the others, Eli says, "That is far enough." His loud voice occupies every inch of the hall, causing me to flinch. He notices the motion and laughs before continuing, "Major Mason, you have done your job well. Thank you for delivering them here to us safely. I suspect you also took care of our other problems on the outside."

"Yes, sir, all threats have been neutralized. The last bus from Alon should be arriving here sometime after midnight, and no survivors were found at the other nearby villages," Major Mason replies proudly.

"And what of the rogue Officers?"

"Disposed of in the woods, sir."

"Excellent! Now, back to the matter at hand. Zayda, you have been quite the naughty girl lately. Sneaking off to explore The Old City several times. *Alone* no less. *And then* convincing your friends to join you. You are extremely lucky one of the mutated Turned didn't show up and make a meal out of you. Don't you think?" Eli says, waiting for me to reply. I just stand still, my mouth pressed firmly closed, and say nothing.

Major Mason smacks me directly across my cheek, busting my lip and drawing blood. I flinch, but do not cry. "You will address The Council when they speak to you. Do you understand me?" I still remain silent. He answers with another blow, and this time a small tear escapes my eye.

"Enough!" Brighton says. Looking up, I see that he has risen from his seat, and his hands are now clenched into fists. "We do not hit women in here, regardless of their crimes. Do *you* understand *me*?"

"Yes, sir. It won't happen again," Major Mason says. Although his words agree, the menacing glare he is giving Brighton does not.

"Okay, everyone just calm down. Brighton, the major was just trying to make our guest a little more cooperative. I'm sure he didn't mean to offend you. Not *everyone* shares your ideas about proper treatment of the fairer sex," Eli says. I can't help but notice how he says the word everyone, and I realize Eli is very much talking about himself. Knowing this, I worry even more about our punishment. "As I was saying, you have been breaking the rules left and right. Making weapons. Trying to get someone to teach you to read. The list truly goes on and on... But, let's not forget, you did not act alone. Which one of you guys was it that set the bomb off in Alon? Camden, right?" he continues. "Step forward, Camden." Cam complies. "I don't know whether to send you to The Pit or make you an officer. Although it was quite stupid and disruptive, your action took some major guts. What do you think I should do?"

"I would rather die than join your Officers," Camden replies. As an act of total defiance, he looks directly into the eyes of Eli as he says it and spits on the ground.

"Moxie! I like it," Eli responds. He doesn't seem to be bothered by Camden's blatant disrespect, and coolly continues. "You will be dead soon anyway. Or at least, dead-ish. Why not spend your last few months living like a king in one of the barracks? You will get all the food you can eat. Plus, a young lady or two has been known to frequent the establishment late at night. *If* you know what I mean." Eli winks as he says this, confirming my earlier theory. Bile rises in my throat, and I struggle to keep from gagging. "Oops, looks like I may have upset poor, little Zayda here. Don't worry sweetie, where you are going there won't be any hanky panky," Eli says with a laugh.

"Don't be cruel, father," Brighton says.

"Honesty isn't the same as cruelty, son."

"No, but taunting a child is," Brighton replies.

The word child hits me harder than Major Mason's hand. Is that how he sees me? "I am not a child." I say. Brighton looks my direction and flashes me a smile, but I cannot interpret the meaning behind it.

"Oh, she does speak. Fantastic news. This will make our time here much more interesting," Eli responds, clapping his hands together excitedly. The other two council members still sit quietly, the only indication they are even alive is their periodic blinking. "Please, dear Zayda, tell me why you so deliberately chose to disobey The Rules?"

Deciding it wasn't worth the extra time I would have to spend enduring Eli's rants, I take a deep breath, try to mask the anger and venom in my voice, and answer honestly,

"After my brother Robinson was taken away to Turn, I began to question the ways of our world. It didn't seem fair to me that he had to face something so scary alone, and I hated you, as I hate you now, for ripping him away from his family. It was then, that I decided the people who could do that to someone were pure evil, and I would not allow evil to dictate my life."

For the first time, the lady of The Council speaks, her voice is high and delicate like a songbird as she says, "But it has always been the ways of The Healers to take people away before the transition. Why did it bother you so much then?"

Her question surprises me, and I think for a second before answering, "I guess because I am a selfish person. I could not see the pain The Turning caused until it was happening to my family."

"So, all of this has happened because of selfishness on your part?" Eli asks. He does this in a way that is neither judgmental nor rude, only confused. "Am I right in taking that away from your answer?"

"You would be well within your right to believe that. And, at first it was true. However, when you took my parents away too...," I pause and look at Brighton before finishing. Something deep inside me wants him to understand that I am more than just a spoiled little kid. "I needed a bigger purpose. A reason to exist, if only for another year. Fighting you and The Healers became that reason. If I could stop someone else from going through the pain I had, then my life would have not been in vain. For years, I have watched people be shuffled around like cattle. Too many people in Alon; bye June. Another teenager about to transition; bye teenager. All the while, we all just stood by and allowed it. So, to answer your question, Eli," I say, adjusting my stance to stand taller and address him directly, "*Your* selfishness is the reason for all of this. Without The Healers, without The Cure, without The Council, none of this would be happening. And now you sit there on your plush chair at your gold-plated desk and decide my future. Perhaps, it is time for you to stop playing god."

"Amen!" Viola says. She has not spoken since we got off the bus, and it is a welcome sound to my ears.

Not daring to look away from The Council for fear of getting slapped again, I stand and wait for one of them to speak. Moments fade into eternity before the young, plain man does. "The Rules exist for a reason. If we allow you to break them without consequence, then chaos will erupt all around the nation. Because of you, your parents were taken away. Because of you, the Officers were killed. Because of you, the little...Julie, was it?...died. Had you followed The Rules, none of this would have happened," he says, narrowing his eyes.

"Julie was killed by a Turned. I didn't create The Turned. You did!" I shout. I hate to admit it, but there is some truth to their words. If I had not convinced the others to join me, they would be safe right now, but Julie, no, she wasn't my fault. "Julie was as good as dead the minute the virus mutated and everyone started Transitioning early. So, once again, that's on you guys." Panic washes over me as I let the truth behind my words sink in. The outside world is no longer safe for anyone. I hear a sniffle behind me and realize that my argument to The Council has wounded Marla more deeply. I am sorry for this, but that doesn't change the reality of our situation.

"How dare you speak to us this way!" the lady says.

"Now, calm down, Abellona. You and Zeke must be careful not to let this insignificant pest get under your skin. In the grand scheme of things, she does not matter. What does is continuing forward with our plans," Eli says.

"Can we please just get on with the sentencing then?" Zeke asks. His face is red, his veins bulging, from his anger. "She has already admitted guilt. There is nothing left to determine for her."

"I agree," Abellona says. Running her long, delicate fingers through her massive mane of hair as she focuses her attention on Reggie and continues, "Plus, there is still the punishment for the others to worry about." The way she looks him up and down as she says this makes me furious and disgusted. I want to claw her eyes out.

"Patience, my dear. We will get to that very soon," Eli replies. Obviously, he enjoys the hunt just as much as the kill, and is not ready to give up his fun quite yet. Huffing in exasperation, Abellona settles back into her chair and assumes her disinterested posture. "Brighton, my dear boy, what do you think we should do with Zayda? You seem to have taken a bit of an interest in her. Though, I can't for the life of me figure out why. Would you have me save her from The Pit?"

Eli does not look at his son when he says this, but nevertheless, Brighton does not change anything about his demeanor when he replies. "It will come as no surprise to you, that I do not wish that for anyone. I have always made my distaste for The Pit extremely clear. We are not barbarians. Therefore, we should not behave as such," he says.

"Then what would you suggest we do? I cannot simply allow her to roam free like nothing has happened. Imagine the fallout if others heard The Council of the Southeast has gone soft," Eli says. He is still staring directly at me; a playful smile has started to spread across his face.

"You know my words will not matter. Stop toying with them and get on with it," Brighton replies. As if he already knows what is coming, he erects himself completely, takes a deep breath, and appears to brace himself for the sentence.

Still smiling sadistically, Eli responds, "True, son, I know you will never be a harsh enough ruler. If you had it your way, these young criminals would skip off into the sunset like a band of carefree idiots. Thankfully, I am still in control here."

"For now," Brighton faintly mumbles under his breath. I do not know if anyone else caught it, but I am again staring directly at him, so I do. A tiny flicker of hope ignites inside my stomach. Even if I am lost today, perhaps someday Brighton can change all of this.

"Let's start with Marla. Poor little Marla, already lost her sister. I bet you don't even want to live anymore. I can't say I blame you. If I were utterly alone, I wouldn't want to either," Eli states. He is looking at Marla with a combination of sadness and sarcasm; she just stares blankly past him without any emotion at all. I hate to admit it, but I think he is right. Marla has given up. "I see no reason to put you through the trials of The Pit when spending the remainder of your lifetime alone and dwelling upon your failure to save your sister will serve as a more formidable enough punishment." Nodding, tears streaming down her face, Marla acknowledges his words as true. She does not even seem bothered by the prospect of spending the next year locked up in a cage. Deep down, Marla's guilt over Julie rules her very soul. "Then, it is done. You will be banished to the cells." Eli says.

Moving his attention to Viola, "Until now, I have not addressed you; that was not on accident. I have come to understand through Posy, that you are not the biggest fan of Zayda. Posy has confided to me that you only went along with these shenanigans because of your brother. Family loyalty means a great deal to me," Eli says, shooting a disappointed look at his son, "because of this, I am willing to go easy on you and allow you to escape The Pit and cells. Instead, you shall serve me until you Turn."

Viola lets out a sigh of relief and quietly says, "Thank you."

Laughing, Eli responds, "Don't thank me yet. You have yet to spend one day, let alone one *night* under my control. I suspect you will be singing quite a different tune come tomorrow."

Viola shrinks back with the insinuation of Eli's words. Not willing to surrender his sister to the sick wishes of a madman, Camden lunges forward and tries to attack Eli. Major Mason, quick on his feet, grabs Camden tightly around the neck and lifts him off the floor. "That was a stupid mistake, boy!" Major Mason growls.

"Moxie!" Eli says again, "I expected no less from you, Camden. You too, will be saved from The Pit. Now, Major Mason, please let our new soldier down."

Releasing Camden from his grasp, Major Mason grunts, "Solider. Yeah right. This boy will never be a soldier."

Camden's body, slumped over, twitches as he struggles to reclaim the air to his lungs. His face is red with effort, and he gasps and wheezes for several seconds before finally regaining his composure.

"Oh, we have ways of making even the most persistent resistor cooperate," Zeke says, pure joy evident in his tone. "Plus, it would be in his sister's best interest if he behaved himself like a good, little warrior."

"You will not touch her!" Camden growls. Despite them having the obvious upper hand, both Eli and Zeke cringe slightly with the venomous delivery of Camden's words. "I promise you, if anyone hurts her, I will kill you all with my bare hands."

"Take him away!" Eli responds waving his hand dismissively. He is obviously annoyed with Camden's continued defiance. "Put him in the holding cells with the other potential Officers from Alon, but make sure he has a private quarter so I can visit him and chat later. We have much to discuss."

Major Mason happily obliges and grabs Camden roughly by the collar. "Let's go see your new home," he smirks, dragging him away. Struggling and kicking, Camden fights vigorously to break the major's grasp, but he is no match for the brute strength of the officer. Soon, both disappear through a small, wooden door in the back of the hall.

I try to reach out to comfort Viola, but she shies away from my hand. "Do. Not. Touch. Me!" she says. The bitterness in the way she says this makes me wince, and I hastily retract my arm and fold my hands together in front of me.

"Now, on to the last two," Eli says. He stands up and walks around the desk to reside directly in front of us. "I've been trying to figure out what would hurt you the most, Zayda. Letting Reggie fight to the death in The Pit," he pauses gauging my reaction, "or giving him to Abellona as a slave?" Again, he stops to read my face. I try not to show any emotion, but I can't stop myself from glaring at Abellona and baring my teeth. Licking her lips in anticipation, she watches with pure elation in her eyes. She is an awful woman, and I know for a fact she will abuse Reggie in horrific ways. "Looks like we have a winner," Eli says, following the trail of my eyes to the retched, female Council member. "Congratulations, Abellona, you have a new toy."

Slightly purring, Abellona responds, "Delightful. If it pleases you, sir, I would like to take him to my wing right away, so he can be properly tended to. I can't have someone serving me who is damaged."

"Yes, please do. I am almost finished here anyway," Eli responds. Abellona rises from her seat and walks toward Reggie, grinning the entire way. Crossing the room, she seems to slither more than walk, and I suspect this is her way of trying to be sexy. However, the beauty she possessed earlier has been replaced by something sinister and dark, and I see the horror on Reggie's face as he takes her in.

"You don't have to do this," I beg. "Please don't."

"Of course, we don't *have* to," Abellona chimes, "We want to." She snaps her fingers and two guards, much larger than Major Mason, enter the room and flank Reggie. Addressing her new prisoner, "Just in case you had any bright ideas about running," she winks. Trying to block their exit, I step in front of them. "Young lady, you can't possibly think you are going to win this fight?"

Standing my ground, I say, "I can try."

"Please, don't be foolish."

Taking a step forward, I smack Abellona across her left cheek. Surprise and fury erupt on her face, she speaks to the guards, "Do not interfere. I am going to enjoy this," and then she lunges for me. Her fingernails, sharp like daggers, tear at the soft flesh of my upper chest, and I howl in pain. I return the favor by intertwining my fingers in her blazing, red locks and pulling as hard as I can. "You little bitch!" she yells, her hands desperately attempting to pull my hands free. Doubling down, I yank her hair as hard as I can and bring her to her knees. Years of allowing others to do her bidding have made her much softer and weaker than me, and I very easily have the upper hand. Grunting, she continues flailing around wildly, unable to break my tight grip, and I drive my knee into her waiting face. Screeching with pain, Abellona gives up, "Get her off me! Hurry, you stupid idiots!" One of the guards rushes over behind me and picks me up, bearhugging me around my shoulders. For a few moments, I am able to hold on to her hair, but as he pulls me up even higher my grip fails. Kicking my legs violently in the air to free myself, I can't help but laugh at the clump of flaming locks in my hands. "You are going to pay for that," she says, before rearing her fist back and punching me square in the nose. Instantly, blood begins to pool down my face, and I choke on the rusty flavored liquid as it enters my mouth.

"Enough!" Eli shouts. "I will not have the Hall of Greats turned into a circus. Abellona, take your leave now. The boy will spend the night in the cells, and you can claim him in the morning."

"I do not wish to wait," she responds.

"I do not care what you wish. The situation is growing out of control, and you know how much I hate when things get out of control," Eli snarls.

Realizing her mistake, Abellona bows and responds, "Yes, sir. I did not mean to offend you. I will do as you wish. But first, please tell me where I can expect to find Zayda tomorrow." Pure hatred flows from every pore of her body as she looks at me. She is lucky the guard is still holding me up, or I would be plucking her catlike eyes right out of her head.

"Do not fret, my dear," Eli states, walking up to Abellona and smoothing down her tattered hair in a fatherly motion. "Tomorrow, our delightful friend, Zayda will be spending her last day on earth in The Pit. Perhaps, one of her old buddies will have the honor of killing her." As he says this, I realize what he means, and my eyes grow wide. "Oh, I see you have put two and two together. Sad for me though, I was looking forward to the surprised look on your face when you got there."

"That's what you do when you take The Turned, you keep them caged like animals and make people fight them?" I ask. Disgust courses through my veins as I process this information. Hundreds, if not thousands of people have been taken over the years. We thought they had been humanely put down. Never in my wildest dreams could I have imagined this was their fate.

"Don't be silly. Only a handful of Turned are given to The Pit. Usually, the most special cases. The rest are being trained, or as close to a braindead is capable of, to help fight the growing resistance," Eli says.

Shocked by his last words, "Resistance?" I ask.

"What? You thought you were the only one? Stupid, naïve girl, if only you hadn't gotten yourself caught. Ah, so sad, now you will never get to truly fight for your cause." For the first time in several minutes, I look toward Brighton. He has his head hung down in defeat. Sensing my stare, he looks up. Eli quickly turns toward his son, his silver ponytail swinging in the air. The two men lock eyes for a few seconds, neither speaking, yet both understanding the meaning behind the gaze. Looking at me, but obviously addressing Brighton, Eli says, "Won't matter anyway. No one can beat me and my army."

"You are sick!" I yell. "How could you keep those poor people alive like that?"

"Maybe I am, and maybe I'm not. One thing is for sure though, after tomorrow, I will still be alive and you won't," Eli says. Turning to Viola, he continues, "You can come with me to my wing of the building, and I will introduce you to the others. You are going to like it there. Hot water, plenty of food, and great company," he laughs. Viola looks mortified but does not make any attempt to shy away from his soft grip on her arm. "Good girl. It will only make things more unpleasant if you fight. As for the three of you, guards, take them to the cells." The guards grab us by the arms, Marla and I sharing one, massive man between us, and begin to escort us out of the rooms.

As we are being half drug toward the same door Camden left through, I can hear Eli laughing maniacally behind us. Brighton still sits in his chair, his face rigid and difficult to read. Part of me thinks he might jump up and save us, but he does not. We walk through the door and into complete darkness. Eli says before we are closed in completely, the madness in his voice rising with each syllable, "Oh, and Zayda, sleep well. You don't want to be exhausted for your big day." Even on the other side of the thick door, I can still hear his hysteria, and I know without a doubt he is utterly mad.

REVELATIONS

Our guides continue forward a few feet to allow the door to completely seal behind us, closing off any possible chances for escape. They then strike a match and light the torches on the wall; there is no electricity in this ancient part of the building. A large hallway stretches out before us, and I can hear desperate cries in the distance. Panic blossoms in me, my knees waver, and I begin to feel faint. The continuous flow of blood into my mouth does not help me steady myself. A firm tug on my left arm pulls me upright, and I am thrust forward into the unknown. The dank smell of mildew permeates every inch of the dimly lit corridor, and a few small rats scurry around our feet. Five bodies are way too many to fit down the passage side by side, so Reggie and his guard walk in front of us. I am trying to be strong for all of us, but it is becoming increasingly more difficult. The mere thought that this is the last night I will spend with my best friend causes a huge crevasse to open inside me. I want nothing more than to be able to hug him and tell him how much he means to me, but the guard's tight grip will not allow me to move even an inch away from him. Mercifully, the walk does not take long, and within a minute we are in front of a row of ten or more cages. Dozens of people sit inside them, their faces and hands filthy from days of captivity; soft moans of both hunger and pain waft out of the spaces.

"Put the girls in this one together," Reggie's guard says, pointing to a small, empty cell all the way in the back of the room. His words alert the others to our presence, and all of them look at us at once. Even through the grime, I recognize a few faces from Alon. No one appears too happy to see me, and a fog of hostility begins to loom heavily in the room. As we quietly make our way back to our cell, I can hear the angry murmurs of my once friends. I know, based on what Viola and the others told me when we met up in The Old City, that I am not very well liked anymore. However, that knowledge did not brace me for the barrage of hatred I encounter.

"Good! Looks like they finally caught the monster. I hope she rots in here until she Turns," our village nurse, Annie says. She is in the first cell with a dozen or more women from the camp, all of whom are nodding their heads in agreement with her words. I hold my head high and continue past them. "She caused all of this with her sneaking around. If it weren't for Zayda, we'd all be back in Alon living in peace," Annie adds. As I pass them completely, an older woman spits on the ground beside my foot. I quicken my pace to get away from them as soon as possible.

The next cell is not much better. It contains the men from our village, and they are even angrier than the women. The vile things they say are too much for me to comprehend, but I still maintain my composure and look at them defiantly. "What are you looking at, bitch?" a skinny man with very little hair left shouts. I do not remember his name, but I do recognize him as one of the farmers from town. He had always been kind to my family and I, but that sentiment is long gone.

Gazing at a row of men sitting on the bench in the back, I try to find any hints of friendliness left among my people. Most men are silently murdering me with their glares, but in the far corner I see a soft smile beneath the dirt. Squinting to see past the darkness encapsulating the figure, I allow my eyes to adjust and pick out familiar features on his face. "Holy crap!" I say as shock runs through my body. Reggie and Marla turn to follow my stare. After a few seconds, their eyes acclimate also.

"Dad!" Reggie yells, breaking free from his guard and running to the bars. Marla and I do our best to block the guard from pursuing him, and Reggie manages to make it to the cell. His father rises from the bench and pushes his way through the crowd toward his son. "Dad, what are you doing in there?" Reggie asks, looking around at the rest of the people in the cells. I do the same and see that almost all the people over forty from Alon are locked up. "Why would they put you in there? I thought The Healers were taking you to safety?"

"So did we, but once we arrived they sorted us into groups and then brought us down here," Reggie's father says, sticking his hands through the bars to grasp his son.

"Where are all of the others? The younger people?" Reggie asks.

"We don't know. There was some talk about an army and soldiers, but no one spoke about where they were taking them," his father replies.

Hitting Reggie in the back of the head with the butt of his rifle, the guard successfully ends the conversation. "Shut up and get back to your bench," he snarls at Reggie's father, "and, you three, stop talking to the other inmates and walk." Reggie, grabbing his head in pain, complies, and we all begin walking toward our cell again. Marla has kept her head down and has not really looked inside any of the cages until this point. Her small frame is still slumped over in defeat. I'm truly afraid she is lost to us for good. The chorus of jeers has abated, and the remainder of our trek is silent. We arrive outside of two cells at the far end of the hall, and our guard, while unlocking the large, steel padlock, says, "Get in, ladies. This will be your home for the next few hours, Zayda." He laughs as he says this, and I can tell he enjoys his job quite a bit. "Marla, might as well get comfortable because you are in for the long haul." He continues laughing as he forcefully pushes us on the back and shoves us into the small, cramped space.

"Hey! You don't have to be so rough!" Reggie shouts in our defense. His face is red with anger and he looks like he is going to explode at any moment. His guard just glares at him, daring him to make a move. Still reeling from the whack on the back of his head, Reggie does not chance another fight. "I'm just saying, they are only girls, so maybe take it a little easy on them."

Getting within an inch of Reggie's face, his guard says, "How about you mind your own business. We will treat them *anyway* we choose. Once you entered this room, you no longer had any rights. Now, shut up and get in your cell." The guard unlocks the compartment adjacent to ours and roughly shoves Reggie inside. A small amount of relief washes over me when I see how close we will be to one another. Deep down, I thought for sure they would isolate us all. At least now, I will have a chance to tell him goodbye before I face whatever horror awaits me in The Pit. "See you bright and early in the morning," the guard says to me, satisfaction brimming his voice.

"Dicks!" Reggie says as the two guards walk away from us and down the corridor we just came from.

"Big ones," I reply. Walking back to sit on the bench, I ponder how I'm going to get out of this situation. There is no way I'm going to be able to open the cell door, and even if I did, where would I go? The only exit is through The Hall of Greats, and I'm positive it is guarded at all times. To say our situation is bleak, is an understatement at best. "Marla," I say quietly, "why don't you come over here and sit beside me, so you can get some rest? You look exhausted." She raises her head and looks at me. The emptiness in her eyes sends sharp pangs deep into my soul. So much loss and pain is visible on her kind face. Not speaking, she does as I ask and comes to rest beside me. I put my arm around her delicate shoulders, and pull her over to me. She allows her head to rest on my shoulder and quickly falls asleep. After a few minutes, I slide off the bench and gently lay her body down.

Moving over to sit on the floor closest to Reggie's cell, I say, "This is some mess I've gotten us into."

Reggie moves over to mirror me on his floor. He glances from me to Marla several times before taking a deep breath and responding. "You didn't get us into anything. We all chose, in one way or another, to join you. Look around,

Zayda, if I hadn't left Alon to be with you, I'd still have ended up here. I'm glad it was on my terms and not theirs," he says.

I do as he suggests and look around. The large, poorly lit room is full of hundreds of people; some I know, and others are complete strangers. The Healers have rounded up everyone who has crossed their path. "I guess you are right. Still, I can't help feeling guilty. I never wanted any of this for you," I say.

He laughs, "Well, that's good to know. I would hate to think all along you were planning on me being tossed into a cage like an animal and being awarded to some psycho as a prize."

Psycho is right. The idea of Reggie having to spend a single moment with Abellona makes me sick. "She means to make you suffer. *A lot*," I say.

"I know," he replies. Despite the simplicity of his words, there is an obvious resignation behind them. Reggie is not going to fight what is coming his way. "If that is the price I have to pay for helping someone I love, then so be it. You must know I would do it all again, even knowing the consequences, to be by your side." I just nod. I've always known Reggie would do anything for me, but the gravity of his devotion had not been clear until this very moment. He truly would follow me to the ends of the earth. "Funny thing is," he continues, "in the beginning, I did this because I thought it would help you fall in love with me." He reaches his hand through the bars, and so do I. Our fingertips barely brush each other, but it is enough contact to offer a slice of peace. "Even up until today, I still thought that. But then, something changed. When we were in The Hall of Greats, and I heard your speech about Robinson, I realized that is how I feel about you. Don't get me wrong, I love you completely, and I always will, but how I love you is different now," he says.

His words spark a revelation inside me. I feel exactly the same way about him. All the mixed emotions I have been warring with are dissolved away with his confession. "I love you too! You are all of the family I have left, Reggie, and I don't know what I'm going to do without you," I say. Tears have started falling freely down my cheeks, and I don't even try to stop them; it feels good to release my feelings into the world. I pull my hand back and place my wet face in my palms.

"Don't cry," Reggie says. He speaks softly but firmly. "Look at me, Zayda." I do as he requests. "No matter what happens to either of us tomorrow or the day after that, I will always be with you. A piece of you lives inside me," he says pointing to his heart. "The only part of my body that can't be altered by The Healers, or The Turning, or anything else this jacked up world tosses at me, is where you will always be."

Placing my own hand over my heart, I simply say, "Thank you!" No other words need to be exchanged between us. We both have found our place together, found our peace within our lives together, and we are finally free from the burden of how our puzzle pieces fit. We are family. Brother and sister. And nothing else matters.

THE PIT

"Get up," a harsh, female voice bellows out. I must have fallen asleep on the floor after Reggie and my talk, but the lack of light in the cell makes it impossible to tell what time it is. Groggily, I sit up and wipe the sleep out of my eyes. Marla does the same from her position on the bench-she must have slept there all night. "It's time to head to The Pit," the woman says shining a flashlight in my face and momentarily blinding me. Shielding my eyes, I avert my attention and look toward Reggie's cage. It is empty. Panicking, I jump to my feet. Noticing my reaction, the woman says, "Abellona came for your friend a few hours ago while you were still sleeping. Too bad you didn't get to say goodbye." The smile on her face contradicts her words, and I realize everyone who works in this place is a complete sadist. Unlocking the padlock, she swings the door wide open and gestures for me to exit. I comply and move to stand beside her. There is no point in putting up a fight; three more guards fill in the mouth of the exit corridor, and even if I managed to overtake her, they would stop me from going more than five feet.

"Where did all of the other prisoners go?" I ask, realizing Reggie is not the only one missing. Marla and I are the lone occupants still left.

"Why, at The Pit waiting, of course. Can't have you performing without an audience," she laughs, as do the men blocking the exit. "Now, if you two will follow me, Eli is waiting with a surprise." She begins walking, and Marla and I reluctantly follow. To my surprise, we do not exit the way we came. One of the male guards pulls down one of the torches lining the walls, and a secret panel opens, thrusting us into daylight. Having been in the dark for many hours, my eyes burn from the sudden onslaught of brightness and begin watering profusely. Beside me, Marla lets out a small yelp and shields her own face from the glare. "Clyde, please take Marla to the viewing area with the others. The rest of you will escort Zayda to The Pit with me," the woman says.

"Got it boss," Clyde says. Brashly, taking Marla by the elbow, he makes a left and they vanish out of sight through yet another door.

The vastness of this complex begins to register with me as my vision clears, and I plainly see what lies ahead of me. A massive wall, hundreds of feet high, barbed wire adorning the top, looms around us, completely closing us in. Lining the wall on all sides, are arena style seats overflowing with thousands upon thousands of people. Some are chanting and cheering eagerly, others just sit stone still peering forward into the center of the stadium. Following their stares, I strain my eyes to make out what they are observing. Dread courses through me as I realize what it is. At least half a dozen bloated and rotting Turned-their arms flailing and grasping, chained to metal posts sticking out of the dirt floor-form a circle surrounding a small body huddled in a ball on the ground. When approximately ten seconds pass, a horn sounds, and the posts automatically move forward several inches, eliciting more excited cheers from the onlookers; the huddled mass squeezes itself tighter together and openly weeps. Looking closer, I see the form clearly; it is a boy. I do not recognize him, but he is right around my age.

"You didn't think you were the only one to break The Rules, did you?" one of my guard asks. "Eli intends to make several statements today about falling in line. Our friend here is just the first. Serving as the main course, so to speak, you will be our last, so sit back and enjoy," he adds. Bile rises in my throat as I think about the massacre I am about to witness.

"Welcome to The Pit," a voice bellows dramatically over an intercom. Exploding from their seats, the crowd reacts wildly and their screams bloom into a litany of profane phrases. My heart pumps viciously as I take in their fervor. "Today is a special day! We have a very important guest. Zayda, please come forward," he continues. Pulling me forward from the shadows, my guard thrusts me into the outside edge of the arena. A chorus of boos echo throughout. Shielding my eyes from the harshness of the sun's glare, I spin in a circle to fully take in the spectators. Many are well-dressed and are apparently the wealthy of The Sacred City. They are the most adamantly engaged in booing. Separate from the wealthy, the tradesmen and women from the street sit, quietly watching. A few of them are jeering, but the majority wear solemn expressions on their visages. "Zayda is our first competitor to have multiple infractions. You may have heard of her from some of the stories floating about the city," the voice says.

Something familiar in the tone begins to register. "Eli," I say aloud.

"Naturally. Master of ceremonies is his favorite job. Now let's get you over to him, so he can properly introduce the games," the female guard says. Amid more shouts from the angry mob, she marches me across the middle of the stadium. A glass bottle lands a few inches from my feet, and I cover my head with my arms to protect it from the copycats in the crowd who all begin bombarding me with trash and other items.

"Now, now, don't injure our prize before she has a chance to fight. It will ruin the surprise I have in store for her," Eli says over the loudspeaker. The mob does not comply, and he continues, the civility evaporating from his voice, "I. Said. Stop. How dare you ignore my words!" With that, a hush settles over everyone; the only sound remaining is that of the boy in the middle. I look back and see that The Turned have not advanced any closer since Eli began speaking, but that has done little to calm the poor kid down.

As we approach the other side, I can see Eli standing inside of a large, gilded grandstand at least ten rows up from the ground. On both sides of him sit the other Council leaders; behind them all, sit my friends. Eli has made good on all his threats, not that I doubted him for a moment. Along with a look of utter disgust, Camden is wearing the uniform of The Officers. Viola looks stunning. She has been adorned in gold jewels and an elaborate, emerald dress; its shade a perfect complement to her alabaster skin and red hair. Marla, just now arriving, is settling into a seat beside Reggie-who has been cleaned up and groomed since I last saw him. A slave collar encircles his neck, a large 'A' is situated in the middle declaring him to his owner. His eyes are locked on me, and I can see the terror behind them. I hold his gaze until I feel the tears welling in my eyes, and then I look away quickly. Unfortunately, I settle on Abellona next. Her face, reminiscent of a cat toying with its prey, makes me physically ill. When she sees me looking at her, she winks, turns around, grabs Reggie by his collar, and plants a large, messy kiss on his lips. He does not return the gesture, but does not protest either. Rage consumes me, and I vow to make her pay. Even if it is the last thing I ever do.

"Well, don't just stand there. Escort our distinguished guest to her seat. I don't want her to miss a minute of the festivities," Eli announces to the guards.

The trip to join the others does not take long, but it is laboring none the less. Not only for me, but also for my guards. They spend the majority of their time defending me from the prying grasps of hundreds of people, all of whom seem to hate me more than Eli. Midway up, we pass a section filled with Officers and their families. Directly in the front row, sits Posy. She does not even glance my direction. "Posy! Look at me! Look at what you've done!" I scream. Only then, does she face me. Shock runs through my body. The vacant look in her eyes is heartbreaking. There is no sign of Posy at all in the deadpan gaze. "Oh, Posy. What have they done to you?" In response to my words, June leans over and whispers into her daughter's ear. Posy's expression changes briefly, but then the mask slides back into place, and she looks forward again. As I am aggressively pushed forward, June smiles at me in triumph. I now know that Posy is lost to me forever. Whatever The Healers have done to her, has erased any remaining ember of the girl I used to love. I just put my head down and continue climbing the stairs.

When we reach the box, they are all seated in, Eli motions for me to come and sit directly beside him. Abellona moves over making space for me, and I take my position between her and Eli. Surrounded by the two people I hate most in the world, I watch in horror, awaiting my turn in the ring.

***

The first boy does not last longer than five minutes. He is seriously outnumbered and does not seem to possess much of a fighter's spirit. As The Turned make their final advance on their poles, the ground around the boy opens and tilts him into the air toward the monsters. They fall on him and begin tearing him limb from limb, digging their teeth into the delicate flesh of his neck at the same time. His cries, despite being loud and desperate, are drowned out by the frenzy of the crowd; these sick people are loving every minute of this. "That was disappointing," Eli announces. He has risen to stand at the front and address his admirers again. Abellona and Zeke also rise to cheer for the demise of the young man. Brighton, however, remains seated, a look of utter repulsion on his face. Even in this moment of immense tragedy, I can't help but recognize the underlying kindness and obvious beauty in him. Brighton is different than the rest of The Council, and he does not care to disguise this. I wish I could have more time to discover those differences and find out who he truly is.

"Poor Randy," Marla whispers. The Council members are standing up and are too caught up in the action below to notice her speak, but all of us perk up at the sound of her small voice for the first time in hours.

"You knew him?" I ask over my shoulder.

She nods, "He was from the village I was going to take you to. Looks like they beat us to it."

"I'm sorry," Reggie says. He reaches over and takes Marla's hand in his, his fingers gently caressing the top in a sweet, comforting measure. She looks at him, the familiar yearning again returning to her eyes. Realizing she is not entirely broken, relief floods over me; Marla still has a chance of coming back. I am surprised when I turn back around and see Brighton staring at us with a slight shimmer of wetness in his eyes. He quickly glances away, the customary blank stare returning.

"Let's keep this party going," Eli says. The excitement in his words hard to miss. "Bring out the next fighter."

The Turned on the rods have been pulled back to the edge of the wall; blood and fresh gore marring their faces. Despite their recent meal, their insatiability can be seen even from afar. A door opens and another small child-a girl this time-is forced into the arena by a group of hulking Officers. She scrambles and claws at the wood as it closes, trying her best to escape the stadium, but it is useless. The crowd again erupts into wicked chants and cheers, and a fresh group of The Turned emerge from an opening directly beside the girl. Caught off guard, she falls to the ground and begins to slowly scramble away. Her haste and nerves make her easy prey, and soon she is engulfed by the horde. Sickening slurping and gnawing sounds travel up to me, and I begin to feel nauseous. I cannot stand to watch this again, so I duck my head low, cover my ears tightly, and block out everything that is happening below. It does not take long for the girl to be consumed, and a group of shabbily dressed people run out to clean up the remnants. This process is repeated, in disgusting variation, five more times over the course of the next hour. By the end, I am emotionally drained, and ready for it all to be over.

Guards appear all around us, and Abellona claps excitedly. "Oh goody, it's time for the main event," she says glaring at me. "I have been waiting for this moment all day."

Jumping to my feet, I lunge at her and clamp my fingers around her slender neck. She chokes and gasps as I squeeze the life out of her, and I can see her face reddening as she struggles to take in air. In a few more seconds she will be gone. Neither Eli or Zeke have the sense to intervene, and I begin to think I might succeed until a hard fist slams down on the back of my head and knocks me to the floor. When I stop seeing stars and roll over to look up, I see the grinning face of Major Mason. "Hello, Zayda. You didn't think I would miss this special event, did you?" He says, seizing me by the waist and hauling me down to the edge of the arena, where I wait to meet my demise.

***

With tremendous fanfare, Eli announces me, "Ladies and gentlemen, it is the moment you have all been waiting for. Let me again introduce to you our main event." The crowd explodes like never before, and the reverberation of their rancorous roar shakes the structure. "I can see you are as excited about this fight as I am, so without further delay, I give you Zayda!" he yells.

Major Mason throws me over the edge of the ten-foot wall. I slam into the ground below with a sickening thud, and my vision blackens slightly. I know I must get up, but my left shoulder, bearing the brunt of the impact, is limp and useless. The sun is blazing overhead, and sweat has made my dirty clothes wet and clingy. I can't hear the approach of any Turned, but judging from how quickly they were introduced to the previous people, I probably do not have much time. Forcing myself up with only my right hand, I stagger to my feet. I am still alone in The Pit for the time being. Okay think, Zayda. There must be something in here you can use as a weapon. Looking around, I see The Turned from the first fight still struggling on their poles. If I can somehow kill one of them and extract the metal bar from the ground, I can use it to defend myself. But how will I kill it? Think. You are running out of time. Wait, what is that? One of the glass bottles the crowd threw in is over by the wall.

"What do you think, folks, has she had enough time to herself in there?" Eli shouts into the microphone. A thunderous cry answers him as I sprint for the bottle. "Then, let's introduce her to the man, or rather Turned, of the hour," he adds. Grabbing the glass in my hand, I spin to look up at Eli. He smiles down at me menacingly. There is no time left, so I strike the bottle on the wall and break the top off, creating a jagged makeshift knife. Eli throws his head back, spreads his arms wide, and bellows, "Open the gate."

I do not have time to run out into the middle of the arena, so I just take a few steps forward away from the wall, bend my knees, and prepare to fight. Directly below Eli, a large, slotted gate opens, and a Turned slowly begins to shuffle out. The platinum tufts of hair shine brightly in the noonday sun, and his gait, although slightly altered, remains the same. "Robbie!" I shout. What used to be my brother, hears my voice and quickens its pace toward me. Panic runs through my veins. I don't know if I will be able to do this. Deep down, I know this is not Robinson. Still, I can't help but picture his smiling face as we ran along the riverbank throwing stones at each other, or when we snuck out late at night and caught fireflies. So many memories of my brother bombard my mind and cloud my thinking. "Please, Robbie, don't make me do this." I beg. His only reply is the hungry, feral sound of The Turned as he continues toward me."

"Surprise!" Eli cheers. He is jumping up and down, clapping his hands with childlike glee. "I do so love a family reunion." Behind him, their hands covering their mouths, my friends all stare in horror. Abellona, still rubbing her red streaked neck, mimic's Eli's delight. She has moved Reggie to stand beside her, so he can have a better view. Reggie, leaning forward and grasping the railing, looks like he is going to jump over the edge at any moment and join me in the fight. I shake my head no at him. There is no way he would survive the fall, not to mention, get past the Officers blocking the entrance. I see Zeke grinning with utter satisfaction. He too, is a madman; they all are, except for Brighton, who is nowhere to be found.

Robinson is only a few feet away from me now-close enough that I can smell his putrefying body-and I still don't know if I can kill him. My knuckles are bulging with the force of my grasp on the bottle in my right hand, my sweat-soaked hair sticks to my forehead and hangs in my eyes, and my left side is still primarily useless. I take a few steps back to put more distance between us. I only have a small area left behind me before I am backed against the wall, and I do not want to be stuck with the only path out being through my brother. Looking around, I see a small corridor to my right that might offer refuge if I can make it there, but I will have to run past Robbie to get there. I chance a quick step to the right, and he mirrors my move. I dodge to the left, again he follows. He moves much slower than me. If I time it right, I might be able to get around him. He is nearly upon me now. I can see every bulbous vein protruding from his translucent body as if they are about to burst open. Any natural color once contained in his irises has long been lost to the gruesome yellow. The open, oozing sores cover ninety percent of his flesh. "Oh, Robbie, I'm so sorry," I whisper, preparing to make my move and taking a step toward him. "I wish they had killed you like they promised. You don't deserve to be like this." Snarling, he takes the last few remaining steps toward me and reaches his long, brittle fingernails toward my face. "I love you," I say, closing my eyes and raising the bottle to thrust into his throat.

Just as the glass grazes his flesh, a deafening boom explodes all around us, knocking Robinson and I to the ground. On my back looking up into the sky, I briefly take in what is happening around me. Bits of concrete, some large enough to pulverize a skull, rain down upon us like heavy snow, and bits of the building crumble to the floor beside me. I roll away quickly to avoid being hit by a massive chunk of the arena wall. Despite the high-pitched ringing in my ears, I still hear the furious shouts of Eli from above. I can see him frantically waving his arms at the guards, but they are too stunned to respond. Regardless of their lack of response, he continues his screeching. I smile at the urgency in his voice; he sounds like he has completely lost the remnants of his sanity.

The shock of the explosion has made the crowd eerily silent, so I can easily make out another voice yelling from the distance. Tracking the sound, I glance over beside Eli and see Reggie screaming and pointing toward the wall, "Get up! Run! Hurry!"

Gazing toward where he is pointing, I see a gaping hole in the arena's wall directly behind where Robbie just stood. In the hollow, stands Brighton. He is frantically waving me to come to him. Not wasting any time, I struggle to my feet. I try to ignore the pain coursing through my body and propel myself forward. The distance to the opening is not far, but it feels like I am running forever.

A few times, I chance a look up toward the bandstand, and immediately regret my decision. The Officers are beginning to move toward my location. I have to get out of here before they make it down to me. "Come on, Zayda," Brighton yells. He is nervously looking from me to his father, and I can see how afraid he is for us both. As Eli continues his rant above me, I sprint faster than ever and close the remaining distance in just a few seconds.

Not bothering to look back at the chaos behind me, I lunge through the opening and into salvation's waiting arms.

EPILOGUE

It has been weeks since we left behind The Sacred City. Brighton and I have been sailing on the ocean in his father's yacht. Living off freshly caught fish and the small cache he managed to sneak away before our daring escape, we have put miles between ourselves and The Sacred City. Despite the distance between us and The Healers, I do not feel safe from their reach, and I'm sure Eli is doing his best to find us. I have tried to block out the terrible memory of my time in The Pit, but the nightmares still linger. I think the worst part of it all is not knowing what happened to the others. Brighton has had some communication with his contact back in the city, but all he has reported is that everyone is still alive. I long for the day we will be reunited.

Brighton has been the only bright spot in all this mess. At first, I did not trust him; he was one of The Council for goodness sake, but now, having spent so much time together, I would gladly lay down my life for him, and I know he would return the favor. Plus, had it not been for his plan, I would be toast right now, and he jokingly reminds me of that every single day. Today, we are moving forward with the next phase of our plan to take back the world from The Healers.

"So, when do I meet this mystery man who can make The New Cure?" I ask, standing on the deck, fresh sea spray misting me in the face. As usual, I am reeling in today's lunch. I am a much better fisherman than Brighton, but he has his hidden talents as well.

"They will be waiting for us when we dock in Alon later today," Brighton answers. He is cleaning the scales off the first fish I pulled in. Thankfully, he doesn't mind completing this task because I barely make it through one slice before I begin gagging. You would think growing up beside a river would have made me immune to the nasty tasks associated with eating a fresh catch, but like many other things in my life, skinning another creature is not one I've become comfortable with.

Looking over at him, his tan skin the perfect shade to make his purple eyes even more stunning, I suck in a deep breath. Even after seeing him day and night for all this time, his beauty still makes my heart skip a beat. I've gotten over the shockwaves that pass through us anytime we accidentally touch, but I don't think I will ever stop feeling this way when I gaze at him. He is spectacular to behold. "They? You never mentioned a they before," I reply, a bit of skepticism in my voice.

"Yes...I *have*. Many times. Too many times, in fact," he replies, stopping his knife and staring at me. "You just only hear what you *want* to hear." Smiling his crooked smile, he shakes his head and goes back to pulling the entrails out of the fish. The gentle rocking motion of the boat, due to an incoming storm, makes his task more difficult than normal, but he quickly filets the first fish and moves onto the next.

"I listen...when it's important," I joke, splashing him with seawater. He throws fish guts back at me and they leave a trail of gore on my shirt. "Gross!" I yell.

"You started it," is all he says back.

Storm clouds are building on the horizon, and a large flash of lightening cuts across the sky in a foreboding arc. I can't help but feel that our times of joking and playing house are rapidly coming to a tragic and permanent end. Suddenly feeling very serious, I ask "Do you really think they can use our blood to keep people from Turning?"

"That's what the doc says. He claims that the reason neither of us have symptoms is because we carry a special immunity, and that when combined, it will form antibodies for everyone else," Brighton says. We have had this conversation a million times before, but it gives me hope and calms me down to speculate about a time without The Turning. "Hopefully, we will be able to find others like us out there, so the doctor can develop the antidote faster."

His words, calm and rational, are a stark contrast to his youthfulness. He has had lots of practice pretending to be something that he is not, and once again I am reminded that he is much younger than I once thought. "I still can't believe you are only eighteen! You and your father did a great job of hiding that from the entire world," I say. Brighton's body goes rigid with the mention of his father, and I instantly regret my words. Eli is a monster, mad with the desire for power. He kept the truth about his son's age hidden away, so no one would know there was a chance for immunity and a cure. Well that, and he wants to amass a Turned/human-slave army to take over the world. He must have thought giving people hope would greatly hamper that task. If it hadn't been for Brighton rescuing me, Eli would have used my own brother to kill me, and I can only imagine what monstrous deeds he had in mind for his son. I understand his hatred for the man better than anyone else. "Sorry. I didn't mean to bring him up," I say sincerely.

"It's okay. We can't avoid speaking about him forever. Eventually, we are going to have to come up with a plan to oust him from power permanently, so I can take over," Brighton says.

"Only if you rule alone," I reply, my blood boiling with the thought of Abellona. God knows what hell she has put Reggie through since we left.

"Maybe not alone, but certainly without her," he says. I love that he knows who I am talking about without me saying so. "Perhaps, you might know someone smart, brave, and worthy to join me. Say a girl around seventeen with platinum hair, blue eyes, and a knack for rebellion?"

"Hmmm? No one comes to mind," I joke.

"Sure, like you wouldn't jump at the chance to be in charge and change the way our world works."

"You know I would, but we need to take it one day at a time."

"True. Today, we worry about lunch and meeting the doctor. Tomorrow, we will worry about staging a coup and ruling the nation. Deal?" he says, wiping his bloody hands on his jeans and offering his right one to me.

"Deal," I say, shaking his hand and feeling the all too familiar zap. Casting my eyes down to avoid seeing the 'look' on his face, I continue, "Do you think it will reverse The Turning?"

"Zayda, please don't do this again. You know every time we talk about Robinson, you end up crying for most of the night. I don't want to see you like that again. Ever!" he replies.

"Okay," I say, dropping the subject and reeling in the last fish of the day. The one thing the two of us disagree on the most it what will and should happen to the people who have already Turned. Brighton does not believe The Turned can ever come back, but I am not willing to give up on them, especially Robinson. A small tear falls down my cheek as I think about my brother.

Taking the fish from me to clean and noticing the tear, Brighton says, "Tell you what, we will make sure to ask the doc what he thinks. Who knows, I could be totally off base here." He reaches up and wipes my face, sending the jolt through us both again. Apparently, the shock is our bodies way of alerting the other that we are immune. Brighton claims it is some sort of Darwinian, survival of the fittest thing, but I have my doubts. A loud crash of thunder makes us both jump. "Looks like the storm is moving in faster than we anticipated. We should hurry this along. Let's cook these fish and head to shore, so you can get all your millions of questions answers," he says, winking at me.

"Smartass," I say, slapping him on the arm.

"Guilty," he replies.

***

A few hours later, we are coasting toward the shore of Alon. I can't help but think about how ironic it is that Brighton and I are taking the exact same journey up the river as he did on the day I first met him. Man, that seems like a lifetime ago, and in many ways, it is. With the thought of going home for the first time in over a month, a combination of excitement and trepidation courses through my body. "Ready for this?" Brighton asks. He has begun steering us in to the dock.

"As I'll ever be," I respond, not really meaning it. I squint to shield my eyes from the raging sun above and try to make out the duo standing on the shore. From here, they just look like tiny bugs waving us in. "Sure you don't want to tell me who it is before we land?" I ask. Brighton just gives me a nervous glance and shakes his head. "Why do you look so freaked out? Is something else going on?"

"Zayda?"

"Yes." I say, gripping the edge of the boat as another clap of thunder booms from the storm cloud that has been chasing us all morning.

"No matter what happens today," Brighton says, pausing and taking a deep breath, "remember that I did all of this to help."

"Why are you suddenly being so serious?"

"Just promise me."

"Okay...I promise. Now please stop freaking *me* out," I reply, turning my attention back to the dock. The couple standing there is slowly coming into view, and I realize why

Brighton is so concerned. "You have got to be kidding me?" I say to him.

"Please, just keep an open mind, and I swear I will explain everything," he pleads.

"You better," I respond, as the boat pulls up to the shore directly in front of Kieran and his father.

ABOUT THE AUTHOR

When A.L. Noble is not sitting at home feverishly writing her short stories or novels, she is enjoying as many concerts as her wallet will support. A long-time lover of many art forms, her passion for reading developed at an early age and quickly blossomed into a love for writing. Last year, she quit her job as an English teacher to formally pursue her dreams. The result of that pursuit lies before you in, *The Turning*.

To learn more about A.L. Noble, www.alnobleauthor.com

www.ingramcontent.com/pod-product-compliance
Lightning Source LLC
Chambersburg PA
CBHW030021180626
46810CB00001B/155